THE WUHAN GAMES

Book Design & Production:
Columbus Publishing Lab
www.ColumbusPublishingLab.com

Paperback ISBN: 978-1-63337-821-6
E-book ISBN: 978-1-63337-824-7

Printed in the United States of America
1 3 5 7 9 10 8 6 4 2

THE WUHAN GAMES

A NOVEL BY
JOHN McGORY

proving press

Preface

The coronavirus outbreak began January 2020 in Wuhan, China. The virus caused seven million deaths worldwide.

I lived in Wuhan from 2014 until February 5, 2020, when an American rescue plane took me and 150 U.S. citizens to San Diego. The U.S. government charged me $1100 to be "rescued."

How and why the tragedy took place remains an enigma. Did it naturally evolve out of a Hankou wet market or did operatives with sinister motives release it on an unsuspecting city?

While scientists, politicians, and journalists debate various theories, no conclusive explanation has emerged. My theory came to me in an "aha moment" as I sat on a bus in Wuhan several days before the government quarantined the city.

The moment evolved from my six years working as a language editor at the *Changjiang Weekly*, Wuhan's largest English newspaper, an English-speaking instructor at Jianghan University, a college in the city's Hanyang district, and a language consultant for numerous large Wuhan companies.

The newspaper job provided the opportunity to get to know the city. Much of the newspaper's editorial focus from 2016 to 2019 involved the 2019 World Military Games. Teaching English to university students and large company executives gave me insight into a changing Wuhan and China. Those elements were crucial in writing this book.

The book is a historical fiction novel but uses actual events and sources to build the book's plot. Accounts from Wuhan newspapers, official releases, personal experiences, or direct quotes from Chinese residents are used in the book's construction.

The book took four years to write, in part, to see if any evidence would emerge to discount my theory. None has.

The book should not be construed as an indictment of China. People cause problems in every country.

Living in Wuhan changed my life. Many kind and intelligent people who live in a fascinating and beautiful city and country left their positive marks on me. For that, I thank them as well as miss them.

The book seeks to answer the how and why questions of one of this century's great mysteries. To quote the 1969 film, *Butch Cassidy and the Sundance Kid*, "Most of what follows is true."

John McGory
May 2024

Main Characters

The following is a list of the fictional characters in this book.

Art Iron-American male-English teacher/journalist from Columbus, Ohio

Jun FuMin-Chinese female-daughter of Jun LiJiao and Hao Gui from Zigui County, Hubei Province

Jun LiJiao-Chinese male-farmer-married to Hao Gui, from Zigui County, Hubei Province

Hao Gui-Chinese female-farmer and real estate salesperson-married to Jun LiJiao, from Jingmen, Hubei Province (Chinese women do not take their husband's name when married.)

Li Shun-Chinese male-farmer and gardener from Zigui County, Hubei Province

Guo Zhenqin-Chinese male-Chinese political leader and developer from Wuhan, Hubei Province

Peng Qiang (aka Wu Qiang)-Chinese male-bodyguard for Guo Zhenqin from YiChang, Hubei Province

Wei Li-Chinese female-friend of Hao Gui

Captain Yang-Chinese male-Wuhan police officer

Wu Tong-Chinese male-teacher-cousin of Peng Qiang from YiChang, Hubei Province

Liz Paine-British woman-English teacher from London, England

Dr. Lui Liang-Chinese medical doctor at Central Hospital from Wuhan, Hubei Province

Chun Fang, Central Hospital administrator from Wuhan, Hubei Province

Zhang Zemin-Political leader from Wuhan, Hubei Province

Hu Jin, Wuhan businessman and Wuhan Communist Party Executive Committee member

Dr. Thomas Christopher, deputy director for the U.S. Centers for Disease Control from Atlanta, Georgia

Greg, bartender, Hideaway Inn, Columbus, Ohio.

CHAPTER 1

Subway Ninja Warriors

Squealing brakes provided the only sound as the subway rumbled into Sixin Station on Wuhan's southside.

Art Iron had a Cleveland Browns' sweatshirt pulled up over his nose and mouth as he counted the seconds before he could get the hell out of the enclosed space.

Panic filled the Wuhan Metro that night in central China's largest city. A mysterious virus had the city on edge a few days before the Chinese New Year. No one moved or talked, only breathing when necessary to lessen the risk of sucking in the invisible killer.

Iron slumped in his seat staring out the window. The station's platform came into view as the train slowed. His eyes began to focus on black-clad figures standing ten feet apart on the platform.

The men wore skin-tight black nylon body suits from head to toe with black boots and a red bandana and sash tied around their heads and waists.

"Ninja soldiers? At the subway station?" Iron stared in disbelief as soldiers positioned themselves before each door of the now-stopped train.

The doors opened and the soldiers simultaneously entered each car carrying a bullhorn. A collective gasp went through Iron's stunned subway car as if a 15th-century warrior appeared out of thin air.

"Get out! Get out now," the Ninja shouted through the bullhorn. The American eyed the Ninja who stood three feet away. Fear seeped out of the frayed eye holes cut into the soldier's mask.

"This guy's either a soldier or a secret policeman. If he's scared, then I'm scared too," Iron thought as he jumped out of his seat.

Old women grabbed shopping bags, mothers put arms around children, and men shoved hands into pockets as they pushed out of the train with heads down.

Wuhan, a city of 11-million citizens, had become the world's public enemy number one the last few weeks. Rumors exploded regarding an unknown dangerous virus spreading through the city's hospitals. Everyone in the city was a suspected carrier.

The Ninjas efficiently evacuated the confused passengers onto the platform. Many passengers rushed for the escalator to get out of the subway station.

Iron stood frozen wondering if the virus was detected on the train.

"No mask on an infected subway. I might be dead in a week," Iron said to no one.

News sources from around the world reported the virus had jumped from animals to man in a Hankou wet market, but no one was really sure.

Rumors or propaganda spread accusing a host of national and international suspects of intentionally releasing the virus on central China's largest city.

Six people dressed in Hazmat suits and carrying equipment exited a platform elevator and entered different cars on the subway.

The familiar three rings signaling closing subway doors echoed through the hushed platform. The train pulled away carrying the white-clad passengers and the Ninja warriors.

A terrified teenage girl stood next to Iron. Her frightened eyes sought comfort. He gave a thin smile as the girl turned her head toward the sound of an empty train coming into the station.

The subway doors opened and less than half of the original passengers got on board.

Iron hesitated before pulling pulled his sweatshirt up tight over his mouth and nose and entered the subway for the short ride to his stop.

CHAPTER 2

Jun and the Dam

JANUARY 1986 TO 1994

Jun LiJiao put more coal onto the fire to combat the crisp January wind blowing through the cracks in his rural Hubei Province home.

He smoked a cigarette near the fire as his wife let out a low moan followed by a scream from the small bedroom in the back of the tiny two-room home.

A few minutes later an old woman walked out of the bedroom with blood on her tattered apron.

"A girl. Sorry," the midwife said in a low, mournful tone. "Do you want me to kill it?"

The farmer's tense face relaxed.

"No! She is our daughter. We will love her. Rejoice," he said with strength. "Everyone is well?"

"Yes, yes. Strong and healthy. Keep the house warm. The cold can kill the young and weak."

The respected farmer had lived in the humble home all his life while his wife and now mother, Hao Gui, moved from Jingmen in an arranged marriage as a teen.

LiJiao's excitement over his daughter ran counter to tradition.

"Don't treat your daughter like a boy," the village elders said several days later. "Call her slave like the other girls. Females are not special."

The elders' wisdom silenced the father, but by the time his daughter reached nine years old, her intelligence and beauty captured the hearts of the small farming community.

"Your integrity and vision will lead a new China," Jun said to her every night before bed. Her name, FuMin, meant rich (Fu) and intelligent (Min).

"I'll do as you say papa. Do women with integrity wear fine silks and meet handsome men from Beijing?"

"Not always," he said with a laugh before tucking her into a straw bed near the stove.

Li Shun, a fellow farmer and Jun's best friend, and his wife joined them on Sundays to share food and socialize. Li usually said little, leaving the women to gossip about the rich, sick, and unhappy.

"The neighbor's cow got sick drinking water. They have no milk now. Someone's dumping poison in the river. We gave them milk but can't do it for long," Hao said in a whisper.

"We'll share as long as we have milk," Jun said. Li just grunted.

"My friend said we will have to move soon. She saw people with strange tools at the river. The government's building something to flood our homes," Li's wife said.

Everyone looked at Jun LiJiao who puffed a cigarette while looking at the floor.

"Yes. A dam will be built. We will leave our homes. But it is a 100-year-old shared vision. Generations will benefit. Millions no longer need to die from an angry Yangtze River."

Hao stood up. "Our family must go? Where? I'm not leaving our home."

"We'll do as the party says," Jun said, silencing the room except for the warm September breeze rattling the cottage's walls. "The dam brings progress."

The river village changed quickly in 1994 as construction of the $22 billion Three Gorges Dam began.

The dam required the destruction of 13 cities, 140 towns, and 1,350 villages. One million people had to move, including the Jun family which had farmed the ground for hundreds of years.

The government budgeted millions of dollars for families to move to cities such as Chongqing or Wuhan. But lax property rights provided opportunities for swindlers, including a few high-profile party leaders.

"The project improves China, but make good choices," Jun LiJiao said to farmers. "The dam will require us to move but don't believe thieves with wild get-rich schemes."

Guo Zhenqin, the Hubei Province party chairman, eyed displacement money to build high-rise apartments by his family-owned Wuhan development company.

"Foolish farmers blow government money on mahjong and opium. We can build thousands of new homes with that money," Guo said to his father. "Money works for the rich. Why give it to drug dealers?"

Guo contacted Peng Qiang, the YiChang Communist Party enforcer, a young loyal party member who got things done without asking questions.

"I need a smart man to convince farmers to move now. Leaving makes sense for a new China," Guo said to Peng over the telephone.

"One family leads the farmers, the Juns. The farmers listen to whatever Jun LiJiao says," Peng said. "They trust him."

"Easy as peeling a ripe banana," Guo said to his new assistant. "We need to....ah....mmm....convince the arrogant Jun to leave and the rest will follow like baby pandas after the mother. I leave the convincing to you. I've heard you can change people's minds."

"Yes, I can. How do you want me to handle it?"

"I don't want to know details. Just take care of him and I'll take care of you."

Jun received a note the next day.

"Come to my YiChang apartment to discuss the construction of the world's greatest project, the Three Gorges Dam. I will serve food and drink. Peng Qiang"

The strong-armed politician's nasty reputation promised trouble. The farmer went to Li Shun.

"Peng sent this note. Keep it. They want to chase me away with hopes of others following," Jun said.

"Stay home. Why look for trouble?"

"Honorable men don't avoid what stares them in the face. Our community must not run away in fear," he said to Li. "Lead them if I don't return."

"I'm a quiet man, not a leader like you. But why worry? Nothing will happen but useless talk."

"One more thing. Take care of FuMin and Hao. They'll need help if I am not here."

"Of course, my friend, we are one."

Peng greeted Jun the next day at his 15th-story penthouse in the beautiful river city. The austere apartment held little charm except for three camel figurines lit by a small spotlight.

Jun tapped his wide-brimmed hat on his thigh, refusing to hand it to Peng's servant.

"Relax my friend. I'm an honest man who doesn't steal hats," the large politician laughed. "We're here to talk about ways for you to buy all the hats you want!"

The servant led them to the living room with a stunning view of the wide Yangtze River nestled in the western foothills.

"We must accept China's new vision. All must do their part to help the future of the young like your daughter."

"Let's not discuss family. My daughter does as her father commands," Jun said with no emotion.

"Zigui County's smartest student, I hear. I was never that lucky," Peng said with a thin laugh. "May you live long to see her prosper."

"The universe decides our fate. Who knows what nature intends? I'm curious to hear your vision of a new China."

"Our leaders plan major changes. The loyal will embrace them. Do you?"

"The dam needs to be built. I will do my part," Jun said with a sharp stare.

"Good. The leaders want you to convince the farmers to begin leaving now. They will pay you $100 dollars for every farmer who leaves in the next two months," Peng said in a low, greedy voice.

"What will they get?"

"A contract saying they'll get paid when the government releases relocation money, minus expenses of course." Peng smiled like a hungry man before a New Year's dinner.

"How can they move without money?"

"That's not my concern. They move or the disloyal will be mowed down like a wheat field. This new way starts today."

"Is that a shared vision or threat?" A rigid Jun stared at Peng.

Peng shrugged but said nothing.

"I cannot cheat my friends."

"Do as you wish but your life changed coming to my apartment. Where and how long it goes depends on your decision."

Jun's face turned red as he looked over his shoulder toward the door.

"I'll pay in cash the day each one leaves. You'll be a rich farmer in no time, rare as a kind Chinese grandmother," Peng said before roaring with laughter.

"No. I'm not stealing money stained with farmers' sweat."

"Be reasonable. You have no choice," a sympathetic-sounding Peng said. "This will happen regardless. Shut your mouth, make a few dollars, and your daughter can go to a decent school in Chongqing and marry an educated man instead of a farmer."

The farmer clasped his hands behind his back before shaking his head no.

"Let's go to the balcony to clear our heads," Peng said, leading Jun outside. "Take a look at the beautiful view. Breathe the fresh air. Relax Jun."

The two walked onto the balcony and Peng let out a long, slow whistle piercing the quiet night. Two men appeared from behind the balcony curtains. The larger man held a baton and approached with careful steps.

Jun pulled a long, shiny knife from his waistband and pointed it at Peng.

"I will not go easy, even if it means killing the local teacher," Jun said in a measured tone.

The three assailants surrounded the farmer, leaving him cornered against the balcony's railing.

"I want to talk to others about your offer. It's time to leave," Jun said with desperation.

"Show this idiot out," Peng said, popping a piece of dragon fruit into his mouth and looking away.

A sweeping lunge by Jun missed the attackers, but a backhanded swipe sliced Peng's cheek. The dragon fruit flew out of the opening.

The man with the baton swung down on Jun's extended arm causing a loud crack. Jun fell to a knee, dropping the knife.

The second man knelt next to the injured Jun, but the baton-wielding man yelled, "Get up. Throw him over." The second man hesitated, reaching for the injured man's arm.

Screaming in pain and covered in Peng's blood, Jun tried to pick up the knife with his broken arm before the first man pinned him to the balcony wall.

"Peng, killing me changes nothing and the rich can't kill us all," he said, struggling to hold onto the balcony wall.

The confused second man watched as the first man peeled Jun off the wall, throwing him over the balcony wall into the darkness of the river city's cool autumn evening.

A muffled thud floated up 15 floors along with shouts as the two men rushed to Peng's assistance, stopping the bleeding with a cloth to his face.

"That idiot. He'll die a hundred deaths," Peng mumbled as he staggered into his apartment. "Don't touch his knife. It's evidence."

CHAPTER 3

Choose Wisely

SEPTEMBER 15, 1994

"Your father died a hero defending the rights of farmers," Hao told her weeping daughter the day after her father died. Peng told a different story.

"Quite distressing. Jun LiJiao became despondent when told the government needed his home, so he slashed my face with a knife before jumping off the balcony. China's loss as well as Zigui County's," Peng said to the police officials who he knew well.

Farmers received an official letter two days after Jun's death, promising a fair price for their land, moving expenses, and a bonus if they signed over their rights and left within a week with the money coming later.

"I completed the request. The tree has fallen, the monkeys will scatter and soon be gone," Peng told Guo in a painful mumble from his hospital bed.

Rumors of widespread murder frightened the confused farmers. Many accepted the offer rather than face a similar fate.

The remaining farmers gathered at Li's request where young Jun FuMin read Peng's offer for those who couldn't read.

"Jun LiJiao is dead. He said to me 'don't let our friends be cheated.' We must remain one," Li whispered to the scared farmers at a secret meeting to discuss the offer.

"And end up murdered. No, not me," a farmer said to a nodding audience. "I've heard 10 farmers were killed in the next village."

Li took a deep breath but said nothing. He had no talent for discussing death.

The group pushed and pulled on what to do before leaving confused and scared.

Li walked home under a brilliant mid-autumn moon, passing small homes with nervous or angry voices spilling out to the dirt path.

A small lake where villagers hauled water gave him a place to mourn.

"My fish friends, soon you will live in my home, and I will swim from place to place," he said to the pond. A small tear rolled down his hard, brown face.

A warm southern breeze blew through the small forest surrounding the lake. Li listened for a long time to the wind whisper many thoughts through the trees.

CHAPTER 4

A Poor Farmer Seeks Justice

SEPTEMBER 20, 1994

"I must go to Wuhan to see the Hubei Province Communist Party secretary to restore order to our village. Talking to our local leaders is like climbing a tree to catch a fish," Li told his wife the next morning.

His wife nodded but said nothing.

The next day Li held a small bag and kissed his wife goodbye.

"Please be careful. This is your first trip away from home," his worried wife told her 38-year-old husband.

"Yes, yes. The wind said Jun will protect me."

The train amazed the wide-eyed farmer who played with the window blinds as it pulled out of YiChang. Soon young people in fine clothes pushed small carts down the aisle.

"Look beautiful with Panda Face Cream," a young lady said to no one in particular. "A gift for your wife," she said to Li.

"She's a beautiful wife without your cream," he said, looking down at his shoes.

The woman laughed while pushing her cart past Li.

"They expect me to buy these things? I only have my return ticket, a few pieces of fruit, a small bowl of rice, a water bottle, and enough money for the bus ride to the Communist Party offices. No money for frivolous items."

A man wearing a hat and tie came next. "This elixir provides energy to work all day and night when you need it," the young salesman said, nudging Li with a sly smile.

"I work hard each day growing crops, not stealing money on trains. Your medicine must be for night workers," he said. "I have no use for it."

The hawker shook his head and moved on, calming Li's nerves.

"They never stop barking 'buy, buy, buy.' Who can afford such extravagances on a train? Maybe if I close my eyes, they will leave me alone." He pulled his hat low.

Li's fidgeted with his seat as the train crept into the Hankou Railway Station at 2 p.m.

"Time to catch a bus to the offices, straighten things out with the party secretary, and make the 6 p.m. train home," he thought as the sight of hundreds of people on the platform worried him.

The huge, bustling station spread far as a great field of rice. Busy-looking people rushed by the ragged farmer without a glance.

Li stood frozen. Everyone knew where to go but him.

Signs in the station pointed in all directions for taxis, buses, trains, luggage, and tickets.

"Excuse me can you tell me where to catch a bus," he asked several people who passed by with suspicious looks but not a word.

A picture of a bus with an arrow pointing down a set of moving stairs caught his eye.

"Are the Wuhan people so lazy they need electric stairs?"

He hesitated before the moving tread pulled him onto the escalator, bringing a smile to his face. A door at the bottom of the stairs led outside to streams of people coming and going in great haste. They carried everything imaginable from babies and boxes to book bags and tools.

Women wore fine wool and leather clothes while men dressed in matching pants and jackets. Vendors sold fruit, dumplings, and kebabs, filling the streets with tempting aromas.

"Don't get distracted," he said while trying to ignore the huge city's amazing sights and sounds. "Find the 208 bus. My cousin in Hankou said it went right past the Communist Party offices."

A small shelter listed many bus routes, but Li couldn't read the confusing listings. Seven buses stopped in the first 30 seconds. People pushed off and on in no time before buses drove away.

Another bus stop across the street sent buses in the opposite direction.

"Ah yes. The bus goes both ways. But which way to the offices? This way or that?"

His heart jumped as a packed 208 pulled up. Fifteen riders formed a tight circle in front of the door, so he waited till all entered before asking the driver a question from outside the bus.

"Excuse me I am Li Shun from Zigui County and I come to..." The bus driver closed the door and drove away before Li finished his sentence. "No time for one question?"

The large clock on the railway station showed 3:45 p.m.

"A homeless night in Wuhan? Maybe. I don't have much time," he thought. "I'll ask this elderly gentleman where to go."

"Excuse me. Are the Communist Party offices this way?"

The man clasped his hands behind his back. "The Hubei Province Communist Party or the Wuhan Communist Party?"

"The Hubei."

"Hmmm. Several stops this way," he said.

"That's not right old man. Take the bus across the street till the end of the route," a middle-aged woman with a young child said.

"I'm right. Women know little of such matters," the old man said in a disrespectful tone.

"Shut up old fool. You can't find your rice bowl without your wife's help," she said. "That way, near the end of the line."

Soon a couple joined, "I think the office moved. Take the 213 bus then transfer on Dongfeng Avenue to the 654."

An arguing crowd grew to 10 people as Li's confusion turned to dread.

"The sage old man's advice must be correct, but the lady and the others seem confident too." A bench gave him a place to think.

"Very challenging. Jun would know what to do," he thought, looking at the clock showing 4:05 p.m. "Not enough money to go wrong. I can find the office tomorrow, finish early, then return to YiChang by 1 p.m. But where can I stay?"

The railway station shimmered in the late day sun. "Yes, that will work. Seats to stretch out plus a bathroom with running water. Better than home."

The moving steps took him up to the large waiting room. He sat next to a smiling young woman with two children.

Her younger child climbed on the seat to play with a toy truck on Li's shoulder.

"Stop it. Sit down. Leave the man alone," the mother said to the child.

"Young ones like to play. It's ok."

"Would you like these?" The small woman held out two red apples.

"Very nice. Did you grow them?"

"No. Are you a farmer?

"Yes, but I don't grow apples.

The woman reached into her purse and pulled out a few dollars.

"Take this for your travels."

"Why are you giving the poor man my apple mommy? He looks scary. Is he a monster?"

"Shh. Be quiet."

"I'll take one apple, but the children need the money. The train offers attractive items for young eyes. My bowl of rice and this delicious apple give me plenty."

"Where are you going?"

"I'm going to see the Hubei Province Communist Party secretary. I have no place to stay so I'll sleep here till morning."

"Do you have an appointment?"

"No. Isn't the secretary's job to take care of the people's problems?"

"The province faces many problems. He may be away solving other concerns."

"No. The wind assured me he'd be there."

"Do you know the office location?"

"No. But I'll find it."

"I work near there. Take the 208 bus across the big street out front. Get off at the fifth stop," she said.

"Thank you. I now know the way."

"Why are you visiting the chairman?"

"To avenge the murder of my friend, Jun LiJiao, a wise teacher. He found me when the clouds hovered low. My selfish world had crumbled. Instead of chastising me like my family, he gave me this," Li said, holding a red ball the size of walnut.

"How did it help?"

"He said, 'The universe, from beginning to end, fits into this tiny sacred space. No room for self-pity or anger. Bring only love and an open mind as you travel.'"

"You come to Wuhan carrying those two items in your heart?"

"Yes. Love for my dead friend and an open mind that the secretary is a just man."

The young mother gave Li a kind, but sad look.

"Our train is here," the young mother said as she gathered her children. "I wish you luck in your travels."

She walked away holding her two children's hands as Li thought of hard decisions on the horizon.

"Who will hold FuMin's hand now? I promised my dead friend I'd watch after her and his wife, Hao, as well."

Holding a child's hand is easy, but a woman's hand creates confusion leading to poor choices.

"I promised to take care of both, but the daughter is more important than the mother," he thought, shaking his head with resolve.

Clouds of street-level pollution covered Wuhan the next morning. The crowded city appeared an unfriendly place as thousands of blank faces pushed onto trains and buses, caring little about FuMin and the loss of her father.

"Jun LiJiao fed and taught many only to be murdered by the rich. He will be forgotten soon. Will the chairman care a daughter will never remember her hero?"

A determined Li crossed the busy street in front of the Hankou Railway Station and pushed his way onto a packed 208 bus.

The green bus soon stopped at a fence with a small, glass-enclosed booth in front of the ornate Hubei Province Communist Party office.

Two serious-looking guards in the booth eyed the shabby Li. A glaring officer slid open a small window.

"I'm Li Shun, a farmer from Zigui County. I want to speak to the party secretary about a serious matter."

"Hey Hong, the esteemed Zigui County farmer Li Shun wants to see the secretary with important business. Do you want to call him?" The two guards roared with laughter.

"What? Are the pigs on the loose again?"

"Get out of here fool. The busy secretary has no time for you. Take your rice bowl and go home. Be thankful we don't put you in jail as a political prisoner." The guard slammed the glass window shut.

"Scumbag eggs. Rot in your little house of lies," Li shouted before hearing Jun's voice, "Please sit down. Be patient."

The angry man went across the street to a bench next to a gingko tree.

"Nature's yellow leaf teaches serenity," Li said as the sun grew warm, then sank low in the western sky.

The two men left their post, turning off the office lights, and closing the gate. Li stretched on the bench, turned up his collar and fell asleep in the cool September air.

A refreshed Li sat eating an apple when the guards returned at 7 a.m.

"Hey farmer, sit too long and roots will grow out of your ass," the beefy guard yelled, laughing, and slapping his companion on the back.

Li said nothing, remaining still all day with his eyes riveted on the small office, only moving to eat a few grains of rice and drink water.

The sun sank low again as the beefy guard talked on the telephone. A third man, dressed in all black, soon approached the booth from the office building.

The small man talked to the guards before crossing the street and sitting on the bench next to Li.

"You've been here two days. What do you want?"

"A poor farmer seeks justice. Peng, a YiChang Communist Party leader, murdered my friend, Jun LiJiao. He steals farmers' homes. The party leader needs to know. I've come to tell him no matter how long it takes. Nature provides the strength."

"Ah. Nature gives much to those who listen. Let's see how we can serve justice. My name is Zhang Zemin. Please tell me more."

The gentleman listened to Li's story of Peng's push to chase the farmers away.

"Peng's invitation shows his evil intent to kill my friend. I seek to preserve his honor as well as his family's honor," he said, carefully putting Peng's invitation into his tattered jacket.

"Can I have the letter? I'll need to show it to the chairman."

Li handed him the letter without a word.

"Let's see if we can have you in Zigui County tonight with your pretty wife. Let me get you food while I talk to the party secretary. You must be hungry. It takes food to be patient," he said, putting his arm around Li.

CHAPTER 5

The Party Understands

SEPTEMBER 24, 1994

The 38-year-old farmer rolled a cigarette at a long fine table with leather chairs and a large screen on the wall. His wife would be impressed but he just wanted to go home.

The clock said 6:45 p.m. The night promised sleep on another bench instead of next to his wife with hair that smelled of roses, so he laid down on a black leather couch along the wall, falling fast asleep.

"Oh, I apologize for waking the esteemed Zigui County farmer and detective Li Shun. Feel free to rest a bit more," Zhang said as he entered the room.

"No, no, no," Li said, rising from the couch rubbing his nose with vigor. "I hope to finish our business and return home tonight."

"That will happen, I promise. Justice and home remain the party's most important principles. You shall have both today."

"I seek nothing more."

"The party secretary knows the disgraced YiChang servant Peng. Your appalling story moved him. The criminal will receive harsh punishment. You and Jun's wife will receive high-paying jobs and free apartments in Wuhan in return for your land, a just agreement. But you must come soon."

"What of the other village farmers? They worry."

"The party secretary promises fair compensation to all. Tell them the good news. I arranged an automobile to return you to Zigui County. You see, a just party listens. Wait here."

"Oh, thank you, thank you. The party does understand," he said with a hopeful look.

Zhang gave a half wave, walked out, and headed toward Guo's palatial office.

An erect Guo read a report behind a large chicken-wing wood desk.

"So how is our farmer friend?"

"Oh, he's good. No problems. He looks handy. You might be able to use him at Baixin. I'll get someone to drive him to Zigui County."

"You drive the farmer home. Then see Peng. Congratulate him on a job well done and give him this," Guo said, handing Zheng a red envelope.

"What do we do about Peng? We need to get him out of YiChang," Zheng said.

"Arrange a trip to Enshi for a few weeks till we find a hiding place. And get Li to tell the farmers they must leave before receiving government money. We'll try to find them," Guo said with a small smile.

CHAPTER 6

A Zeal to Succeed
1998

A determined Hao embraced Guo's promise of housing and a job when her small family moved to Wuhan from Zigui County.

Baixin, a massive condominium project, rested along the Yangtze River in downtown Wuhan. Guo needed cheap labor and the farmers provided it.

Her job started as office help, but soon expanded into sales as a kind demeanor and farming background enticed many flooding the city to buy apartments.

Soon FuMin passed out flyers on weekends to the hordes of people seeking housing. The young girl noticed that Wuhan women wore different clothes than those in Zigui County.

"Mom, the clothes in Wuhan make girls look like television stars."

"Yes, many more options here. I can now afford to buy you a few new dresses and shoes."

The words, "let's go shopping" soon electrified the young girl. Mother and daughter explored the new malls springing up like flowers in the growing Wuhan.

Soon every morning began with, "Mom, can we go shopping today?"

"Not today. Too many customers want to buy units and I need you to pass out flyers. Now, if you help, I'd have time tomorrow. I'll buy you new clothes as payment."

"New clothes," she screamed and ran around the dining table waving her arms. "Yes, yes, yes."

Jun attacked the job of passing out flyers with zeal. Her attention to detail never wavered whether standing in the driving Wuhan rain or its sweltering summer heat.

Li's effort as a Baixin gardener paled in comparison to the young girl. He had turned bitter after his 36-year-old wife died of stomach cancer after living in Wuhan several months.

"Why so angry? I understand the loss of your wife hurts," Hao said. "I still grieve about my husband. But can't you do your job without fighting with everyone?"

Only Sunday afternoon walks with the now-fashionable FuMin brought a smile to the farmer's face.

Each week new stylish clothes adorned her body accompanied by a colorful umbrella to protect her pale skin from the hot Wuhan sun.

Ferry rides to WuChang or visits to JieFang or Zhongshan Park revived Li's memory of his past pastoral life of soil, ponds, and trees.

Love blooms in Wuhan on Sundays. Hundreds of single people and aggressive mothers pin dating profiles on dozens of large boards in city parks in hopes of attracting marriage partners.

Photographs of men next to automobiles or women in tight-fitting clothes lined the boards. Mothers mill about with phone numbers and stories about beautiful daughters or rich sons.

"You should put up a profile," FuMin said to Li as they walked past hundreds of Zhongshan Park listings.

"The universe is orderly. The earth travels in the universe at the same speed for millions of years as do all the planets and stars. Only humans have the freedom to choose the speed they travel. We must protect that independence and not give it away to a billboard."

"Well, when you do choose, wearing those rags won't help. Your beauty remains hidden."

"Choose me for who I am, not what I wear. Those who pick with care understand. You marry the person, not the clothes."

"Wondering eyes see a lazy, poor man. Your gardens are very tidy and neat. Why not the gardener?" Jun gave a small, sweet smile.

"Ah, you are sly, like your mother."

She walked a bit before looking at Li.

"When we walk in the park or along the Changjiang, my father is here." the young girl said. "When you go, he goes, and I walk alone."

"No. His blood is your blood. His strength and intelligence live inside you."

"But will the elderly give me the freedom to show his strength and intelligence? A young girl gets told to keep such traits hidden," she said with a quizzical look.

"If done with a proper serious attitude a young Chinese girl can achieve great things. But I see your mother's silly interest in clothes and red hair in you too. A waste of time to one who wants to change the world."

"I love my mother. Plus, I like her hair. She's taking me this week to her hairdresser. I'm so excited. I may go blonde!"

"The strong and intelligent yellow-haired Chinese girl wearing fancy dresses while fighting the powerful! Hmm, not your father's path, indeed," he said shaking his head.

CHAPTER 7

Your Eyes and Ears Open

2001

Jun's clothes and aggressive flyer efforts grabbed the attention of Baixin community's most important resident, Guo Zhenqin.

Endearing sweetness wrapped in an enticing slender body with exquisite features captivated the aging political leader. Lively, engaging eyes and an energetic mind set her apart from the many tall, thin, long-black-haired Chinese girls.

Guo began stopping by the development's guarded gate on Saturday mornings to discuss the comings and goings of the Baixin community with Jun.

"What are people doing and saying today little darling?"

"Zheng left early with a woman I do not know" or "Visitors complaining about the high price of housing" provided him intel while she built trust with the powerful man.

"Good work. Keep your ears and eyes open and your mouth shut," he replied each week before giving her a small treat, her only payment from the company. "People will pay you great sums of money for such information one day."

The young girl soon understood the power of building relationships by sharing salacious information with the rich. The Chinese term, guanix, requires two people to build a closed and caring relationship built on trust before any business can take place.

Jun began to see the excitement in the old man's face when he arrived promptly at 10 a.m. every Saturday morning. Each week she whispered rumors to feed Guo who lapped them up like a thirsty dog.

Years of Saturday morning conversations paid off for Jun as Guo's influence led to her acceptance and eventual graduation from Wuhan University, one of China's prestigious universities.

Jun's family and friends occupied the Wuhan University auditorium's front row to see the class's top student graduate 10 years after passing out her first flyer.

A decade of coy smiles and whispered rumors taught her to artfully fend off the powerful man's inappropriate suggestions while encouraging him to return every Saturday.

The placid Guo sat in the front row imagining the young beauty's undergarments while her mother sat next to him, worrying if the hairdresser dyed her hair too red.

Li stood in the back of the auditorium wearing patched pants and an ill-fitting shirt.

"A free seat next to you. Let me get Li. Jun wants him up front," Hao said to Guo.

"No. I'm not sitting next to stench. Garbage gets dumped in the back for a reason," he growled.

The graduate with a bright future wore a Guo-purchased printed yellow flowered dress from Musier Paris with Chanel pumps under her graduation robe.

Recruiters from China's top companies lined up to snatch the university's talent, but Guo had secured the top graduate.

"Do a good job and you'll be in the mayor's office in no time, no matter who the mayor is," he said, telling her of a job in Wuhan's economic development department.

Jun had a simple graduation plan involving clothes, money, and the rich.

"Clothes attract attention. An ED job will bring the rich into my office every day," she told her friends who had jobs lined up at Huawei,

Tencent, and Alibaba. "From there it is simple math that adds up to a paid ticket to the west's freedom and money."

"The rich only share money with corrupt government workers," a friend said with a laugh.

"Oh, I'll get it out of them," the confident graduate said with a smile.

Guo introduced her to the future mayor within weeks of the appointment.

"This is the honorable Tang Wong, mayor of Xiangfan and the next mayor of Wuhan."

"Hello Tang," Jun said. "I'm in the economic development section.

"Oh, my favorite. They call me Mr. Dig-Dig in Xiangfan."

"Good and you'll keep that name in Wuhan," Guo said. "Jun will be your chief of staff and report to me. You'll end up in jail for stealing money on your own."

"I appreciated your support in the past. That dust up in Xiangfan? A simple misunderstanding created by extremists."

"It cost a lot to get you off. I'm not paying anymore. Got it," Guo said.

Guo had stepped down as province chairman to become the Wuhan Communist Party chair several years earlier. Wuhan's explosive growth gave the new mayor and local chairman the opportunity to develop elaborate schemes to siphon millions of dollars from new construction.

The two experimented with different ways to steal money. They included sharing bid information with favored construction companies, inflating public job specifications that only a preferred company could meet, or allowing companies to cut corners by using inferior products and building techniques. Whatever way, the construction companies provided healthy kickbacks for the assistance and swore allegiances for the right to pay for acquiring city contracts.

Mr. Dig-Dig promoted the city, Jun unknowingly handled rigged specs and legislation, and Guo collected the payoffs through an old friend, Peng Qiang.

The schemers' buried secret details in blizzards of reports justifying decisions provided by the benefitting companies.

Jun never stopped getting necessary documents approved through various boards, committees, and legislative bodies, unaware of Guo's side deals.

Stunning gifts showed up at Jun's home after an approved development or building contract.

"Last month a jade necklace. Today a Macau vacation. The old man's sexual fantasies never stop. But he never mentions the gifts so who cares," she thought with a laugh.

The kickback train worked until a young engineer asked Jun to dinner after winning approval of a contract.

"My father owns the company receiving today's contract. We are most grateful for your assistance. He promises to deliver his thanks next week as agreed to with Guo," the man said to Jun as they ate hotpot.

"Thank you, but your father and Guo's dealings are not my concern," she said, hiding the questions spinning in her mind. "My job involves city legislation. I'm not involved in outside agreements."

"Sorry for my ignorance. Please forgive me, I thought you knew. Let me buy dinner as thanks for your hard work and nothing more."

"Nothing more means something more for Guo and the mayor. They're stealing money," she thought as she smiled and nodded at her dinner companion.

She quickly connected the dots. Contractors got public works' contracts with spot-on proposals or no competition due to the unique specifications. Inexperience and self-flattery put her at serious risk.

"I'm holding the bag. Crooked legislation passes and I get gifts. I'm not going to jail for Guo and the mayor."

Two days later the city's environmental committee tinkered with specifications for rebuilding portions of a park along the Yangtze River. The committee almost awarded the contract to Guo's preferred contractor, but then selected another one. Jun said nothing.

Guo called her 10 minutes after the meeting ended.

"I heard about the changes."

"That was fast," Jun said with a bit of surprise.

"Please come to my Baixin penthouse tonight? I want to discuss a promotion."

"A promotion? Oh, no, no, no."

"Yes. I have a special job for you. No one else will do."

"I must work late. How about tomorrow? Oh, several meetings including an important discussion regarding construction specifications for Metro Line 3. Maybe next week?"

"No! Tonight," Guo said with anger.

The calm Jun again refused. The old man softened his tone.

"Please meet me for 10 minutes at the Starbuck's next to your office at 4 p.m. Ok?"

Jun agreed but walked in an hour late.

"Thank you for meeting. I know the city's Metro system needs your valuable attention. Can I get you a latte?"

"No thank you. I only have a few minutes. Meeting at 5:30 p.m. with a city engineer who has suggestions on the Metro's plans."

"The plans will remain as submitted. No changes. This is an order from the Wuhan Communist Party Executive Committee."

"Small changes save millions in construction costs and improve safety. I'm sure the executive committee wants to know about this important information."

"Their deliberations do not involve you. The committee has reasons for its decisions. You have your orders. Carry them out."

Jun smiled at the elderly gentleman. "Oh Guo, let's not play games. Our relationship can't blossom if I get sent to jail for getting a few small gifts for helping you steal millions of dollars," she said looking down at the table with a smile.

"Rumors of you receiving gifts float around city hall," the old man said with grim face. "What if the wrong people find out? Many difficult questions to answer. A heartbreaking situation."

"You don't want bad things to happen to me, do you?" She leaned forward to stroke his arm. "I know you send the gifts. And I think it's sweet."

"You're mistaken," Guo said. "Why would I send gifts?"

"You know why." She dropped her head and blushed.

"So young and innocent. The party loves to swat the fly. I'll protect you as a friend and mentor.   But Jun, no more changing specs or legislation, OK?"

Jun nodded in silence.

"Here. A small gift. A peace offering," Guo said, giving her a jade bracelet.

"No. No more gifts."

"A gift from me. My name's engraved on it."

Jun put it on and held it near Guo's face, letting her perfume linger.

"It is nice. Thank you. But we have more to discuss."

CHAPTER 8

We Love Shopping

FEBRUARY 1, 2014

Li Shun loved farming, from tilling soil in the blazing Hubei Province sun to listening to the joyful patter of drenching rains on planted fields.

Li yearned for the glorious Zigui County days with Jun LiJiao and the bountiful earth.

Now, the gardener spent afternoons envisioning his tall thin body sailing off a 20th floor Baixin condominium, gracefully picking up speed as it hurtled toward the short wall surrounding the rose bushes.

Nightly suicides happened in Wuhan. Thousands of tall buildings enticed the worn down to jump off convenient condo balconies, ending many sad stories.

A recent suicide scene attracted the talkative who whispered, "he was sick" and "no job" to rationalize the death.

"He chose suicide. Why live in chains?" Li screamed at the whisperers who turned their backs.

"A pitiful world," he thought. "A world run by cold, hard men who believe they control the universe. How insane. I don't blame the man for jumping to his next life. I'd jump if I had the courage."

His only joy, weekly Sunday walks with FuMin where they laughed and cried about her late father, had dwindled to 20-minute affairs every couple of months, consisting of Li watching FuMin on the phone.

"I'm sorry. This is the last call then we'll talk," the 34-year-old beauty said the last time they had met before she left in an excused rush, her glittering jewelry flashing in the bright sun.

The disappointing walk had left Li's moist eyes watching the water lap against the Yangtze River ferry that took him to his empty apartment.

"Bit by bit life no longer needs you. Loved ones move on to new lives or disappear into the void, leaving nothing but the freedom to regret a wasted life," he said to the gray-green water.

Hao stood with other women from the development waiting to start their Sunday evening dancing in the courtyard when Li returned.

"Your daughter chases dirty money. She owns more than other government workers," he told Hao, arms folded across his chest.

"Oh Li, such fabulous tales. We love shopping on Taobao," the red head laughed. "You're just jealous she spends more time with Guo."

Li's sullen look shifted her tone.

"Be happy. Her father would be proud of her, as I know you are."

"Hao, we grew up buying clothes with government coupons. Blue or grey was the only decision."

"China's richer today. That's good," she said adjusting her colorful headband matching a flowing dance outfit.

"Your daughter travels east but will only find the west. Those consumed by money find poverty," Li said in a loud voice creating a stir among the anxious dancers.

"Calm down. Why are you always angry? One minute you're arguing with condominium owners and the management company and the next minute it's FuMin."

"The owners are thieves. Guo lied to me. The Zigui County farmers never received any money. It came here to build. Now, you have red hair and eat food until your dresses don't fit as our poor friends die in Chongqing."

"My dresses fit fine you blind old man. The rest, all lies told by competing developers. Don't believe them."

"I believe what I see," he said, scanning the 55-year-old dressed in a swirl of colors highlighting her vivid red hair.

"My family works hard. Don't question our honesty without more proof than we dress better than you," Hao said with a snap as the dance music started.

Two weeks later, Li invited Jun on a trip.

"Life means more than a cellphone or purse. You've lost your way as the young do. A visit to a humble Zigui County will bring back the spirit of your father," Li said.

"So sweet," FuMin said with an uncomfortable smirk. "Let's try to fit it into my schedule. Can I let you know next week?"

Three weeks of calls found her voice mail full. Then, late one night, the phone woke him.

"I haven't forgotten my promise. How about this weekend sweetie," FuMin said in an enticing whisper. "I love visiting those trapped in pens like cows, pigs, and farmers' wives. We must go."

Li coughed before spitting out, "I'll purchase the tickets tomorrow. We can leave on the 7 a.m. train Saturday."

"Dreamy. Now, don't get any funny ideas. I'm not a child anymore," she said with a giggle. "We must get two rooms at a nice hotel."

The comment flustered Li, denying the insinuations before stopping. "You need sleep FuMin. See you Saturday at 5:30 a.m."

A typed note slid under Li's door Friday evening.

"Sorry but work makes it impossible to go tomorrow. We will go soon, I promise. Here's the money for the tickets. FuMin."

Ten red Chinese 100-dollar bills fluttered to the floor, landing next to a satchel packed with snacks and a small gift for FuMin.

Li tossed and turned in a dark bedroom.

"Maybe I'm the one who needs the trip? The fresh country air will do me good. I can visit Hong Yi's knife shop. A sharp new blade may come in handy one day. The young learn at their own speed as I once did."

CHAPTER 9

I've Made It

MARCH 8, 2014

Jun traveled early Saturday morning to a private WuChang garage. An attendant opened the door to a new sky blue 2013 Mercedes-Benz SLC 300 Roadster.

Peng Qiang and Guo walked up behind her. "Admiring your good fortune?" Guo raised his eyebrows, widening his eyes.

"Oh. I didn't hear you."

"That's it, Wu. I'll call Monday morning," he said to his bodyguard. "Let's go Jun. You want to drive?"

"Such a beautiful car. Are you sure?"

"Of course. Need to find out if you like it," Guo said with a small smile.

The sports car soon sped past Wuhan's Third Ring Road toward Shanghai.

"Don't worry about the cameras. I'll take care of the tickets," Guo said with a wave at the continual highway cameras.

"The Four Seasons, I'm so excited. But Li needs an apology. He'll be disappointed."

"Don't worry. I gave the pig farmer enough money to keep rice wine flowing for a month. Why waste time worrying? He belongs in Zigui County. I can get him a job there."

"No, he belongs near my family," she said.

"Now, now. Just a suggestion. You're going to be busy with a new

Wuhan project. I plan to discuss it tonight. Maybe over some champagne in my suite?"

"We can discuss it in the hotel's dining room."

A red leather case with a script *Cartier* across the top caught Jun's attention as she glided to a table in the spectacular Shanghai Four Season's restaurant. Guo tried to look casual, a thin smile plastered on his tense face.

"Sorry I'm late but preparing for such an elegant dinner takes time. But I've made it finally," Jun said with a sparkling smile.

"And well worth the wait. Here is a taste of the future," Guo said sliding across the table a leather case containing a white gold necklace, set with 135 brilliant-cut diamonds totaling 7.5 carats, costing north of $350,000 Chinese dollars.

"For me? Why?"

She knew why. The same reason for all of Guo's gifts since promising "more treats in my home" to the then-13-year-old who passed out housing flyers.

A light-headed sensation overcame Jun as the twinkling lights in the world-class restaurant blended with the jewels. She tried to focus on Guo who was rambling about another way to make money.

"Richer than anyone in Wuhan except me and this week's software titan. Custom French dresses, purses, pieces of jewelry, and pairs of shoes will soon turn the farmer's daughter into a princess."

"What? Richer than who?"

"Please, let me put this necklace on your exquisite neck." Guo said, standing behind her, clasping the latch, and then placing both hands around her delicate throat.

Her right shoulder and arm jerked to dislodge Guo's hands from the suggestive position.

"Thank you," she said, looking annoyed.

A flushed Guo sat down. "Let's go upstairs to continue the

discussion. They'll bring the food to my suite so we can talk in private."

"Let's have dinner in this beautiful dining room. We can have a drink upstairs later."

"An excellent idea. I'll send up a bottle of their best French wine. I've thought about this moment many times over the years, one that deserves kindness and respect."

"I hear the stir-fried lamb is excellent," she replied without looking up from the menu.

CHAPTER 10

Wuhan: Different Every Day

MARCH 8, 2014

"Wuhan, a world power. My father's vision. Now, the dream comes true, but at a price."

Guo told her Wuhan's story.

"The city's strategic location deserves world attention. We have it all, manufacturing, high tech, no immigrant problems, and creativity, fed by one million college students from 50 universities."

"Nobody cares about Wuhan. Business owners walk through my office everyday looking for one thing, cheap workers," Jun said.

"You can't blame them. Wuhan makes people money because we control our workers. We're the backbone of the world economy."

"So that's what we are. Isn't that enough?"

"No. We think too small. We belong in the same class as Beijing, Shanghai, Guangzhou, and Shenzhen."

"We try. We have a slogan and civic improvements."

"People laugh at the city's slogan, 'Wuhan: Different every day!' They changed it to, "Different traffic jam every day" or "Different rain every day," Guo said with a wave of the hand.

"The mayor understands that the rich want to grow the city. We do our best," she said in a defensive tone.

"We need more. Wars and floods ruined our three old cities of Hankou, WuChang, and Hanyang. We'll never be a historic Xi'an or Beijing attracting tourists with ancient temples, palaces, and pagodas," Guo said.

"Maybe in time things will improve," Jun said.

"And that's why we're here. To put Wuhan on the map," he said.

"How? The Olympics?" Jun asked.

"No, Beijing holds the 2022 Winter Games."

"A film festival, football tournament, or events like Spain's running of the bulls might work but it takes years to cultivate a following," Jun said.

"A waste of time. I discovered the perfect event, the 2019 World Military Games. A military Olympics, attracting teams from 140 countries including the United States. Soldiers serve as the athletes."

"In Wuhan?"

"Yes. Wuhan can highlight China's growing military power on a world stage. A winning combination for the city, the country, and Xi Jinping."

"Never heard of it. Who'll come?"

"Many people. We'll create a spectacular event, impressing organizers of other events," Guo said with pride. "Wuhan's efficiency, beauty, and capabilities ensures the Olympics by the 2030s."

"How did the committee respond?"

"Our secret report to the mayor says Wuhan gets the 2019 Military World Games. We won't be outbid. He agreed. Our plan starts tonight."

"A sports' event requires a lot of money for new stadiums, housing, road projects, Metro lines, and parks," Jun said.

"Exactly. With our team handling specification, contract details, and collections, the 2019 Wuhan World Military Games will be like printing money," Guo said with a smile. "I have assurances of Beijing's support."

Jun reached behind her neck to unclasp the necklace before putting it into the case.

"Little gifts won't work anymore. I can buy my own jewelry if I get my fair share," she said without emotion, sliding the case back to Guo. "Send dinner to my room. Good night."

"You'll get paid. Just focus on your part without getting greedy.

Remember, a purse is just a rag until you put something in it," Guo said. "Good night, Jun."

Her tight-fitting Paris original glittered in the chandelier's light as Guo watched her swish away.

"A farm girl needs respect. The lesson's coming soon." He picked up his chopsticks to taste her lamb.

CHAPTER 11

The Lotus Flower

Li groomed the peonies, orchids, chrysanthemums, roses, and azaleas gracing Baixin's grounds with the care of a father. The development, however, had no body of water to grow his favorite flower, the lotus.

Chinese lotus flower culture grew from thousands of years of Buddhists' belief that it represented purity, long life, humility, and honor.

Li related to the lotus, known as the gentleman's flower, because it grew pure and unstained out of the mud, much like he did.

The countryside trip without Jun allowed him to relax among the lotus flowers.

"Thank you, Zigui County, for the order you bring to my life. I miss that in Wuhan. The countryside blends the lotus flowers, silent forest, and gentle waters into a peaceful paradise."

Wuhan's 24-hour-a-day noise and confusion prevented Li's conversations with nature. His spirit belonged on the bank of the small silent lake.

The shimmering water's wisdom reverberated on this early spring day as the bright sun shone through the cold, naked trees.

"How do we choose what is right?"

Li picked up a pebble and tossed it into the water. "I can pick up another stone or not. Does it really matter which one I choose or if I choose?"

"Nothing lasts, including life's choices. Make them and move on, they'll soon decompose to feed a hungry universe," the waters said in a low voice.

"I guess you're right. I chose to be a farmer and now the only thing I grow is old," Li said to the water with a faint smile.

"Yes. But choose life while you can. Don't be in a hurry to die. Embrace passion, beauty, and strength while your world still spins."

A bright reflection from the sun-struck waters blinded the farmer for a few seconds. He blinked several times trying to refocus his eyes by looking across the lake. Through the luminescence he thought he saw his wife and Jun LiJiao waving.

"Hello. Hello, dear friends," Li yelled, rubbing his eye. "I have much to say and ask."

But the glare subsided, and the vision faded. A second wave brought no response.

Li meditated for a long time before his face broke into a broad smile. The western sun rolled its light up the mountain side and the time had come to return to Wuhan.

CHAPTER 12

Cut of What?

MARCH 8, 2014

The Mercedes sped through Changshu on the G4221, the Shanghai-Wuhan Expressway. Neither Guo nor Jun had spoken for an hour.

"Let's talk. The committee and city want you to organize our World Military Games' effort. You'll manage the development proposal to attract and prepare for the games and receive a nice raise."

She blinked several times and took a deep breath. "What's my cut of the kickbacks?"

"Cut? Cut of what? We have nothing to divide. Get the games and we'll talk."

"Oh, a simple snap of the fingers? This requires a lot of work. That's part of the deal."

"The party rewards success. Make it happen and money flows into Wuhan like the mighty Yangtze."

"A proposal includes new stadiums, housing for the athletes, new highways, Metro projects, and much more. Projected costs can vary by a significant amount. Without, ah, incentive, the proposal might be conservative," she said.

"The committee adjusts costs as it sees fit. Your input serves as a starting point. As committee chairman, I have final say."

"We work well together," she said with a Hollywood smile behind her Saint Laurent sunglasses as the Mercedes sped past several cars. "Why ruin a good thing?"

The old man watched the Chinese countryside fly by for a few seconds before answering.

"Three percent of the take, net, and I'll throw in the Mercedes," he said with his palms open to the sky. "Take it or leave it. You're replaceable."

"So, let's say, the city builds a $100 million stadium. A 10 percent kickback brings in ten million. You get $9.7 million. I get $300,000 minus trumped up expenses like the retail cost of the car. No," she said shaking her head. "I want half, or I'll turn you in."

His hand crumpled the siren on his Starbucks' cup before throwing it out of the speeding car.

"Half for planning and a couple contracts? Stumble into a deal then you want to get fat. You'll disappear before anyone arrests me."

"Stumble into a deal? That's a joke. Nothing got done without me for five years. You need me. I'm the public face. Deal with it."

"Again, the game's contracting remains unclear so why negotiate now. Let's keep my proposal on the table. Get the games then we'll revisit it. OK?"

"We've played this game a thousand times. Dreams die hard old man," she thought as she nodded yes.

Guo smiled, handing over the necklace, "Now that's a good girl. Take this, you deserve it."

Her bright white teeth flashed as she slipped the Cartier box into a Speedy purse.

CHAPTER 13

Kill it Now

MARCH 9, 2014

Hao rolled over in bed, putting a pillow over her ear to block the hard rap at the front door.

"Go away," she moaned before the doorbell rang five or six times, shaking her from a deep 6 a.m. Monday sleep.

A sleepy-eyed Hao put on a robe, expecting one of her employees.

"Oh, you Li. Mad before the roosters' crow?"

"The roosters crowed long ago. Does the good farmer's wife forget the time?"

"Tell me what you want so I can ignore it and get on with my day."

Li threw 1000 dollars on the table. "Dirty money."

"Are giving it to me? Dirty money spends the same as clean."

"Guo gave it to me to forget my Zigui County trip with Jun. Only the wolf throws this much money at guilt."

"What trip? She went to Shanghai for business. She said nothing about Zigui County. You dreamt it. Be careful, old men get heart attacks chasing young women."

He drew a long shiny knife from his coat pocket, its two edges curving upward to form a fine point. He walked toward Hao.

"Put it away," she said in a whisper, clutching her nightgown.

"Don't worry. Eating pork will kill you. This knife will slit the bastard's throat."

"You're nuts! Murder a high-ranking party official? They'll kill you without a trial."

"Your husband visited me in a Zigui dream. He said 'A silky gray animal stalks my daughter. Kill it now.'"

Hao's wide eyes stared at the calm Li, shaking her head in disbelief.

"I will do what my friend asks," he said before walking out of Hao's apartment, leaving the money behind.

CHAPTER 14

I've Killed Enough

2014

Wu Tong and his cousin, Peng Qiang, grew up in the same village near YiChang.

Peng's father worked Yangtze River freighters before moving to Pacific Ocean vessels bound for the west. The letters and money soon dried up, leaving Peng's mother to raise the boy.

Wu Tong's father supported his sister and Peng on a meager teacher's salary. The small community struggled, like many in China, trying to recover from the famine of the late 1950s and early 1960s.

"Do I have to play with him? He's so big and pushes everyone around," Wu complained to his father.

"Families need support. My sister washes clothes and doesn't have time. Maybe he'll teach you something."

Wu learned a simple lesson: steer clear of his hot-headed cousin.

The poor boy's one gift, physical strength, grabbed people's attention including the YiChang Communist Party, which needed young strong men to solve problems.

The cousins drifted apart as teens, Peng becoming active in the Red Guard faction in YiChang and Wu studying 12 hours a day.

Then, murder opened doors for Peng.

The imposing man acquired Guo Zhenqin's life-long support by throwing Jun LiJiao off a balcony in 1994.

The party boss smoothed over the murder with a bogus suicide ruling. The rich man liked people who did the dirty work without complaint.

Peng had potential.

After the murder, Guo sent the violent young man to a school run by ex-Chinese secret police who trained security staff for the powerful.

The school encouraged patrons to send violent men instead of loyal ones. Loyalty comes with money while killing requires a certain innate talent. The training facility, located in the mountains near Dali, considered the young man an excellent student.

The curriculum included eliminating people without suspicion. Poisons, household and car accidents, and drug overdoses aroused less alarm than throwing farmers off balconies. Peng understood the lessons but still believed violence sent a more effective message.

Guo whitewashed his past by "killing" him in a plane crash near Tibet. The crash burned a political opponent of Guo's beyond recognition. The airplane pilot parachuted to safety, identifying Peng as the dead man. Peng then changed his name to Wu Qiang.

The strong man's main tasks involved intimidation, extortion, blackmail, and murder, if necessary, along with Guo's protection.

His work after hours included finding young girls for Guo's sexual habits. An efficient Peng delved into the active trade of young girls from Chinese farms or orphanages and Thailand and Cambodia refugees.

Cleaning the mess left him cold, but those deals paid best so he didn't complain over blood stains or half-dead kids who he threw back onto the streets.

Hints of a new business deal needing his collection skills trickled out from Guo, promising a fruitful retirement if things went well.

"I want to return to YiChang to collect ceramic camels. I've killed enough," he said to Guo when discussing the promises.

Shaking down Guo's clients was easy money. Clients paid without much trouble since Guo mostly dealt with business owners.

His scar convinced feet-dragging clients.

"Dragon fruit popped through the hole when I got slit here. Hate to see that again!" He'd show a knife and laugh. They paid.

CHAPTER 15

He's Struggling Right Now

The Hideaway wasn't hidden at all but sat on an outparcel in front of a busy shopping center on Columbus' northside.

Twinkling bottles of high-end whiskey and bourbon on glass shelves behind a long oak bar greeted patrons searching for pleasure, relief, or amnesia.

Art Iron walked in at 5:05 p.m. on a Tuesday, missing the start of happy hour by five minutes.

"Traffic's bad tonight. Central Ohio drivers suck! A little rain and it's 'Grandpa you better slowdown.' Hey Greg," he said, sitting in his usual stool, halfway down the bar.

Greg put a glass of red wine in front of Art without a word.

Half the glass went down his throat before he exhaled and looked around at the regulars, nodding or giving a half wave to the few who didn't avoid eye contact.

Greg eyed him five minutes later. "You ready?"

"I thought you forgot about me."

A bottle of the house wine appeared in the bartender's hand. Art was off and running on another Tuesday night.

Full-tilt Art kicked in around 6 p.m. when two attractive women sat next to him.

"Nice necklace," he said with a nod of the head to the dyed-blonde woman next to him.

"Do you think so? My husband bought it for me when we were in New York."

"I'm sure he cried himself to sleep that night."

"Well, as far as I remember, we had quite a time," she said with a laugh to her friend.

"Yeah, that night. What about tonight? I don't see him around. Looks like he needs to buy a jewelry store."

The woman shook her head and turned back to her friend.

"God damn women just want you to watch them spend your money. That's love to them," he said to Greg. "Whatever happened to romance?"

"Yeah Art. Marriage is tough. It takes work," Greg said.

"Was tough buddy, was," Art said with a sneer. "Now I only cry at the 15th of the month when the check's due."

He turned back to the two women.

"So, do you only sleep with him if he buys you something? You know, like flowers gets him a kiss." Art looked toward the ceiling and laughed.

"Cool it Art. She's not your ex. Two open seats down at the end of the bar ladies," Greg said with a tight smile. "He's struggling right now."

"Thanks. More room down there Lucy," the woman told her friend as Greg moved their drinks to the end of the bar.

"Struggling? Really," Art said to Greg when he brought him a new glass of wine.

"Chase my customers away and you're goin' be gone dude. Stop being an asshole."

"Hey Greg, that's what journalists are trained to be. I got a new idea. We should change the Constitution to one amendment."

Greg winced. "Alright, I'll bite. What amendment?"

"The freedom to obey. That's going to be the only freedom we'll have in a few years. The freedom to obey the government, the police, and, of course, women."

"Man, I had a woman here the other night who I'd obey," Greg said with a laugh as he poured a draft beer. "She loved some kinky stuff."

"Get serious. Everything's tapped. The government knows our every move and it's just going to get worse. We're no better than China."

"Stop the hatin' amigo. You get divorced and now you're a counter-revolutionary. One woman screwed you. Not all of them. Don't go over the edge and turn into a women-hating Hitler. It's not a good look."

"Hey, I'm no…," Art said, pounding the bar with his fist, hitting his wine and spilling it on the bar. "Sorry man. Spilled some wine."

"Time to obey me and I say you gotta go Adolph," Greg said, taking the empty wine glass away and wiping up the mess. "I won't charge you for that one."

"Yeah, yeah. Too many smart people telling me what to do anyway."

Art wobbled toward the door and the women at the end of the bar.

"Good night, ladies. Sorry for being rude. It is a nice necklace," he said, bumping into the door frame as they looked away. "Your husband's a lucky guy."

A splitting headache greeted him the next morning.

"Man, got to get up before 11 if we want to survive Tony." His dog cocked his head as if agreeing while Art sat on the edge of the bed trying not to puke.

He laid back down to calm his stomach while leafing through his laptop. An Internet ad caught his eye: *Teach in China and see the world.*

"Ha! China. It's no worse. Why not? It'll surprise the hell out of those Hideaway clowns," he said clicking on the ad. "Always can say no."

Twenty minutes later the phone rang. "Hello, this is the Royal Dragon Recruitment Company. This is Bob. So, you want to go to China?"

"Well, that was quick. I didn't expect a call this morning but, yeah, I'll play along."

"When do you want to go?"

The immediate offer stunned him.

"Oh, maybe in a few months. I got a house and stuff to take care of before I can leave. Fall semester? I want to teach at a college in a big city."

"We can do that. Are you a teacher?"

"I was. Taught three years. Now I work for a newspaper about to go under."

"Beautiful. You'll love China."

Art laughed before letting out a loud burp as he hung up the phone.

"Tony, it's China baby."

The Hideaway crowd laughed at the news too.

"Moving? To China? Really? You Ok?" Greg peered at his customer with a bartender's sincerity.

"Dude, out of the blue. Cornered here. Need to stop obeying and start doin'. Maybe I can find a Chinese wife. They're hot and like to obey. That's what I need."

"Ah, you ain't going nowhere. More wine? This one's on me."

CHAPTER 16

A Little Late to the Party

FEBRUARY 1, 2015

Art kept busy the next nine months by selling everything he owned, renting his house, flying to China, getting diarrhea several times, getting lost and confused many times, and finishing his first semester teaching English at Wuhan's Jianghan University.

A 10-day vacation to Thailand's sunny international beaches following the semester left both China and The Hideaway behind.

"Man. a little late to the party but who knew? More to life than a Columbus barstool. Thailand was spectacular," he told a confused Asian Air stewardess before the jet touched down Super Bowl XVIX Monday in Hong Kong.

"A subway to Shenzhen then a train to Wuhan. Might catch a bit of the game and still be home by 1 p.m. Should be perfect," he thought as he walked into the train's ticket office.

"You speak English?"

"A little," came out of the small, round mouth of the Shenzhen train station clerk as he glanced down behind the smudged window.

"Good. One ticket on the next rain to Wuhan," Art ordered. The clerk's head nodded. The short slender man tapped on the computer at a rapid pace.

The ticket seller's eyes widened. He looked up, "Sorry. All tickets sold today."

"Really? Today's 10 trains sold out?" Art's eyes now widened. "How about tomorrow?"

"No seats. Next three days except one seat for $1700," he said, shrugging his skinny shoulders. "Ticket brokers buy them all for holiday travel."

"Well, that ain't right. Seventeen hundred?" Art winced. Things began to melt on the warm day. China veterans had warned him not to travel during the Chinese New Year.

"You want ticket?"

"No. I don't have $1700. Where's the bus station?"

"Go out and turn right. Straight to big building," the slight ticket seller said without emotion.

An energetic 20-something stopped Art as he walked into the blinding sun.

"You need bus?"

Art grabbed his wallet, squinting at the street hustler.

"Uh, yeah. Where can I get a ticket to Wuhan? Wu-HAN." Art looked back to the ticket office then turned to the hustler with a look of disbelief.

"Wuhan?" He placed a hand on Art's shoulder.

"Yeah, Wu HAN. Bus."

"Come," he said weaving through the crowd until reaching a small office. Twenty metal chairs lined two walls. Twelve people sat among piles of luggage.

The salesman went behind the counter, tore out a scrap of newspaper, and wrote.

"Wuhan. 2.2-2.3, 10 am" with a crude drawing of a stickman in a bed. "Bed," he said to Art, pointing to the drawing with a smile. "Get there tomorrow."

"The Chinese gray dog." Art pulled out his wallet, smiling at the young man who nodded with glee.

The salesman took his seven-hundred-Chinese dollars before leading him to a chair next to a beautiful young Chinese woman.

"Wuhan," the young salesman said pointing to Art.

"Wuhan," he said again, pointing to the young woman.

"I guess we're going to Wuhan," Art said with a smile.

She lowered her eyes and said nothing as the salesman waved and left to find more fresh fish at the train ticket office.

A buzz of "Wuhan" reverberated through the waiting room several hours later.

The young woman stood, so Art did too, following 12 Chinese bus riders and a stern-looking gentleman through the immense Shenzhen railway/bus/subway complex to a backdoor and a standard-size van.

"No way 12 people, all this luggage, and a driver fit," Art said to the woman who looked away. But homemade benches along the van's sides provided seats while the driver stacked the luggage to the ceiling between the two sides.

The driver yelled then punched the gas pedal, sending suitcases flying as passengers ducked or covered up to prevent broken noses or busted teeth. A flying suitcase smashed into the window above Art's head.

"Jesus Christ. Watch it," he shouted at the driver who laughed while speeding down a wide palm-tree-lined boulevard.

Fifteen minutes later the van pulled into a shopping center. A large Chinese man dressed in a bright blue suit met the van with an impatient look. He led them into a large room resembling a bus station where others waited.

Twenty minutes later the large man received a large sum of cash from the van driver before waving 35 passengers toward the back parking lot.

A new bright blue bus drove into the lot and parked in front of the passengers.

"That's not too bad," Art thought as the shiny bus stopped.

Ten seconds later a 30-year-old canary yellow double-decker bus chugged into the lot bellowing smoke before lumbering into a spot next to the new bus.

Two shady characters got off the bus, greeted the big man, then looked around to make sure no one recognized them.

A wave went to the travelers to get on the dirty yellow bus.

"The odds of that bus making a twenty-hour trip is 50/50 at best," Art thought, sensing an adventure not quite as fun-filled as Thailand.

The drivers threw the luggage into the bus storage area except for Art's duffle bag. The big man tossed it near the bus door, flicking his finger first at Art then toward the bus door before wiping his hands clean.

"No white privilege on this trip," Art said with a laugh, giving a get-screwed smirk.

The passengers entered the bus to find 36 beds, three rows of upper and lower steel bunks, singles by the windows and doubles in the middle, separated by two aisles. A quarter-inch pad and dingy brown blankets covered each bed. The bus contained no toilet, seats, or storage space.

Art stumbled down one aisle looking at the hostel on wheels before deciding on an upper berth next to a window.

A metal ladder took him up to his bunk. He swung his luggage over the railing, jumped into the bed, and hit his head on the ceiling. A crew member yelled, pointing at his shoes.

"Yeah, yeah, sorry. Don't mess up the mattresses," Art said, pulling a tennis shoe off. Patong Beach sand flew out of the shoe and onto the bed. He brushed the sand once before the guy across the aisle brushed his hand toward Art's bunk.

"Sorry. I guess I own the sand." Art said with a wave and smile.

"Swishing sand in a coffin-sized bed along with a duffle bag between my legs for 20 hours. A diabolical Chinese torture," Art thought with a laugh.

Each two-foot wide and six-foot long steel bunk provided an incline at the head of the bed to create a place to sit up, creating a small cubby hole for feet for the bunk behind.

"Home sweet home for the next day. I don't think I'm claustrophobic," he said, touching the bus's ceiling with his elbow while lying in the bed.

The bunk had no pillow, so he pulled out a dirty t-shirt to cover his duffle bag which worked except for the buckle jamming into his neck.

The double-decker rolled out at 2:15 p.m. The large dirt-caked windows dimmed the bright southern China sun as the bus hit the 12-lane Shenzhen highway.

Art tried to sweep away any hard feelings over the sand with the young man in the next berth.

"Hello," Art said, leaning up on his elbow with a smile.

"Ni hao," he said back to a disappointed Art who had hoped for an English response. He laid down and watched the palm trees fly by.

"Did I get hustled? That hustler jumped on me like he knew what I needed. I'm probably on a bus to KuMing. Oh well, another Chinese adventure."

The double-decker bus hit the open road with increased speed. Curves and changing lanes made the bus sway like a pine tree in a stiff breeze.

"It's on two god-damn wheels," an alarmed Art muttered as the big yellow bus sped around a sharp bend.

Bus crash headlines filled his mind …"37 killed in fiery Chinese bus crash. Only driver survives."

Last month a Chinese TV program showed a bus interior during an actual crash. People flew around like lottery ping pong balls. Art looked from side to side.

"Do I want the bus to roll onto my side where the large windows cut me to shreds or the other side and a 15-foot fall into several steel beds? Hmmm."

Dusk approached as the bus headed into the mountains. Sharp curves and downhill speed increased the G-force on the double-decker bus, making sleep impossible.

Art's damp palms gripped the bed's railing as night descended. A vivid imagination turned steep curves and flashes of light into spectacular crashes over cliffs.

He closed his eyes to shut out the car lights flashing in the front window. A semi-conscious dream took him on a stroll with his wife on a sunny Ohio day. A vicious argument erupted between them as her head turned into a sudden, violent storm that ripped the fabric of the universe into pieces.

Art jerked up in terror, letting out a scream before hitting his head on the ceiling.

His buddy across the aisle cleared his throat, an international sign of, "Shut up you crazy fool."

An audible sigh of relief flowed through the bus with a midnight pitstop at a rundown concrete building near the peak of the mountainous highway.

A cold, strong wind swept down the ridge, smacking passenger faces as they trotted across a gravel parking lot into a crude restroom.

A line of men stood along a wall to urinate, letting the steamy yellow liquid trickle into a small trough and out into the parking lot. The strong restroom odors brought Art back to reality like a punch to the face.

The hungry passengers then went into a small restaurant with pans of hot food set on tables. The owners, a young married couple, took six dollars for the food that diners piled on tin plates.

"Please eat as much as you want," the man said to Art in excellent English. "Are you from America? Do you like Chinese food?"

Art laughed. "Every Chinese person asks me those two questions. Yes, I am and do. Thank you so much."

The tapping of chopsticks on tin plates created a melodic symphony in the mountain-top hole as the hungry American inhaled the surprisingly excellent food.

The satisfied passengers drifted back toward the bus as the stars shone bright in the clear, cold mountain air. A fellow passenger offered Art a cigarette.

"No, thank you," he said. "Shi-shi." A woman passenger offered candy.

"They're trying to calm my nervous ass down so they can sleep," Art thought while smiling at the woman and tilting his head like Tony had done to him many times.

The 20-hour bus ride ended when a crew member yelled "Wuhan" into Art's sleeping face. He grabbed his duffle bag and scrambled off the bus with four people bus including the young woman from the bus station.

Art stepped off the bus at a crossroad where farm fields stretched in every direction. The bus pulled away.

The American looked in each direction only to see fallowed fields.

"Where's the freakin' bus station? Wuhan must be miles away in who knows what direction."

He pulled out his wallet and counted 47 Chinese dollars and a Wuhan Metro card. His shoulders slumped as he closed his eyes.

The young woman walked down the side road to a man standing next to a car so Art began to follow her.

The Chinese man waiting shouted to Art, "You go to Wuhan? You share taxi?"

Art exhaled, jogging toward the car with a large smile.

"Yes. Yes. I can help pay. Thank you very much. Get me to a Metro stop and I'll be fine," he said patting the young man's back.

Ninety minutes later the duffle bag and part-time pillow landed with a thud on a slate gray couch in a freezing apartment. The bedroom had opened drawers and materials from a bookcase strewn about the room.

"Guess I was messy when I left," he thought, shaking an exhausted brain.

A knock on the door surprised him. His neighbor, Jack, looked upset when he opened the door.

"Did they rob you too?"

CHAPTER 17

We Work as a Unit

FEBRUARY 6, 2015

"How do we know you had money?" Ann, the Jianghan University International Office supervisor, peered at Art with resolve.

"Why would I lie? Somebody took 500 US dollars from my apartment. Maybe the crooks wanted money, or someone wanted to look around. Either way, it's gone."

"The police report said someone broke into your apartment the night you left. They climbed onto your second-story balcony."

"Or walked in using a key. Somebody knew I was gone thanks to your office. Refund my money."

Ann shook her head no.

"Whatever," Art said, walking out of the office, knowing an argument caused her to lose "face," guaranteeing failure if not repercussions. "That money's gone."

Keeping his mouth shut paid off. Five days later the university offered him a side job teaching English in the Wuhan mayor's office starting in March. The job paid $500.

Jianghan University served as the local Communist Party's employment agency. The university provided the party teachers or volunteers when asked.

The mayor's office wanted an American teacher for three female employees who dealt with English speakers from time to time.

The students included Chao, a kind, thoughtful, and quiet

accountant, Bo, the pushy head of the city's business office, and the mayor's stylish chief of staff, Jun.

"Hello, hello, hello," he said with wide eyes and a smile when the three attractive English-speaking adult women walked into class. These were no off-limits' 18-year-old coeds who populated his university classes.

The class soon evolved into trips to nearby restaurants, parks, and museums. The Chinese countryside served as "extra credit" on free Sundays.

The women enjoyed the class as it provided a break from the 9-9-6 work schedule, 9 a.m. to 9 p.m., six days a week.

"Today's English lessons was very good. The mayor is happy," Jun said at the end of a class after several weeks. "I work many hours each week, so this is my only free activity other than Sunday walks with my friend, Li."

"Well thank you. I appreciate your kind words Jun, And, thank you too, ladies," Art said to Bo and Chao with a brief nod while staring at Jun.

Bo and Chao whispered as they left the class.

"She's so innocent when the teacher comes but acts like a Shanghai whore when he goes," Bo told Chao, glancing behind her to make sure no one else heard her. "You know she fucks Guo for money. Where do you think she gets those clothes?"

"Please, say nothing," the nervous Chao pleaded.

A weekend English class to Hanyang's Tanghu Park provided Art an opportunity to approach Jun as Bo and Chao searched for photo opportunities.

"Why don't just the two of us go to lunch one day? I'd like to learn more about you. Our own private lessons. On the house. You can teach me about Chinese culture while we practice English," he said, leaning in close to the young beauty.

"The blossoms is very pretty. No?" Jun took a close look at a low-hanging branch as the sun reflected off her beautiful silk blouse.

"Are very pretty. Yes. Lunch maybe?"

"The Chinese work as a unit," Jun said. "No time for private lunches."

"I'll ask again," he said with a smile. "I hear the Chinese refuse gifts or invitations two or three times before accepting. I might turn your no into a yes."

The woman flashed a smile without answering.

"Teacher, please come now. Chao looks beautiful in the garden. Please sit with her and I take photo for you," Bo yelled from 50 yards away.

The scream ended the conversation. Stuffing his hands into his pocket, Art marched back to the rest of the unit as Jun took out her phone.

CHAPTER 18

You're Here to Learn

MARCH 17, 2015

"Not today Teacher Art. Too many meetings," Jun whispered into the phone, trying to keep her intentions private. The phone line went silent for a few seconds.

"I can schedule a special class."

"No. Class meets Tuesdays at 2 p.m. Do not change." She hung up without a goodbye.

Art punched the end button with the twist of his index finger before turning to Bo and Chao.

"Just the three of us today. No Jun. Get out your workbooks and turn to page 23," he said without looking up from his phone.

"You said we'd go to hotpot today," Bo said. "Chao wore a very pretty dress."

"I changed my mind, page 23," he said, leafing through the workbook.

Bo feigned sorrow before whispering to Chao. "She's too busy for these classes. Now that he no longer smells her expensive perfume, he'll start paying more attention to you."

Chao just shook her head while staring at page 23.

"Workbook for two hours? We never do that," Bo said. "I know very nice restaurant. Very fun. We can learn names of all the vegetables. I'll buy."

"You're here to learn, not take a holiday."

Ten minutes later Jun sent a text: "Teacher Art my schedule does not allow me to attend class anymore. The city will pay the same for teaching two students. I enjoyed your class. Please forgive me. Jun"

A coal barge sailed down the Yangtze River outside city hall as he shoved his phone into his jeans.

The next week a part-time job as language editor for the city's English newspaper became available. Art accepted the job with the hope a change back to journalism would do him good.

CHAPTER 19

A Newspaper Echo Chamber

MAY 21, 2015

Wuhan's English newspaper, the *Changjiang Weekly*, served the city's expats, foreign diplomats, and visitors.

English-speaking editors polished stories written by Chinese journalists highlighting the city's tourist destinations such as the Yellow Crane Tower and East Lake, local fashion, international music shows, Chinese culture, and non-stop appeals for foreign investors.

The newspaper was beefing up its staff to target a new audience, the World Military Games Selection Committee. The military leaders had started visiting the city in its quest to find a host for the 2019 World Military Games.

The newspaper covered the game's selection committee inspections like a visit from Queen Elizabeth.

"These military con men could make a forty-year-old bride feel special," Art told the editor after six months. "They just want your money. No one's coming to those games."

"The party and city believe hosting the World Military Games puts us on the international map."

"No one's ever heard of it in America. Who wants to see a bunch of soldiers pretending to be athletes?"

An echo chamber went into high gear. The paper quoted games' officials and city leaders who exchanged love notes before, during, and after visits all commenting on the beauty of a generous and grateful Wuhan.

The newspaper paid Art extra to provide journalism and editing lessons to the Chinese editors which were promptly ignored.

"Why not publish actual news instead of propaganda? If pickpockets work a busy shopping area like Jianghan Road, then the newspaper should warn its citizens. That's news," Art told the newspaper's chief editor.

"A police matter. People don't want the truth. Our readers want what they believe. We publish news people will read."

"Not so sure about that. Did you ask them?" Art laughed.

"People believe a great sports event is coming to the world's most beautiful city," the editor said, ending the conversation.

The committee, after squeezing the last concessions from the city, announced on page 1 of the *Changjiang Weekly* the news Wuhan craved:

"On May 21, 2015, Bahrain Colonel Rafael Al-Sharma, the president of the International Military Sports Council, made the announcement at a congress of the organization in Kuwait City that China's megacity of Wuhan, central Hubei province, has been picked to host the 2019 World Military Games."

Yu Kaiping, head of the Chinese military delegation, pledged Wuhan "will do all it can to make the sports event a success."

CHAPTER 20

Lies and Jealousy

MAY 21, 2015

"Li wants to kill Guo. He believes LiJiao sends him messages in his dreams," Hao told her girlfriend, Wei, after dancing in the courtyard. "He'll pay full price for those dreams."

"A man like that needs a woman to calm him down," Wei said.

"Wei, he's too far gone."

"Everyone connects you two. You're in trouble if he kills to protect FuMin," Wei said, patting Hao's arm.

"Guo's relationship with her drives Li crazy. Maybe she can help. She has a way with him."

"With many men, including an American I saw here once," Wei said, letting out a snort. "Get her married, raising babies like my daughter. Let me show you the new photos of my grandson. He's so cute."

Hao ignored Wei's photos, staring out across the river.

"A murder stirs up the rumors of her beautiful clothes and jewelry. The neighbors talk about it. What they say is not pretty," Wei said as she put away her phone.

"Lies and jealousy from people who just complain about others' good fortune."

"Murder investigations lead to talk about good and bad fortunes. You don't want that to happen," Wei said with a shake of the head.

Hao nodded without a word.

"Get your daughter to talk with Li. He'll listen to her like all men do."

C H A P T E R 2 1

You're Just Hustling Me

M A Y 2 2 , 2 0 1 5

"WUHAN TO HOST 2019 WORLD MILITARY GAMES."

The *Changjiang Weekly*'s cover shouted in 96-point type the city's spectacular achievement.

Two 14-hour days produced a 36-page games' special edition. The Chinese staff editors and the Wuhan Communist Party, spearheaded by Jun, approved final copy touting the massive investment by the city.

Guo set up a congratulatory meeting with her at a small Thai restaurant in the International Plaza in midtown Wuhan. Many of Jun's gifts had been purchased at its upscale retailers such as Gucci and Burberry.

"My friend, I miss you," Guo said as she strolled in 35 minutes late. "How are you?"

"Givenchy is having a sale. Had to stop in. Hope I'm not too late," she said flashing a smile.

Bright, white teeth and a classic Balmain double-breasted blue blazer captured Guo's hungry gaze.

"Yes, a gift is appropriate for your fine work on getting the games. Let's see if something catches your eye after lunch," Guo said in a warm tone.

"The trinket days are over Guo. Are we partners or not?"

"You know I need your help. This will be the same as the other jobs. I'll write the specs for the job with the help of our contractors, you get them through the city."

"For what? You steal millions from the city, and I get a purse or a pair of shoes? No more. I've learned a lot. It's time to fly away. Maybe Beijing."

"You can't run away from those gifts you received. Enough people know."

"Some old rich man tried to bribe me for something he'll never get. Judges will feel sorry for you," she said without a smile. "You're just hustling me."

"Those gifts will put you in jail. A fair agreement with me makes your great grandchildren comfortable for life. Arrangements will be made one way or another."

"So, you, Guo Zhenqin, have stolen money and will continue to steal money from the city?"

"Don't act surprised. I get paid for my work. All the necessary arrangements have been made. I'd hate to see your wonderful career end for failing to follow through with the Wuhan Games."

"I understand. What arrangements have been made?"

"I'm not going into details. Let's just say when the time comes, no one will care about Wuhan's World Military Games."

"Really? How will that happen?"

"Not your concern. Let's negotiate another day. Keep in mind, your tastes far exceed your servant's salary. Is life worth living without silk and Italian leather on your beautiful body?"

"Oh, you old fool. I've been offered three jobs this week alone exceeding my servant's salary."

"Young child, jobs are for the poor. I'm talking real money."

CHAPTER 22

She Wants Something

Snow Beer poured down Art's throat, washing away Wuhan's low-hanging smog.

This Friday night's entertainment consisted of watching African students chase a ball on the soccer field outside his apartment as a festive crowd danced to blaring Afrobeat music.

Art popped another 16 ouncer as a tall athlete with a world-class physique sprinted past a defender on a break for the goal 70 yards away.

The crowd rumbled with anticipation as the superior athlete's long strides outpaced pursuers. The goalie, an older, overweight man, waited certain embarrassment in the box.

The striker neared the net before the goalie pounced, attacking the ball with unanticipated quickness. The surprised forward tried to pivot past the goalie but was a step late, causing a tremendous collision like a Porsche hitting a dump truck at 50 mph. The forward went flying while the goalie dropped in his tracks. The ball dribbled out of bounds.

"Ohhhh," the crowd roared as Art took another sip of beer. "Way to take one for the team old man," he yelled as an unrecognized cellphone number rang.

"Teacher Art, this is Jun. How are you?"

"Great Jun. I didn't know the number. Almost didn't pick up. Thought it was another Chinese spam call," he said with enthusiasm. "Nice to hear your voice again. It's been a minute."

"Been busy. You doing anything? I'm leaving a meeting in Hanyang. Have you had dinner?"

"About to start cooking."

"Well don't. Meet me at Gate 1 in 20 minutes. We'll catch up over food."

"A random Friday night call after eight silent months? She misses me. No. She wants something. Women don't call without a reason," he thought while walking back to his apartment to change clothes.

A black Buick Regal pulled in front of Gate 1 as a tinted rear window eased down. Jun's blinding smile burst out of the car like a flashlight in a dark alley, a phone plastered to her ear.

Curious students stopped to watch the driver jump out to open Art's door.

"Thank you," he said to the tired man who gave him an ugly look.

"Yes, yes, yes, bye-bye, bye-bye," Jun said while smiling at Art with lively eyes.

"Jun. How are you?"

"My dear teacher, it's been too long. I missed you," she said, grabbing his elbow like a seasoned politician or pickpocket.

The smooth material on her black sleeveless Carolina Herrera bateau-neck sheath cocktail dress aroused him. A string of pearls glistened around her neck.

"You're beautiful," he said, feeling like a slob wearing black jeans and a knockoff Polo golf shirt.

"Just coming from a Honda party in the Hanyang Economic Development Zone. One of those 'so-glad-to-meet-you affairs' where everyone wants to be somewhere else on Friday night except the boss who'll work till midnight."

"Nice car. Driver looks like he wants to slit my throat."

"What do you want to eat? Fish?"

"Is that a rhetorical question? Every Wuhan meal means fish. Sure."

"I know a place you'll like."

She switched from sweet to a basic training Marine sergeant, barking orders to the weary driver who said nothing while pulling a U-turn on busy Taozhi Road, stopping traffic.

The car cruised to a restaurant near the campus in the Little Broadway district where an elevator whisked them to a private second-floor dining room.

They entered a room where a chef, wearing a European-styled 12-inch pleated white hat, stood behind a large grill.

A waitress appeared, giving Jun a wine list. "A bottle of red or white? Let's get one of each," she said to Art with a relaxed smile.

"What? When did you start drinking?"

"Just a little. I'm stressed. My life's so busy. I see no one, not even my mother. And I live with her. The mayor's chief of staff works too much."

"Stealing money keeping you busy?" Art laughed and gulped down half a glass of red wine.

"Why would you say that?"

"Thought it was funny. Covered government while working for American newspapers. Governments and crooks blend like a sweet chili sauce. Spice and honey make for an irresistible temptation."

Jun shook her head. "Let's not talk work. It's Friday night. How've you been? Are the freshmen girls in love with their cute American teacher?"

"A few photos with the teacher. Good kids. Just like you!" He laughed, as Jun's right hand drummed her manicured nails on the table while her left brushed her hand through her long silky black hair.

"I'm my mother, a mean, old lady," she said as her phone buzzed and rang. She looked at the message and number before turning the phone off. "Let's have a quiet night."

Enthusiastic talk ensued as the chef grilled an array of dishes from fish, shrimp, lamb chops, beef tips, to asparagus, and Bananas Foster complete with a four-foot flame.

Art's red wine bottle went dry before Jun put her ruby-red lips to her first glass of white wine.

"I need your help," she said between tiny bites of Bananas Foster.

"I was waiting," he said with a look of apprehension. "Will I become a Chinese political prisoner?"

"Jail? Oh no, no, no. It's simple. Just keep five small packages and mail them if, for some reason, something happens to me."

"If something happens? What in the hell does that mean?"

"Let's not go into it. The less you know, the better. Just promise me you'll mail them."

"How will I know? I haven't seen you in eight months."

"I'll keep in contact," she said with a wry smile. "Plus, my friend Qin will call if necessary. Please say yes?"

"Geezus, I don't know. I'd ask why but who wants to listen to bullshit. Ok, on one condition."

"What's that?"

"The two of us meet once a month, visible proof of your well-being. I think that's fair."

"I was hoping you'd ask."

CHAPTER 23

A Delicate Matter

MAY 28, 2015

"How's Wuhan's best salesperson? I hope well," Guo asked Hao in an upbeat tone over the phone.

"Oh, I'm honored to speak to you. I haven't done anything wrong, have I?"

"No, no Hao. I want to take you to lunch to thank you for your great service to Baixin. You made us rich. I should have done it sooner. Can we meet tomorrow?"

"Of course."

"A car will pick you up at the office at 11:45 a.m. I look forward to seeing you."

The driver arrived at 11:30 as Hao prepared in the office's restroom.

The mirror reflected no flaws as heavy pancake makeup covered a pock-marked face that she blamed on malnutrition as a youth.

Her feathered red hair, cut in a layered bob, took 10 years off her age. "I'm still sexy in short bursts," she said, laughing in the mirror.

The spanks under her tight black leather pants produced a slim illusion but two or three pounds needed to go. A Kobi Halperin one-button red leather jacket over a low-cut blouse intended to distract if not entice the richest man in her life.

A quick head shake produced a carefree look that turned the driver's head when she walked into the office's waiting room.

"A celebratory lunch with Guo? He celebrates making money or getting laid by young women, not lunch with a fat 55-year-old employee," she thought as they left the office.

The car headed to a Japanese sushi restaurant near the New World Trade Center in midtown Hankou where numerous bars and restaurants attracted the city's westerners on weekends.

Guo strolled in 40-minutes late, dressed in all black but with a rare smile.

"So good to see you. Thank you for joining me. You know, I've trusted you since Baixin's early days."

Stress-induced dark circles around his eyes blended with dyed jet-black hair near the ears to create an illusion of a mask.

A sushi platter for two and plum tea arrived without saying a word to the waitress.

"This hidden gem sits among the despicable bars like the Belgian Bar across the street. Westerners prey on our young girls there. I've tried to close them, but others say we need such places to be an international city."

Hao said nothing but nodded her head.

"A delicate matter needs your guidance. I trust you'll help a grateful party."

"Of course. What can I do?"

"Your daughter is now a powerful party member with my help. But, as with many young successful people, they want too much, too fast. Headstrong and uncooperative with elders. Perhaps you experienced this?"

"Since she was 12, when I stopped her from playing basketball with the boys. She's headstrong, like her father. That makes her successful, no?"

"The great Chairman Mao said, 'Service to the people.' Our youth must serve a strong China. Independent thought and a fixation on material possessions lead to weak minds as in America."

Hao shifted in her leather pants and jacket. "What can I do?"

"Talk to her. She doesn't listen to me, her most trusted mentor. Tell her to be patient. Money and power come from loyalty. China hammers the nail that stands out."

"I understand. I'll straighten her out."

"It's the best for all, including you."

Hao winced as she chewed a small piece of octopus.

One piece of salmon and a sip of plum tea finished Guo's meal, leaving a large platter of sushi for Hao to take back to share with coworkers.

"Hao, don't ignore this conversation. Remember, a good dog doesn't block the road."

CHAPTER 24

Do You like Me?

Five addressed packages, each about the size of a small book, sat on Art's table. He shook one.

"Who asks a friend to do this kind of shit?"

He picked at a corner of one before stopping.

"She's not a blackmailer, is she? Maybe she knows something big. Whatever it is, it's in Chinese so no need to open one."

A copy of *Changjiang Weekly* sat on his desk with a cover photo of Wuhan's new biosafe laboratory which held the world's most dangerous viruses.

"Hmm. Chinese Communist Party extremists dabbling in germ warfare. Hell, for the right money she'd support that. Who knows? I'll just wait for the call."

Jun held up her end of the bargain, meeting Art on Sunday afternoons once a month when she used to meet Li.

"This is nice," she said as they strolled in Zhongshan Park. Art's face turned red with a silly grin when she grabbed his hand after a few minutes.

"Will you carry my purse?"

He laughed, taking it in his left hand.

The park's aging Ferris wheel spinning in a grove of trees drew a line of fidgeting youngsters.

"They are sooo cute," she said. "Do you want to be a father?"

"Sure, but time slips away. Finding a willing and desirable partner isn't easy!" He squeezed her hand.

"I know someone who's willing." She dropped her head for a second, avoiding eye contact.

"Anyone I know?"

"Let's go ride on a swan," she said, pointing to the rental peddle-driven boats on the park's lake.

Soon the day melted into a silent memory of her sweet good-night kiss on his cheek.

"I have a surprise for you," Art said the next month, sliding a small poorly wrapped gift across the coffee shop table. "Something for the future."

She laughed tearing open the package.

"A baby rattle. Oh, Art, I love it," she cooed as the light blue toy's small beads swished with a soft sound as she shook it close to her ear.

"Your first baby toy."

The rattle came out of her purse during a lunch of fish soup and mixed vegetables, shaking it in Art's face.

"You want a baby, don't you? I bet you'd make a great dad."

"Who knows? Probably never find out. The women I like don't like me and I don't like the women who like me. Quite a dilemma."

"Do you like me?"

"Yes, very much. You know I do," he said with a stutter.

Jun smiled but said nothing.

The next Friday afternoon she called Art. "Can you make dinner tonight? I want to see you but I'm tired."

"Of course. What do you want? Fish?"

"I'll try to come by 8."

Cold WuChang fish and rice waited as Jun buzzed his apartment from outside the building at 10 p.m.

"Sorry for being late," she said. "Work never stops."

Her tired eyes drifted around the small apartment.

"Let's watch television," she said pointing to the apartment's dingy couch. "The mayor brought in food so I'm not hungry."

"Let's turn off this nasty overhead florescent light. Makes everyone look green," Art said with a laugh.

"I feel cold," she said in a soft voice.

He wrapped a blue blanket around them, trapping her sweet perfume under the covers as the flickering television cast a dim light.

"I have another gift for you. A book. It's by Herman Melville called *Moby Dick*."

"It's a long one," Jun said, holding it in her hand like she was weighing a tomato. "What's it about?"

"Ruining your life by chasing crazy dreams. An American classic," Art said.

"Does he chase money?"

"No, a whale. We all pursue something. I want a family. What do you chase?"

"I spend too much time shopping for purses, but what I want is freedom," she said with a laugh. "My father believed in dreaming with a purpose too. I'll show you."

She pulled a small red rubber ball out of her Gucci handbag.

"My father gave me this. I always have it with me," she said in a solemn tone. "He said the whole universe is no bigger than this tiny ball. Chase your dreams with care because not many will fit."

"Yeah, we all chase too many dreams and rarely succeed, but you're close," Art said with a wry smile before handing the ball back to Jun.

"A successful dream costs a lot," she said putting the ball in her handbag and pulling out a tissue to dab her eye.

The talk of fulfilled and unfulfilled dreams silenced the conversation, leaving the television to fill the void. Jun's body soon went limp, slumping into Art's chest with a soft breath.

"Let's go to bed," he whispered, helping Jun up.

'No. I must go," she said with little enthusiasm.

"No. You're staying here."

She nodded before walking into his bedroom.

CHAPTER 25

Mom? You Awake?

Emergency Couple, a Korean soap opera about two medical students who fall in love, mesmerized Hao on Tuesday nights.

Tonight, the table in front of her large sectional couch held the usual seaweed flavored chips and packaged sausage snacks.

"I need you," the young male doctor said as Hao gripped the edge of a blanket and pulled it up to her chin.

"No. My family expects me to complete my internship. Love doesn't play a part," his female counterpart replied.

"We can't escape love," he said, pulling her hand to his lips to kiss it.

The weekly show stirred the aging-beauty's memory of the 24 years of heartache since the death of her husband. The man she loved remained her beacon of light.

"My life changed so much. Would I still be happy as a farmer's wife? His death brought this life," she thought, looking at her well-furnished penthouse.

Large real estate bonus checks brought a jumbled blend of celebration, guilt, and longing.

"Does money matter without love? Would I trade my success to be an old farmer's wife tending chickens?"

Love won on this Tuesday night as the evening's warm breeze blew in memories of sitting by a lake, kissing her lover under the stars.

"Why did they take you? So young and handsome," she said to the television actor who she thought resembled her young husband.

The show's ending let her eyes close on a game show with clownish characters until Jun slipped in the door after 10 p.m.

"Mom? You awake?"

The sleeping woman stirred, rolled onto her back, and coughed.

"Yes. Dozed off watching my show, waiting for you."

A half-eaten bag of chips and a couple magazines on the table told Jun about her mother's evening.

"Didn't you dance tonight? The weather's perfect," Jun asked as she opened the refrigerator to a few bottles of water and last night's noodles. "No dinner again? Keeping me skinny mom. I need nourishment."

"Evil chased me away. That mean-spirited old woman who lives downstairs kept spitting out ugly questions."

"What did she say?"

"Where is your daughter tonight? How does a government worker acquire such beautiful clothes? She must work overtime doing who knows what?" Hao laughed at her witch-like imitation of the woman.

"Those who have nothing, know nothing," Jun said, grabbing the noodles and chopsticks.

"Old windbags made me so mad I couldn't stay. Talk, talk, talk about you. Who knows if they have a cousin or friend who wants to buy a unit? It is hard work maintaining our reputations."

Jun shrugged as she slurped the cold noodles.

"How was work? Did you see Guo Zhenqin today?"

"He wants to meet. No free time right now."

"We had lunch yesterday at the sushi restaurant across from the Belgian Café. We had a nice talk," Hao said.

"Good. Let him try to get into your pants so he'll leave me alone."

"Now FuMin. Respect Guo. He wants what's best."

"For him. What's he stealing now?"

"What? Such talk about a gentleman."

"He's nothing but greedy gluttony," Jun said. "Don't trust him. He devours everything. Did he threaten you?"

"No. But things might be better by working with him. I don't know what he's referring to but I'm sure you do."

"He'll get his chance. Go to bed. I have work to do."

"One more thing. Li's getting jealous of Guo. He bought a knife on his visit to YiChang. Threatens to use it on him for leading you down dark paths."

"Ahh. I love Li. The sweetest man. He's not killing anyone. Against his nature. He just loves dad and me. But I'm not so sure about you!"

"He loves to say I look fat so I'm not so crazy about him either. Just make sure he doesn't act like a stupid farmer."

"Stupid? Not so sure." Jun stared into the carton of noodles.

"Just talk to him. You're exhausted and don't make sense. Go to bed soon."

"Sure mom," she said, knowing the clock would say 2 or 3 a.m. before sleep. Planning and shopping came first.

"She's got her father's arrogance," Hao thought as she changed into her pajamas. "That got him killed."

A smile crossed Hao's face as she climbed into bed as thoughts of *Emergency Couple* retreated into the darkness until the following week when a big-screen television in a spacious living room left her feeling small and alone again.

CHAPTER 26

Watch Me

"My Reign Hotel suite. Excellent service. Food, drink, no interruptions," Guo said over the phone as he stretched his painful back.

"An excellent hotel but a private room in the Zhifang Excellent Restaurant on Eryao Road works better. I'd feel safer," Jun said.

"We need to be disciplined in how we finish our business. Going to unknown restaurants puts us in a bad position," he said, smacking his hand against his thigh in a rhythmic pattern.

"Being near city hall allows access to more information if needed. Han Street is so far away," she said. "Being close helps. Please?"

"My back hurts due to recent rains. The comfortable hotel will make me a generous negotiator."

"Let's postpone to a later date when you feel better."

"No. This needs immediate attention. Arrangements must be completed so we can move forward without delay. Meet me at the hotel at 10 a.m. tomorrow."

"I meet with the Sports Center people for stadium renovations at noon. You're going to want me there. That only gives us 45 minutes."

"The yo-yo goes back and forth. You win. I'll come to the restaurant in the morning. Be prepared to deal. No time for wild requests or indecisive attitudes. We have a lot of work to do."

Billowy clouds of pollution hung low over the nearby Yangtze River at 8 a.m. when the restaurant owner unlocked the front door.

"My friend, we are ready for your important meeting," he said to the young woman who he treated like a daughter.

"Thank you for getting up so early. You are always too kind," Jun said with a child's smile.

Audio-visual equipment, charts on easels, and printed documents filled the room. A spread of steamed buns, fruit, hot water, tea, and hard-boiled eggs sat on a white tablecloth, compliments of the owner.

Peng weaved Guo's Buick Regal through Hankou's buzzing streets as mothers with children zipped by on motorcycles, store clerks trudged to the pedestrian street to sell sneakers, jewelry, and clothes and city employees, dock workers, and museum ticket-takers headed toward the river.

"Park nearby without drawing suspicion. Sit outside the meeting room. Who knows what that crazy bitch will do? I'll send a message if I need anything."

"Good luck boss."

"Being smart creates luck," Guo said wincing as he got out of the car's backseat, his back sore from falling onto a WuChang hotel marble floor two days ago trying to whip a teen.

"How's your back? The restaurant provided a chair," Jun said, pointing to a large leather chair.

"Let's get this over with," Guo said, sinking into the comfortable chair that left him several inches below Jun.

"My staff prepared charts and graphs outlining projects and projected costs. The World Military Games' cost exceeds ten billion dollars," Jun said, pointing to an array of material circling the room. "Not all projects need our attention, just the solid ones."

"I know how it works. Move on."

A 200-page book titled "The Wuhan Games" outlined projected costs for 13 new sports' facilities, 17 remodeled ones, and five temporary venues along with an athletes' village, a new four-story media building, 1300 kilometers of renovated roads, two new Metro lines, 360,000 new trees and countless beautification projects such as lighting the bridges and buildings throughout the city.

"Coordinating 70 to 100 projects requires care. My staff will provide logistics, but I worry about you. A three-year project at your age and health may be challenging."

Guo jumped up before flinching in pain. "My family helped build Wuhan for 80 years. I'll do my job. Do yours," he said through clenched teeth.

"That's never a problem. I'll handle legislation and specifications, but we need to be flawless."

"How can you put a price on 80 years of construction experience? Each contractor a long-time acquaintance with much guanix built. Without this necessary element we approach strangers who place us in harm's way."

"Success comes with today's performance not what dead men did years ago. What's your proposal?"

"Again, three percent of any money made, minus expenses plus gifts as well. That gets you three million dollars. Quite a haul for a farm girl. And the Mercedes is yours." He sipped a glass of plum tea, hiding a small smile.

Jun stood, closed her notebook, and began packing.

"Thank you but we're too far apart. Why waste time? I'll do my job as the city and party require. Nothing more."

"The foolproof plan involves more sophistication and cost than you realize. You know too much to let walk away."

"Watch me soar like a bird."

"Let me tell you a story about a city employee who received many gifts for questionable actions. A violation of Chinese law. Questions came up, embarrassing the family. Several key witnesses testified. The employee received a long jail sentence and the shamed family suffered. A sad tale."

"I might not do that. Listen to this." She pushed play on a recorder on the table.

Jun's voice spoke: "So, you, Guo Zhenqin, have stolen money and will continue to steal money from the city? Is that right?"

"Don't act surprised. I get paid for my work. All the necessary arrangements have been made. I'd hate to see your wonderful career go down in flames due to failing to follow through with my plan for the Wuhan Games."

She stopped the tape. "There's more but why waste time? Thought you might want a taste before arresting me. Might get messy in Beijing."

"Wise move. Two percent of the project cost is my new offer along with all copies of the tape. Our Beijing insurance costs serious money. Our technical advisors want upfront money that I must pay out of pocket. Hard to estimate the costs right now," he said as his thumb and index finger held his chin.

"Five percent of total project costs after paying Beijing."

"You want half? Harsh considering the plan's built on my money, ideas, and contacts."

"Three percent. That makes it 70/30. Plus, ten percent interest for your financing costs," she said smiling. "I'll give you the tapes when I get paid. And I get the Mercedes."

"Hmmm. Realize no money till one year after the games conclude and I'm repaid in full for out-of-pocket costs at 20 percent interest. A British Virgin Islands' account will be set up in any name you'd like. That's a long time for a tape to hang over my head but I'll survive."

"Twenty percent interest? Ok, but I want one million dollars in U.S. Treasury bonds upfront as insurance in case you cheat me. My Sports Center meeting takes place in 45 minutes. Thank you for all you've done."

"Treasury bonds? If it's necessary. One piece of advice. Stay away from the American, an immoral man who draws attention from party leaders."

"Don't look," she said with a disarming smile.

"You've been warned," the old man said with an unforgiving look before leaving.

"She has me on tape. Find out who's holding them for her Peng."

"Won't take long," the burly guard said, holding the door open for the hobbling Guo. "She's no crook."

CHAPTER 27

No Need to Worry

Peng tracked the tape's likely location within several hours to either the American or Jun's friend, Qin Leiho.

A China Mobile manager building guanix with Guo pulled Jun's cell-phone records. Evening calls went to Qin's number and occasionally Art's with day calls going to city officials, vendors, businesspeople, restaurants, and her mother.

"Start with the American," Guo said. "Get his teaching schedule from the university then search his room."

Peng nodded.

"Photograph the tapes if you find them but don't take them. Leave the room as you find it," Guo said.

Guo cited security concerns when getting the room key from a university administrator and party member.

Peng found four packages sitting on Art's desk, addressed to a newspaper editor, police detective, and two city hall employees.

"A voice-cloning expert will create a tape to put in its place. Jun and Hu Jin discussing a plan to steal money," Guo said to Peng when he returned from Art's apartment.

"Why you screwing Hu? He's on the executive committee. What he do?"

"Don't trust him. Need to shut him up. When she panics, her idiot American friend will mail the tapes. That'll fuck her better than he ever could," Guo said with a forced laugh.

"Not sure a fake tape will fool anyone."

"It's not me on the tape, you idiot. That's all that matters. When the tapes are ready, wrap them in the same paper. Make sure the American sees you near his room. Fear will chase away other emotions in his small heart."

The bodyguard paid off the apartment superintendent for his second visit. A borrowed toolbox gave Peng the look of a repairman.

The tapes remained on Art's desk in the small living room. Peng admired the resemblance before placing them in a new location on the desk.

Music played in the apartment across the hall, so Peng knocked on the door.

Jack, a Canadian English teacher, answered.

"Fix toilret," Peng said while pointing to Art's door. "Tell him."

"So what," Jack said, slamming the door in his face.

"Asshole," Peng said with a smile.

The big man talked with the superintendent outside the building when Art arrived.

"Key. 2B," Art thought he heard Peng say as he passed the hulking repairman with a scar across his face.

"Hey, that's my room. Was this guy in my apartment?"

"He fixed water pipe," the Chinese woman said. "All fixed."

Peng nodded with a look of disdain as Art shook his head, "Nothing better be missing."

The next morning Art received an official request for an afternoon meeting in the school's International Office.

The office secretary told Art the police needed to do a check-up on foreigners.

"No need to worry. Officer Ling from Wuhan police wants to ask a few questions. Please go to conference room."

A smiling policeman sat near a video camera set to tape the conversation when Art entered the room.

"Please sit here," Officer Ling said in excellent English, pointing to a chair in front of the running camera.

"Now your passport shows you are American. Is that correct?"

"I am."

"The university provided your resume. At one time you worked for the American government. Do you still work for the government?"

"My government didn't want me anymore. I came here to marry a Chinese woman."

"I see. How long do you plan to stay?"

"Long as I have a visa."

The officer shifted in his seat, then continued, "Now Mr. Iron, how long did you work in the Wuhan mayor's office?"

"Eight months. You should know that Officer Ling."

"I do."

"Then why ask?"

"We want you on the record."

"On record? What record? Am I under investigation?"

"This is a regular procedure with all teachers."

"They're on record and videotaped as well?"

"That's not your concern. Now let's move on. Who do or did you tutor in the mayor's office?"

"You know that too. Why are you wasting time asking silly questions? Can I see your identification?"

"The university will verify my position. Do or did you spend private time with any of them?"

"We went to parks and restaurants to practice English. Many teachers do that. We consider it teaching."

"Do you know Jun FuMin? Is she a student of yours?"

"She was."

"Do you or did you spend private time with her?"

"As I said, as a teacher."

"Are you sure that's your answer?"

"Of course, and what business is it of yours what adults do with private time? That's not against the law."

"Just making sure our guests are safe Mr. Iron. Nothing more."

"Safe? She's dangerous?"

"Now one last question. Do you provide tapes or any audio-visual materials to your students?"

"Each instructional book has such materials that students use."

"Nothing that you provide?"

"No."

"Thank you for your time. Goodbye."

"Sure, buddy boy."

CHAPTER 28

What Insurance?

The large white face twitched on the Reign Hotel's big-screen television.

"A repulsive terrorist. Makes me nauseous," Guo said shaking his head. "Probably a fat CIA operative."

"A guilty look," Peng said as they watched a replay of Art's International Office performance that Officer Ling dropped off.

The officer's son had his eye on attending Wuhan University the following year, so a favor by Officer Ling might build a little guanix and help the odds.

"Maybe he'll remember our relationship next spring," the officer told his hopeful son. "Helping our leaders succeed leads to our success."

"Quite combative. Typical. He fooled the naïve Jun that he loves her and will take her to America," Guo said, bristling at Art's performance. "He just wants to screw her."

Peng grunted. "Looks like he got home. You need to see this. The school's surveillance camera shows Jun entering his building at 10 p.m. last Friday and not leaving till early the next morning."

"She spent the night with the American pig! I expected more," Guo said, pounding his fist on a table. "A woman's virginity shows good character. Virginity shows love, responsibility, and virtue. The whore needs punished."

"Let's take out the American. An accident maybe? Not a problem," Peng said.

"Let's not try to catch two frogs with one hand. Jun remains an asset while any harm to the American brings trouble. Especially if he's secret police. Accidents can wait. Turn that fucking TV off."

Guo gazed at the busy Han River bridge next to the hotel for several minutes before turning to Peng.

"Let's walk through this. Jun thinks the tape screwed me, so she'll do her job in hopes of a huge payday that's never coming. You do a solid job collecting. The insurance price is the only deal killer."

"What insurance boss?"

"Nothing you need to know. Just a plan that assures success."

Guo smiled at a pensive Peng.

"Let's toast to our plan. Pour two glasses of champagne. A drink to our bright futures," Guo said pointing to the Dom Perignon and crystal glasses. "Let the Wuhan Games begin."

The bodyguard's wide smile stretched his scar across a beefy face.

CHAPTER 29

Honest People Fear Nothing

JULY 12, 2015

Chinese families come together on Sundays. Long-distant trains to and from Wuhan fill up with grandparents, grandchildren, farmers, and college students heading home to see loved ones.

The city's subways overflow with families arguing and laughing at persistent grandmothers trying to corral mischievous grandchildren who run and hide behind train riders.

A bright July Sunday provided a perfect time for Hao to host a dinner for Jun, Li, Wei, and her daughter's American friend.

The menu included pork ribs and lotus root soup, steamed fish cakes, fried Hongshan caitai, and Hubei duck.

Wei arrived early to help Hao, whose cooking skills had diminished in recent years.

"Pay attention to the heat when cooking fish cakes," Wei said shaking her head at Hao. "The water evaporates under high heat, burning the fish."

Small beads of sweat formed a ring around Hao's red lipstick. "My mind's not on cooking. Should've ordered food from Junlin Fish. I look awful."

"Worrying about Li?"

"Jun considers him family, but I always thought my family didn't kill people," Hao said.

"Li's like a child," Wei said as they prepared the duck. "But a child needs models, not critics."

"Scolding men never works. A gentle touch works best. Can you help? His talk about my weight makes me angry."

"Bad child? Guilty parent," Wei said, as the two laughed. "You get used to it."

Hao winced. "A difficult man. A nice woman like you would help. Men need wives."

"Handsome, but angry. Flowers make him smile, not women."

"Keep him calm if you can."

An inpatient, hungry man arrived at exactly 6 p.m.

"Hao, I am ready to eat. No interest in idle chatter with foolish women," he said, entering the penthouse.

"Jun's not here. Let me get you a nice glass of rice wine while we wait. You remember Wei, right?"

"No wine," he said. "I've come to eat, talk to Jun, and leave as soon as possible."

"Jun brought it home, very expensive. Try a little."

"She lives at the mercy of money," he said.

His erect motionless body sat in the straight back chair, resembling one of Hao's collection of antique teapots on the living room's glass shelves.

"Talk to Wei while I finish in the kitchen. Jun will be here in a few minutes," she said, not knowing when her daughter would arrive.

"What do you do with your time Li?"

"That's my business. Why do you care?"

An undeterred Wei continued. "You grow flowers, right? Hao said you grow Baixin's most beautiful gardens."

"This summer's rain helps. But children throw balls and crawl around, knocking the petals off fragile peonies. People need to watch their children," he said, taking a sip of rice wine.

"Would you like almonds? I brought them."

A guttural answer sounding like yes came out, so Wei patted off to the kitchen.

"Not the easiest man to talk with but he loves flowers and that's sweet," she said to Hao, preparing a bowl of almonds on a tray with an embroidered napkin.

A stilted 30-minute conversation ended when Jun and Art arrived. Jun's stunning black Alaia Jersey cross-back knee length dress perked up Li more than a second glass of rice wine.

"Leaving your father's best friend at the mercy of two cunning women? I was lucky to survive," he said to Jun with an alcohol smile.

"Two beautiful women serve wine and nuts as they cook in a hot July kitchen, and you complain? Women are not slaves in the new China," she said, as everyone laughed.

Art nudged Jun. "Does anyone speak English?"

"No. I'm sorry Art," Jun said.

"I'll act like the Buddha, smile and say nothing."

Hao and Wei brought numerous bowls of food from the kitchen to the seated guests.

Jun, the seasoned politician, wasted little time in confronting Li as the dishes of food spun around the table.

"What are your plans for the knife you bought in YiChang? Killing Guo brings dishonor to us, including your friend and my father, Jun LiJiao," Jun said in an icy tone.

"Your father died because he had the courage to say no. You lack his strength, so others take advantage of you. I'm only protecting you as your father asked me to do."

"The government will put you to death. My father wants your knowledge and wisdom to protect us, not your knife."

"A violent man only understands violence."

"Guo is a difficult man, but he has been good to me," Jun said, hands spread wide as if pleading before as court.

"No fancy perfume covers the stench of sleeping with a pig," Li said through clenched teeth.

"I am a free woman. No man touches me. We work together for our great city," Jun said.

"You have too much money for such a young woman with a government job. Wei and all the Baixin cackling hens talk about it."

Wei lowered her head, "Yes. People ask questions during evening dancing."

"Our family's finances don't concern busybodies," an indignant Hao barked. "I do well, as does Jun. Honest people fear nothing, right Jun?"

"A rich old man gives me gifts. But I refuse his advances. I accept the gifts or lose my job. What would any of you do?"

The dining room went silent as the click of chopsticks on the bowls stopped. Li folded his arms across his chest.

"That bastard's blood will drain into the sewer."

"Please do nothing for one month," Jun said. "I will not accept gifts and stay away when possible if you agree to not to kill him."

Li unfolded his arms, looking at his bowl and chopsticks. "Thirty days. Then if nothing changes, I will do what's necessary."

"More rice wine Li?" Wei smiled, trying to calm the agitated man.

"Enough strange talk." Li rose from the table, giving Jun a withering look. "Your father, the great Zigui County spirit, told farmers, 'The teacher opens the door but the enlightened must enter on their own.' The door remains open. Do you have the courage to enter?" He walked out.

"He could have said thank you for dinner," Hao said to Wei as her daughter stared into a bowl of rice while the ladies cleared the plates in a busy clatter.

"Jun, we need to talk," Art said.

"I'm so tired. Can it wait?"

"No."

"Let's sit on the patio so we don't interrupt the others."

The magnificent penthouse view overlooked the dark, choppy

Yangtze River. The two admired the view for a few seconds before Art took a deep breath.

"Let me tell you a story. This week I interviewed 42 students who are going to America's Duke University for a three-week visit. I privately interviewed each student to check on their spoken English skills. I asked each to give one word to describe America. Do you know what each student said? Freedom. Forty-two separate times. That blew me away."

"Yes. I would say the same," Jun said. "But what does that have to do with me?"

"Well since I received your tapes, suspicious people hang around my apartment. Someone broke in and stole one of them. Then, the police interviewed me about teaching in the mayor's office. I love freedom too but feel like a political prisoner in Wuhan."

Jun gazed out at the river, not moving but breathing fast.

"The police asked about our relationship and the use of audio recordings for teaching."

"Now you're in it. Give the tapes back. It was a bad idea. Did you tell the police about the tapes?"

"No, but it's too late to run. They've searched my apartment and interviewed me. My phone must be tapped. Yes, I'm in it."

"We must stop seeing each other. It will remove suspicions of you in time. I know what's going on. You don't need to know."

"My freedom's threatened. I need to know!"

"Stay out of Chinese politics. America's freedom doesn't make a difference in our world."

"You can't get rid of me. I love you."

She patted Art's hand before slipping through the screen door.

CHAPTER 30

Throw Him Out

NOVEMBER 8, 2015

Unnecessary noise distracts star employees. Guo, the efficient boss, eliminated the turbulence in Jun's life.

"You need a penthouse," Guo said, letting her move into a beautiful WuChang condominium near Han Street and the Reign Hotel. Her mother found it hard to complain about her daughter moving into a condo more spectacular than her own.

Next, the Jingmen Communist Party boss got a call.

"I need a job for a farmer, Li Shun. Make him a local government farming assistant," Guo told his friend.

Soon the Jingmen farmers heard 40-year-old planting advice from the new employee. "The great Zigui County farmer, Jun LiJiao….," a resolute Li said to farmers who played on phones or slept.

Guo's development company opened two new projects, including where Jun now lived. Hao's new role as sales manager kept her busy so promised get-togethers with her daughter dwindled.

Lurid rumors of Art harassing Jun, Chao, and Bo with inappropriate comments during English lessons circulated around city hall and Jianghan University.

"Yes, the American discussed sex and religion. We were quite embarrassed and upset," Jun told the mayor when he questioned her about the rumors.

"Freedom-crazed Americans will not corrupt our employees! I will begin the process of throwing him out of China."

"His unrestrained freedom doesn't understand the way of the Chinese. But I've heard no complaints from the *Changjiang Weekly* editors," Jun said to the mayor. "We do need his skill at the newspaper to succeed."

"Keep your opinions to yourself or face serious consequences," university officials warned Art two days later. He smiled and nodded.

Art missed Jun but her blocked number and new address eliminated his late-night drunk calls or visits to harass or beg. City hall guards knew to keep him out.

A tired-looking Jun occasionally appeared in a *Changjiang Weekly* photo with military men from various countries at a bridge opening or city function involving the games.

The elimination of friends and family combined with a 9-9-6 life began to take a physical and mental toll. Seventy-five-hour work weeks left Jun with only one friend, Taobao.

Their conversation started every night at 11 p.m. with the question. "What should I buy today?" The two friends got little sleep, spending nights exploring fashion from around the world until the sun rose on another day of manipulation.

Good for You

M A R C H   5 ,   2 0 1 9

The black Buick Regal sped across Wuhan's First Yangtze River Bridge as a coal barge sailed toward Shanghai.

Jun laughed as the barge belched smoke like an overweight man after a large dinner. "I wonder if he's a fat American? Three years is a long time."

"Don't flirt with these generals tonight. Just be the classic mysterious Chinese woman," Guo said while looking at a report. "And don't go looking for that American."

"Another command performance."

Guo called Peng.

"You there? Good. You know what to do? Yes, yes. Tighten the noose. We needed westerners at the show for the games' officials, but I don't want him getting comfortable again," the old man said with childish glee.

The car headed toward an evening's musical performance by Moscow's Tchaikovsky Music Academy at Wuhan's beautiful Qintai Music Hall.

The hall stands near Moon Lake where, in ancient times, lovers cuddled while enjoying flowing water melodies from Guishan Mountain to the east, the Han River to the north, and Meizishan Mountain to the south.

"The forgotten lover returns tonight from a long voyage, smarter but colder and lonelier than ever." A tear gathered in the corner of Jun's eye as it watched the barge disappear into the hovering river smog.

The music hall attracted international classical and jazz performers.

Tonight, the audience included World Military Games' dignitaries who spent a full day inspecting Wuhan's finishing touches for the fall games.

Jianghan University trotted out its 30 international teachers like show ponies at the bequest of Guo and the local Communist Party. The western teachers created the cosmopolitan feeling the party craved to impress the games' officials for the special Qintai concert.

Enthusiastic audiences enjoyed the quiet elegance of Qintai, a cross between two historical music halls, Vienna's Wiener Musikveren and Boston's Symphony Hall.

"Let's sit together," Art said to his friend, Liz Paine, a tall, attractive woman from London. The raven-haired woman always grabbed the attention of the Chinese.

"Of course. Maybe it'll stop the Chinese chavs from drooling on their shirts," the statuesque woman said.

Skin-tight black pants, a crisp white shirt, and a black waist-length coat, showing off her long, slender legs grabbed the attention of many at the show.

The most ardent watcher caught, a large, bald Chinese man, wore a military-styled outfit that gave him an official look. He stood next to the escalator leading to the hall's seats.

The scarred face looked familiar to Art. When Liz reached the stairs, the man moved in front of the escalator, giving her a wicked smile along with an inappropriate touch to the shoulder.

Art reached around, trying to remove the man's menacing hand.

"Excuse me," he said, showing their tickets and pointing up the escalator. The hulk stepped around Liz, jumping into Art's face with the look of hair-dragging caveman.

The teacher stared at the imposing man before holding up two tickets and pushing past him with an air of privilege.

Peng grunted while turning to gaze at Liz as she went up the escalator.

"Who's that beast?" Liz turned to make sure he stayed behind.

"A repairman, I think. But I wouldn't recommend him. Doesn't always let you know he's coming."

"What?"

"Nothing. Just a jerk. Don't let him into your apartment. He has light fingers."

"That's not happening. Going to the loo. Will you wait?"

Art's second-level view let him see a commotion outside the five-story glass entrance. Security guards formed a corridor from a black Buick Regal to the entrance, holding back the pushy crowd trying to enter.

A familiar-looking chauffeur hustled to open the door for the VIPs.

"That's weird. Looks like Jun's old driver. I wonder…," he thought as his heart raced.

Jun, dressed in a black dress and mink, slid out of the black car followed by a gentleman who looked like her grandfather.

"Oh man. This is too much," Art said with a cynical laugh.

Her beauty and grace provided a red-carpet moment as the bald repairman now stood outside the front door like a military honor guard.

The escort looked familiar, maybe someone from a *Changjiang Weekly* photo. He glided into the building like a seasoned politician, waving at several patrons while grabbing elbows and whispering into the ears of others.

Art clutched the second-floor railing with one hand while running his other hand through his hair as he thought he saw Jun's twinkling eyes flash toward the second floor for an instant when entering the building.

"What's wrong? You look balls up," Liz said.

"An old friend came. The lady in mink down there. Haven't seen her in three years."

"Quite elegant. Meet in the school cafeteria?"

"Tutored her in the mayor's office. I told you."

"You mentioned a mousey clerk. Not that! A bit dishy for you, don't you think?"

High-ranking officers representing several militaries greeted the couple near the escalator before turning down an adjacent hall to the elevator for the private boxes. Jun and her black dress disappeared behind the closing elevator door as the bald guard stood ready.

"Come on, let's go. Show's over," Liz said, pulling Art by the arm and pushing past four Chinese gentlemen standing too close for her comfort.

"Looks like we're in the front row," Art said, looking at their tickets.

"Why have props if you can't see them. We'll be the only ones in the theatre to know we're not important," Liz said as Art glanced at the private boxes.

"Stop looking like a heartbroken schoolboy," Liz said. "Act your age. She wants you to suffer."

He shrugged, staring at his fingernails before biting at his thumb.

The Russian orchestra played the hits from Tchaikovsky and Rachmaninoff to Prokofiev and Shostakovich. An usher approached Art as intermission neared.

"Excuse me, Mr. Iron?"

"Yes."

"This for you," the usher said, handing him a perfumed lavender envelope.

"Please see me in the lobby during break. I have something to tell you, Jun." Liz, leaning over his shoulder, smiled, nodding her head.

"Get your arse in gear, don't need me hanging around," Liz said as the orchestra walked off stage. "Be still my heart."

"Get me in 10 minutes. Brief is better."

The audience inched toward the rear doors of the auditorium as Art pushed the stragglers aside like an aggressive local bus rider in line outside the mall.

The atrium lights sparkled off Jun's black sequin dress, her right arm draped on top of the second-floor railing.

"Jun! What a surprise," Art said, feeling disappointed with the bland greeting.

"Teacher Art, thank you for visiting me. I missed you so. We think of you often."

The two exchanged a brief, light hug. Her French perfume acted like a magnet, bringing the American closer.

"I missed you Jun. I always hoped we'd meet one last time," he said in a whisper.

"Ah, so sweet."

An immediate electric charge erupted as the two babbled like three-year-old children, interrupting, finishing sentences, and touching each other's arm when talking.

But Jun's talk of her past three years soon left Art feeling like a rain drop pushed aside by a car's windshield wipers.

"You're doing well. Life seems much better without me hanging around. Good for you," he said with an edge. "A limo, a box, and a fur. Your performance tonight as arm candy for the rich fits you like that designer dress."

"Don't be that way. I need to tell you…."

Art saw the bald repairman striding toward them with purpose. The three-year wait for this brief chance to recapture their relationship had come and gone.

"Mr. Guo awaits your return for an introduction to DongFeng's president," Peng said without waiting for a break in their conversation.

"Hey asshole, give me a minute." Art gave Peng a withering glare.

The bodyguard stepped closer, but Jun held up a hand as if controlling a trained dog, "One minute Wu, please."

"That's the guy who broke into my room and messed with your stuff."

"I know. It's ok."

"Ok? You're friends with people who break into my apartment? No," Art said in a loud voice, causing the people around them to stop talking and move in closer to listen.

"Time to go Art," Liz said, grabbing his arm from behind.

"You don't understand," Jun said as the ladies nodded like two mothers blaming each other's kid for the fight.

"Get a leash for your slag," Liz said, pointing at Peng. "He's a tosser."

Liz put her arm around Art's shoulder. "Hi, I'm Liz Paine."

"My name is Jun FuMin."

"Nice to meet you. You should come visit us sometime. Take care. Love the dress."

"Nice touch," Art said as they walked away arm-in-arm.

"How was my timing?"

"Couldn't have been better," he said shaking his head as the elegant Jun walked away as if nothing happened.

CHAPTER 32

More to Tell

"Hello. I'm Li Shun." The tall, lean man wore a wide-brim hat, standing with an apprehensive look at Wu Tong's door.

"Please come in. I'm his wife. I contacted you," she said in a quiet worn voice. "He is not well. Maybe you can bring him peace while discovering information about your friend."

"He seeks peace? An elusive emotion these days. I can't promise it."

"Thank you for coming. Meeting at a restaurant might harm him. The doctor says he needs rest."

"I'm a busy man so let's say what must be said," the farmer said with his arms folded across his chest.

A frail, shirtless man laid limp on a straw bed in the corner of a small dark room.

"I didn't do it. Please believe me," he said to the wall as Li entered the room. The wife placed a small wooden chair next to the bed.

"Please sit," the wife said to Li. "He talks to himself a lot so don't worry about it."

"Hello," Li said in a loud voice.

"Oh. Yes. Oh. Please excuse for not getting up," Wu said, turning over and straightening a bit.

"Please relax. I am Li Shun, friend of Jun LiJiao. Your wife says you wish to tell me a story."

The man looked to the door and yelled, "Wine. Wine!"

Wu's wife brought two glasses of cheap rice wine, placing them on a table next to the bed, saying nothing.

"Drink," Wu said licking his lips with anticipation.

Li put his lips to the cheap wine as the sick man gulped it down.

"People die every day. I'm about to die. I saw your friend die."

Li clenched his jaw before speaking, "Life and death come as one."

"How is young FuMin? My best student at the middle school has not been to class in several weeks. Do you see her? Does she keep up with her lessons?"

A few seconds lapsed before Li replied. "She misses her excellent teacher, but her health is good."

"Good. Good. Education never stops. She will continue to learn."

"What do wish to tell me? My time is limited."

"Let me tell a story.

My father taught to respect your family. My family includes my cousin, Peng Qiang. I always responded to my cousin's requests as he rose through the YiChang Communist Party ranks.

Simple tasks came without danger. He'd say, "Hey college boy, deliver this package without being seen. You're smart enough to do that, aren't you?"

He wanted to be the local Communist Party secretary.

"I have a good chance. I knock heads together for rich people. They like that approach," he'd say.

Peng's political influence assisted me in assuming my father's teaching position at the village's school, so I always helped him when asked. He called one September day.

"I want to invite you to my new house tonight. It is important to come at 5 p.m. Don't be late. You can make 500 dollars." This was more than my monthly salary.

His 15th-floor condominium overlooked the Yangtze River. I figured he needed help moving furniture. Peng and another man who held a baton greeted me when I arrived.

"Thank you for helping on a special project," he said. "No need to know this man's name. A dangerous man is coming. If he becomes belligerent, then we'll need to control him."

The stranger said, "I handle most men. This baton does damage, but it never hurts to have help. Lend a hand if I say something. Ok?"

I nodded but was nervous. I'm a Buddhist and don't believe in violence.

"Hide behind the curtains on the balcony. I will let out a long whistle if help is necessary," Qiang said, giving an example of the sign. "If not, just hide and you'll get $500. But if I whistle then follow the lead of my friend. Do whatever he asks."

I shook behind the curtain as the doorbell rang. A familiar voice came from the apartment, a man I knew, Jun LiJiao, a farmer and father of Jun FuMin, my best student. Not a dangerous man.

Sweat rolled down my face. Shouts about farmers and land escalated from the apartment. The argument sounded as if my Buddhist beliefs might get tested.

The two men stepped onto the balcony.

"Take a look at the beautiful view. Breathe in the fresh air. Relax," Peng said, but his words sounded threatening.

"Empty words Peng," Jun said. I won't help you steal farmers' money."

Then came the slow, long whistle followed by Peng saying, "Show this man to the street."

We came from behind the curtains. Jun looked surprised, shaking his head as if chastising the teacher.

A long knife came out of Jun's waistband. "I will not go easy, even if it means killing the local teacher." I could tell he didn't mean it.

A swipe at me missed by several feet before going after Peng, making a deep cut down the cheek of his face as a piece of dragon fruit flew out of the hole.

The other man smashed Jun's extended arm with the baton, dislodging the knife from his hand.

I was confused. Jun and Peng were both screaming, but the other man *threw down the baton, yelling at me to "throw him over the balcony."*

My mind went blank. I froze as the first man grabbed Jun, throwing him off the balcony without my help.

I went to my cousin's aid, applying pressure to the hole in his cheek.

"Tell the police he attacked me and then jumped. Nothing more," Peng said as he left for the hospital. I followed orders.

My best student, Jun FuMin, failed to come to class the next day or ever again. I never forget that evening.

My cousin soon disappeared, dying several years later in an airplane crash, according to newspaper reports.

I try to forget by drinking rice wine, but it only leads to more wine and more remembering.

Only my wife knows this story. Every night she listened to my rants of "I didn't kill him. Why don't you believe me?"

One day at the market my wife heard of a stranger in town. "A man who was Jun LiJiao's friend works in Jingmen, but often visits YiChang. Maybe you should talk to him," she said.

Now I have.

Tears flowed from Wu's eyes. "Why did they kill him? I don't know."

Li tilted his head to listen. "Tell me, what didn't you know?"

"Why they threw him over the balcony. My cousin said orders from Wuhan. Why did they kill him?" The man's small brown wrinkled face looked for forgiveness.

"Another old man regrets his life," Li thought as the man's story added nothing new except the phrase 'orders from Wuhan.'

"More to tell," Wu said in a whisper, looking around the small room. "Peng visited before disappearing, trying to give the $500 but I refused. My cousin pleaded his innocence. I don't know. I tried to help Jun! You must believe me!" The teacher grabbed Li by the shirt.

"I believe you. A wise teacher never lies."

"My cousin warned Wuhan people would kill me and my family if I ever spoke of the death. My wife thinks I'm a babbling fool about to die. She doesn't care what I do."

"Did he say who gave the orders?"

"No. But he said they would kill me."

"Do you believe your cousin is dead? That may not be true."

"The newspaper said…." The sick man's voice trailed off.

"Who believes newspapers? Do you have a photo of your cousin?"

"It is old, taken when I graduated from high school many years ago. My wife will find it."

A tattered photo showed the large sullen teenager towering over the petite Wu.

"He'll have a large scar on the left side of his face if he's alive. But I think he's dead. My cousin saw him several years ago at Hankou Railway Station, but his poor eyesight makes him see things no one else does."

"Does your cousin live in Wuhan? I want to talk to him."

"My wife will write down his address."

"May I keep the photo? I will return it."

"I don't need photographs anymore. No children, and my wife wants me to die," Wu said with a relaxed smile before yelling, "More wine."

"I must go."

"You deny a dying man a final drink?"

Li pursed his lips, looking at his half-full glass. He wanted to study the familiar man in the photo but said, "More wine."

"More wine," Wu said with surprising vigor.

CHAPTER 33

Pin It on Anyone but Me

AUGUST 5, 2019

"We need to finalize a few details," Guo said on a secure phone line at the Wuhan Communist Party headquarters.

"Before you start, the price is now $25 million in US dollars. The two scientists are fine, but a few other people got greedy."

"Ridiculous. What am I paying you for? It was $10 million six months ago," Guo said with anger.

"Things change. Call it off, but then I expect a few more accountants to show up in Wuhan during the two meetings to look at the Military Games' books and ask a few questions."

Guo grumbled before spitting out, "When do you want the money?"

"October 1 for half. January 20 for the rest," the contact said.

"Can we trust the white coats to keep their mouths shut?"

"We know their families."

"And I know yours. How's it going to work?"

"The virus gets released in November at a wet market. Tell the newspapers to call it a mysterious pneumonia. Don't cancel the January meetings. We'll plant rumors of a virus. That will cause a distraction. No one will give a shit about the games' budget with a virus circulating. When the meetings end on January 18, we'll discover the virus and take the necessary steps to halt it. We'll blame the Americans for planting it during the games." The contact laughed.

"Blame anyone but me."

"No meeting delays. Finish on time. January 18. Don't want this virus circulating too long."

"How dangerous is it? I don't want to make money just to die."

"Scientists say a few hundred people will get sick. Steer clear if you can. A few old people may die, but they would anyway. Control the hospitals' comments. We'll discover the virus after the 18th. The chaos gives you time to walk away with $200 million dollars."

"That's bullshit. I'll be lucky to make the same as you," Guo said.

The contact let out a loud cackle. "Sure Guo. The wheels roll on October 1 when the money shows up."

"You'll get your $25 million but no more. No need to talk again."

CHAPTER 34

The Chinese Can Keep Secrets

AUGUST 15, 2019

Pink lotus lined the banks of SanJiao Lake next to the London Bus Coffee and Florist Shop on the Jianghan University campus. Patrons enjoyed cappuccinos and lattes while watching flying fish leap out of the water.

The owners, a middle-aged couple, loved Art even though neither spoke English. The barista always sang "cappuccino" with a big, toothy grin when the American entered the shop.

Art ordered a latte and the wife brought it 15 minutes later and repeated the hearty 'cappuccino' call.

The teacher thanked her with a mumbled "shi-shi" as his mind focused on Jun.

"I still love her after three years and all she cares about is money," he thought as a fish leapt out of the water, snatching an insect with a graceful swish of the tail before diving back down.

A young Chinese man walked up to his table.

"Hey dude, what's going on?"

"Living a bug's life Daniel. Keeping busy in a pointless world," Art said with smirk. "Nice to see you. Thanks for coming."

The meticulously dressed young man nodded and sat down. He owned an English-consulting company but admitted he had no clients or income. He either had rich parents or the authorities paid Daniel to keep tabs on the university expats. Today, Art bet on rich parents.

"I need a favor. You can't tell your girlfriend, your parents, or any other teachers. Ok?"

"The Chinese can keep secrets," he said with an unbelievable sincerity.

"If you don't want to take the risk, I understand."

Daniel just nodded.

"Can you translate a 10-minute tape from Chinese to English for me?"

"Sure. Buy me a coffee and we can do it right now."

"No. Don't want to do it in public. Not sure what's on it. Might be hot."

"Like a Chinese love poem?" Daniel laughed as his face turned red.

"Political stuff. I need to know what's on it. We'll do the translation in private tomorrow at my apartment."

The next day Daniel showed up at Art's apartment with a new tape player. He handed it to Art.

"Did you just buy this?" Art examined the device before handing it back.

"Thought it might help."

"We'll use mine. Just return it."

Art peeked out the window as he reached for his tape player. Two unfamiliar middle-aged Chinese men chatted near the building's front door. One looked up, making eye contact with him before looking away.

"Were you followed?"

"Man, what's wrong with you? You know me. I'm not the secret police. Nobody cares what I do."

"Let's forget this. It's a bad idea."

"Dude, I'm no Chinese spy." Daniel laughed for a few seconds before folding his arms across his chest. "And if I am, I know you have the tape, so what difference does it make? Maybe I can help."

CHAPTER 35

People Get Sick

"Today, we discuss plans for the 20th Baixin Potluck Family Dinner Banquet, the best ever," Chairwoman Hao said to the planning committee, a group of 20 residents of the condo project. "This year's ambitious goal: Attract 40,000 family representatives, the largest potluck dinner in history and a place in the *Guinness Book of World Records*."

"Ahh," committee members said, nodding heads in support of worldwide recognition of the banquet Hao started planning in 1999 to attract buyers to the development.

The plans for the record-setting banquet, the crowning achievement in her surprising career, included 15,000 food dishes along with musical and dance performances, dignitary speeches, and community news.

The media sent reporters to the committee meeting, thanks to orders from Guo and the Wuhan Communist Party.

"Don't forget our other developments and the Wuhan Communist Party but don't mention me," Guo said to Hao before her remarks. "CCTV will highlight our company in a follow-up story. Don't screw it up."

"Should I look at the camera?" Hao dabbed a tissue around her nose to dry the sweat rolling down her face on the steamy August day. "It's my first television appearance."

Guo had already hung up.

"Are you excited for this great event? It's quite an achievement," the CCTV news reporter asked her.

"Guo Zhenqin has been very helpful in creating our honorable event that honors family, yes. And I'm excited about the kindness of the Wuhan Communist Party," Hao said staring at the camera while tugging on the red, white, and blue scarf, hiding her wrinkled neck. "Wuhan will remember the January 18, 2020, 20th Annual Family Potluck Dinner forever."

The live interview flickered in the Reign Hotel.

"First thing she says is my name," Guo said shaking his head as Peng spit out the shell of a shrimp onto the coffee table. "Well, the banquet serves our purpose."

"Why boss? A bunch of old hens clucking about the place falling apart. You complain about building maintenance costs after each year's event," Peng said, changing the television to a football match.

"You miss the big picture. The event takes place January 18, 2020, the day the Wuhan and Hubei Communist Party meetings end. A perfect time."

"What difference does that make?"

"We'll put the Wuhan Games to bed while the talk will be about the banquet and how it shouldn't be held because of the pneumonia. The confusion allows us to walk away happy and rich."

"Talk about pneumonia? What's confusing about pneumonia?"

"People get sick in January. Predictions say it will be bad year."

"Oh, then I can go on vacation after the banquet?"

"Yes. In fact, I'd recommend leaving Wuhan as soon as the banquet ends. You can take a month off for the New Years' holiday."

An excited Hao met Wei after the interview. "Did I look ok? I could feel the sweat rolling down my face. Hard to believe I was on television throughout central China as the leader of a great event."

"Service to the people Hao, not the ego. You deserve credit, but not too much," Wei said to the red head. "Many people helped, including me."

"Of course," Hao said remembering the countless hours of organizing the first few banquets without help.

"The television didn't make me look like an old, fat woman with hot flashes, did it?"

"Not fat, but well fed," Wei said with a laugh.

CHAPTER 36

My Protection

Dreamy thoughts of a New York City life high above Central Park drifted through Jun's mind like wispy summer clouds.

The World Military Games' last contract, involving flowers at Tianhe Airport's International terminal, ended the gravy train. The time arrived to plan a new life.

"Out of Guo's prison," she said lying on the couch and kicking her feet into the air to the beat of Tchaikovsky's 1812 Overture, an album she listened to daily since the Qintai concert months ago. "Time to bring Art back into the picture. Our meeting after three years shook him, but he still loves me."

New York City museum brochures, condo project floor plans, and city maps littered the table in front of her.

"Yes, please get the car ready. Tonight, it's Broadway then a bite to eat in Chinatown," she said to the imaginary butler. "Then take the night off. Arthur and I want to be alone. The nanny will watch the baby." She giggled.

The thoughts faded as memories of Guo's pawing her in the limo following the concert and his rambling demands to "give me what the American got" unsettled her.

His aggressiveness toward her had only increased since the concert. The inappropriate touches and talk of "farm-girl discipline" worried her.

"Just an object for his disposal. Used and thrown away like tissue paper. I'll kill him before that happens."

The tape of Guo confessing to stealing city money served as her evidence and protection, even if it could put her and a lot of other people in jail.

"Where are those tapes? I need to check them."

Never-worn shoes, dresses, and nightgowns stacked into large piles in one of her walk-in closets hid the tapes. She flung the clothing into the air searching for them.

"Ah, my protection," she said when finding them under a pile of Italian silk lingerie.

She ripped off the wrapping and popped the tape into the recorder near her phone.

The beginning sounded unfamiliar with her voice, or what sounded like her voice, saying, "Yes Hu Jin, this in Jun FuMin, and you know I have been processing contracts for the city."

"Yes, and from what I hear, you are a fine employee," Hu replied.

A startled Jun stopped the tape. "I never talked to Hu about contracts." She examined it before starting it again.

"Have you ever wondered how I have all these fine clothes? I know many people have. Fixing city contracts is quite easy and I've done it for years. If we work together, then I believe anything is possible considering the citywide construction for the World Military Games. We can make a lot of money together."

Jun pushed stop. "Doesn't even sound like me. And why Hu?" Guo's friend served on the Wuhan Communist Party Executive Committee.

She grabbed a box holding years of recorded phone calls, frantically digging for the original tape, finding it at the bottom.

"Hello Jun. This is your mother. Can I come over to see your new apartment in WuChang?"

"No," Jun yelled at the recorder. She ripped open the three other addressed packages only to get the same recording.

"Art," she yelled, picking up her phone and dialing his number.

"Oh my God Art, I'm going to jail," she screamed.

"Huh. Why?"

"The tapes! I now know why they broke into your apartment. They switched tapes, making one with me admitting to stealing money from the city."

"Did you?"

"What?"

"Steal from the city."

"They're trying to frame me."

"Who? The jokers you were with at the music show?"

"Yes."

"No surprise. Don't you have the original?"

"No. I accidently taped over it."

"Now that's too bad," he said staring at the fifth tape that had sat on his desk for three years.

What's Important?

The farming village restaurant on the outskirts of Jingmen served a breakfast of mantou, steamed buns filled with bean curd.

Hao's cousin, a local tea farmer, complained to Li between bites of the popular morning fare.

"I want to move to Wuhan. Live like a rich man, like Hao," the farmer said. "But my tea crop gets smaller and smaller."

"You must deliver tea leaves to the factory for processing as soon as you pick them. You can't eat lunch, take a nap, or go later in the week. Cut an apple and it turns brown. The same with tea leaves," Li said to the farmer who looked at his phone.

"My son moved to Wuhan last year when he heard of Hao's good fortune. He now has a good job, but I have no help. I'm old and my legs and back get tired and need rest."

"Tea farming alone is difficult, but why do it if it's not done well?"

"All the government does is take money from my hard work and give it to you. Work, work, work are my orders."

The stubborn man angered Li who wanted to think about Wu Tong's story and the photograph.

"The truth's in Wuhan," he thought as the farmer rambled on.

"Hao's apartment has four toilets and running water in every room? Have you been there?"

"What? Yes, all true. Hao's rich. She eats pork every day. Visit her and stay a month."

"Maybe after the summer growing season."

"I'll pay for your mantou, so go. We both have work to do."

"Government thieves eat in fancy restaurants while ordering poor farmers to work in the sweltering heat. The working man stands no chance. Just slaves for the fat man," the farmer said heading to the door.

"I work for you," Li said as the door closed behind the farmer.

The cheap restaurant chair groaned as Li leaned back to watch the farmer walk across the thousand-year-old rock bridge crossing the village's small stream.

"Wu Tong's story will soon turn brown as well. I must decide whether to die a loyal worker or a loyal friend."

But I Love Her

SEPTEMBER 10, 2019

A blues singer from Tulsa, Oklahoma moaned about a cheating woman on a satellite radio station as Liz and Art sipped Johnny Walker Black and water from tall glasses in her cozy living room.

"Do you love her?"

"Who?"

"Stop it."

"We were close for a short time then one day, boom, she's gone. She just blurted out, 'stay out of Chinese politics' and disappeared."

"You shagged her once and now can't walk away? Was she that good?"

"Love and sex aren't the same thing."

"But it sure helps if they talk to one another," Liz said with a laugh.

"A big bank account turns her on."

"Oh, she's more of a 'love that money' kind of girl. I'll let you in on a secret, most women are," Liz said in a stage whisper. "You're daffier than I thought."

"Love is blind," he said staring out the fifth-story window.

"And deaf and dumb. The tape doesn't make her look like Snow White, does it?"

"No. She can be a princess in the right environment."

"I can be Queen Elizabeth if I drink enough," the tall English woman said pouring half her drink down. "Leave well enough alone. You were barmy for letting Daniel listen to the tape. Chances are you'll be exposed like a park pervert."

"I need another drink."

"Help yourself but stay away from the window. The secret police will get a clean shot and I'll be cleaning up blood for a month. I'm going to the balcony for a fag," she said with a laugh.

A tall Johnny Walker Black and water joined Art on the couch as they waited for Liz and the smell of cheap Chinese tobacco.

"Hey, are you having a laugh?" Liz glided into the room and grabbed her drink.

"You love it when Americans get in trouble, don't you?"

"No, I love Americans. It's America that's daft."

"I'm thinking of selling the tape. Squeeze some cash out of someone, make a buck or two and blow China."

"Please! Put it up for the highest bidder? You'd be dead then arrested in five minutes. Plus, you love Jun. You want little Juns running around a middle-class shack in Ohio. Just sayin'."

"She deserves jail. Why get her ass out of trouble when I can make money off it?"

"One. You don't have the balls. Two. You want to help her. Guys always think if they do something nice for a woman their dicks will get a prize. This ain't Ball in the Bucket."

Art nodded and took a healthy swig of Johnny Walker.

"She has dangerous friends. Don't fuck with them. Throw the tape away, keep your mouth shut, and live to see your mother again."

"I'd feel awful if something happens to her."

"Listen to Jun, stay out of Chinese politics. Me and your ma will feel bad if something happens to you sparky."

CHAPTER 39

How's the Games Going?

OCTOBER 18, 2019

A jammed Wuhan Sports Stadium roared to greet Chinese President Xi Jinping and military athletes from 140 countries on October 18, 2019, in the spectacular opening of the 7th World Military Games.

The newly renovated stadium, costing $100 million, held 50,000 flag-waving fans. Guo and Jun ate a catered Reign Hotel dinner as they watched from a stadium luxury box built by their friends and business partners.

Swirling light electrified the stadium, creating a mosh pit of colors and patriotic images. A replica of China's bullet train circled the field as Jianghan University dancers and flag wavers whipped the crowd into a frenzy.

An astronaut descended into the stadium as if walking in space as the raucous crowd held LED lights to simulate stars, letting the city embrace its brief but expensive moment in the sun.

The huge foreign crowds for the two-week extravaganza, promised by the military games' promoters, never materialized. Not even Chinese residents cared to see sporting events between Tunisia, Mongolia, or United States soldiers.

Free tickets flooded the city. A few dripped down to the Jianghan teachers who saw a volleyball match between Brazil and France at the university's new gymnasium. The professional Brazilians trounced the short, fat French team that resembled a pick-up squad from a southside Paris brasserie.

Art ran into three U.S. soccer players and their coach perusing the WalMart's liquor department in the Wuhan Mall two days into the games.

"Hey. Fellow Americans! You're here for the Games?"

"Yeah. The soccer team," a bright-eyed young soldier said.

"You going to kick some ass?"

"No way. We lost our three games as fast as possible so we can drink for the next ten days," said another player.

The coach, an overweight, glassy-eyed military lifer, focused on liquor bottles calling his name.

"Hey, I'm Art. An American teaching…"

"I got no time to chit-chat with a Commie-loving American. Blow asshole," the coach said without taking his eyes off the scotch selection.

Art laughed as he walked away with his Johnny Walker, fist bumping the young soldiers who were in a fierce debate on how many bottles of liquor to buy.

The games ended October 27, 2019, with the United States' team finishing 35th in medals, behind Tunisia and Mongolia, along with sports' powerhouses North Korea and Morocco.

CHAPTER 40

Others Aren't So Sure

NOVEMBER 5, 2019

"Captain Yang of the Wuhan Police Department is here to see you, Jun," the city hall secretary said around the office door. "Shall I send him in?"

"Give me a minute."

"He says it's urgent."

Random thoughts flew through her mind. "Guo's phony tape. Stealing money. Arrested in city hall. A life in jail."

She dumped her purse onto the desk. A bottle of sleeping pills fell out. She shook the bottle, hearing 40 pills rattle.

Fleeing to the mountain cities of KuMing or Dali in western China had crossed her mind, but her conscious got in the way. Now the result of that decision came knocking on her office door.

The bottle popped open with a flick of the wrist. She poured a glass of water.

A framed photograph of a 9-year-old girl in a yellow-flowered dress with her smiling papa sat on her desk. Jun loved the dress more than any she ever owned, wearing it to family holiday dinners till the hem was mid-thigh.

Her fingertips grazed the photograph. "Dad, I'm sorry. Your daughter failed," she said before taking a sip of water and pouring a handful of pills into a sweaty palm.

A shaky hand brought the pills to her mouth before her head fell to the desk, scattering the pills in all directions.

She moaned, bringing her elbows to the desk to hold her head. A moment passed before she stood to wipe away the tears and head to the door.

"Hello. I'm Captain Yang. Wuhan Police. We need to discuss a delicate matter."

"I'm prepared." A shaking hand dabbed a tissue in the corner of her eye.

"Can we step into your office?"

"My office?" Jun looked back to the door before turning to the captain. "Yes, of course."

A bewildered look crossed the officer's face as he followed her.

"Please sit down," Jun said, pushing loose pills into the desk drawer as the police officer picked one up from his chair and set it on her desk.

"Jun, Central Hospital detected an infectious disease in Wuhan. A mysterious pneumonia is what I was told to call it. They believe it's controlled but others aren't so sure."

Jun straightened. "Pneumonia?"

"No one is sure yet. If it spreads as some predict, then the city will need to coordinate drastic measures. Planning needs to begin for widespread infection."

"Should we contact Beijing?"

"The city and party decide the answer to that question. You've been informed. Please contact the Central Hospital administrator for updates. We will help any way we can. Thank you for your time."

The captain walked out as Jun picked up the phone.

"A serious problem Guo," she said. "Central Hospital detected a mysterious pneumonia. It might spread through the city. What should we do? Contact Beijing?"

"Beijing knows. Doctors have it under control. I'll make sure the police step on anyone spreading erroneous information."

"What about the upcoming Hubei and Wuhan party meetings? Should I prepare a discussion or should we cancel them?"

"No public discussions! The meetings will proceed and end on

January 18. The virus or pneumonia will not stop our government from doing the work of the people. That's our priority until the 18th. Nothing else matters till then."

"Ignore it?"

"The hospitals will handle it. We're not doctors."

"The police say prepare for a full-blown health emergency."

"Millions of reasons to keep your mouth shut. A few people may get sick, no big deal. That happens every January. We must move forward with our work. For now, we'll let the hospitals control the pneumonia without distraction."

CHAPTER 41

The Wolf in the Open

NOVEMBER 26, 2019

Li watched the countryside fly by at over 200 miles an hour on the bullet train heading to Wuhan.

Memories of his 1994 trip where colorful hawkers sold beauty cream, elixirs, and snacks danced in his head. New fast-train technology eliminated some of the travel time from the trip while big business phased out the hawkers and the fun.

"Maybe I should have bought cream from that young girl. I never bought a gift for my wife and now she's been dead 20 years," he thought. "When you focus on the future, you forget today."

Wu's picture stared at the farmer as the train rolled through the Hubei Province. The elusive murderer in the graduation picture taunted Li, smiling with smug disdain.

"Wu said his cousin saw him at the Hankou Railway Station. Who knows, I might get lucky? Maybe he works there."

The train pulled into the station. Hundreds of people waited on the platform to board the incoming trains.

His shoulders slumped after scanning the crowd. "Insane. Too many people to get lucky."

Wuhan's warm polluted breeze cleared his head as he stood at the taxi stand.

"Baixin," Li said squeezing into the back seat of the smoke-filled taxi. The driver grunted and lit another cigarette with the one he was smoking.

The mega-city's insane rush of millions of people sunk in on the 30-minute, smoke-filled ride to his home. Li slammed the taxi door shut and took a deep breath of semi-fresh air.

"Take a rest," he thought, heading straight to his favorite Baixin bench to enjoy the enticing November foliage before going into his empty apartment.

The osmanthus trees produced a late-fall sweet smell from now-dying yellow petals. Several deep breaths of the hypnotic aroma and the beams of sunlight streaming between the surrounding condominiums calmed his racing mind.

"Developers began building Baixin in the mid-1990s," a familiar voice said, shaking Li from the meditation.

A well-dressed gentleman with his back to Li led a group of 10 on a tour of the development.

"The marketing program attracted those displaced from the construction of the Three Gorges Dam, bringing waves of families seeking Baixin's location and educational opportunities," Guo told the listeners.

"The wolf in the open." Li clenched his teeth and opened his suitcase. "Nature provides an opportunity."

Li reached into the bottom of his bag and grabbed the slick handle of the new knife he purchased in YiChang. He slid the blade under his shirt, closed the suitcase, and slowly moved behind Guo.

"Our gardens provide a rural western Hubei feel as residents enjoy the flowers and ginkgo trees. The beautiful park setting brings peace to our residents. In fact, our best gardener, Li Shun, stands with us now. Please applaud him for his fine work."

The tour group turned toward Li, clapping and waving. The gardener's face turned bright red. He froze for a second before running away.

"As with many gardeners, a shy, sensitive person," Guo said, leading them away while looking over his shoulder.

Li's chest heaved after the several-minute jog. "Yes, the sly wolf has keen eyes. A dangerous foe indeed."

A calm breath returned as he rested on a bench, but he continued to watch for the tour group.

A large, impatient-looking man walked toward Li. The farmer pulled his hat low and slumped on the bench as if sleeping. The man walked by, letting Li take a soothing breath of the sweet-smelling flowers before heading to his empty apartment.

CHAPTER 42

He's a Dead Man

NOVEMBER 26, 2019

"The farmer's eyes flashed murder. That bastard wanted to kill me," Guo said to his bodyguard. "Before we kill him, I want to know why he returned. He had the perfect job."

"Maybe Jun brought him back to kill you. Did she know you were leading the tour? He'd do anything for her. I'd be afraid of you if I was her."

"Why go through three years of guilt then kill the payoff. No, she loves money too much."

"Then ask her."

Guo picked up the phone. "Hello. I have a question. Why did your friend, Li, come back to Wuhan? He tried to kill me today at Baixin. I won't tolerate such behavior."

"What? I haven't talked to him since he went to Jingmen. Kill you? I don't believe it. Peaceful men who grow flowers don't kill people."

"Men who carry knives do. He's a dead man," he said before hanging up.

The farmer's daughter sighed before dialing Li's number.

"Hello Jun. I'm back in Wuhan. Can we meet soon?"

"Did you see Guo today?"

Li hesitated. "Hmmm. I did at Baixin, but nature prevented bloodshed."

"Yeah, your blood. He wants you dead. Please, go back to Jingmen."

"I quit. Evidence about your father's killers has come to light. I want to share it."

"Not now. Guo's watching. He'll cool down in a few weeks. You can't stay in your apartment. My mother just bought an apartment in Hanyang. Stay there if you won't return to Jingmen."

"The wolf cannot chase me from my home."

"Li, for me and my father? Please? A dead person can't find anyone. My mother will meet you. Pack your things and meet her outside Gate D at the Sports Center Metro stop at 8 p.m. And don't bring your phone."

"Only because it's you. Justice will wait, but not for long."

CHAPTER 43

Are the Masks Necessary?

DECEMBER 1, 2019

The Hankou Catholic Church opened a medical clinic in 1880 in the city's Jiang'an District. The facility served the foreign concessions and western sailors traveling to the Yangtze River trading port established in 1861 by the British government.

The church expanded the facility into Catholic Hospital in 1893 before renaming it Central Hospital. The facility serves the center city's residents including those living in the nearby Baixin development.

Dr. Lui Liang started working at the facility in 2013 as a virologist after graduating from Wuhan University a year after his friend, Jun FuMin.

The two met in a computer club at the prestigious university, forming a lasting friendship.

The yinyang relationship matched Lui, an intelligent but shy scientist who wore drab clothing but distinctive circular glasses, with Jun, a sparkling jewel whose designer clothes lit up the campus.

Dreams of dating the beautiful Jun lingered, but the excuse of studying hid the intellectual's bashful ways while Jun's attention never strayed from acquiring clothes, shoes, power, and money.

"She can have anybody, so she wants nobody," Lui explained over and over to his jealous university roommates who had all been rejected by her.

Infrequent reunions occurred after graduation, but today marked the first business meeting. The hospital's sterile white meeting room held six doctors, two hospital administrators, and Jun. The doctors wore masks while the others did not.

"Dr. Lui, you're handsome as ever even though you still wear those funny glasses," Jun said, looking stunning in a Neiman Marcus burnt orange cashmere sweater and matching skirt.

"You never change. Always a flirt. Here, put this mask on," the doctor said handing her one.

"The mask ruins my makeup. Is it necessary?

"Stubborn as ever," he said with a laugh. "So, you're not married with a child? Oh my, a forgotten woman. My wife and I have one child and expect another soon."

"My child will come after the right rich man does," she said with a shrug.

"Guo Zhenqin, secretary of the Wuhan Communist Party, called this meeting to discuss the mysterious pneumonia spreading at Central Hospital," Fang Chun, hospital administrator, told the group. "He'll be here soon."

Guo arrived 20 minutes later with his bodyguard, Peng. Both stood at the door looking around the room before sitting.

"Are the masks necessary?"

"We recommend it," said Dr. Lui, handing him one.

Guo looked at Jun, who held her mask, before throwing it on the table.

"The pneumonia panics some. The Wuhan people look to us for strength. The party has full faith Central Hospital will cure it."

"Panic never cured a disease," Dr. Lui said. "But neither does ignorance."

"So, you believe it's not pneumonia?" Guo looked around the table to the other doctors. "Maybe the esteemed doctor can tell us what it is?"

"The answer will come soon. But as patients increase, including hospital personnel, precautions against human-to-human transmission by wearing masks and cleaning infected spaces need to be implemented in all Wuhan's hospitals."

"The party will control the situation. We've decided on two rules for the coming weeks. One, no information to other hospitals. Two, the party will report new cases to the Wuhan Health Commission. Doctors cannot report new cases," Guo said, causing whispers from the doctors.

"The policy makes little sense when dealing with an unknown disease. Delays increase the risk to hospital personnel and patients and the city," Lui said. "We must protect hospital workers."

"We'll continue to call it pneumonia. No discussion with other doctors or hospitals until proven facts show it's not pneumonia. Spreading false information becomes a police matter with those responsible facing jail time."

"The city understands Dr. Lui's concerns, but I agree with the secretary. Panic serves no one. Your excellent skills will eliminate the risk," Jun said. "The city will provide necessary supplies to combat the pneumonia."

"What are you hiding? China's best experts, the World Health Organization, and even America need to help us identify what we have here. Without help, many will die, including people in this room," Lui said.

"You've heard our orders. No experts, especially Americans. Quietly take care of it or go to jail," Guo said, before leaving the white room with Peng, both covering their mouths.

The "tick, tick, tick" of the large wall clock echoed as the doctors sat in silence before the administrator broke the hush.

"Doctors, you have patients to handle, charts to fill out, and operations to perform. The party expects you to do your jobs."

Lui turned to Jun. "These foolish rules will kill Central Hospital staff. Why?"

"Wuhan needs you here, not in jail. Please try."

"It's not pneumonia. Hospitals need to protect themselves until we know what we're dealing with."

"I'm on your side," she said, patting his arm and giving him a weak smile before leaving the white, sterile room.

CHAPTER 44

Clothes Just Hide Us

DECEMBER 3, 2019

"No. You're out of your mind," Hao said to her daughter. "He's nothing but trouble."

"Your new apartment is perfect."

"The man tried to kill Guo. Why risk our lives for a crazy man?"

"Because he came to Wuhan years ago to help us, that's why."

"Can't you find another place?"

"No one knows about it. Just for a few days then I'll find a place. Please Mom."

"Till Monday. Cleaners are coming and his clothes will make the apartment smell like pig shit."

Jun laughed. "Ok. Meet him at Exit D at the Sports Center Metro at 8 p.m."

Evenings at the busy intersection of Taozhi Road and DongFeng Boulevard brought thousands of people on subways, buses, and taxis. One of the busiest intersections in the Chinese megacity always had streets filled with Wanda Mall shoppers, automobile factory workers, and fans heading to the sports stadium.

Hao's taxi crawled through the insanity, arriving 10 minutes late. She jumped out trying to find Li among the crowd. Her eyes scanned the street like a hawk looking for a squirrel. She spotted him near a food cart selling shish kabobs.

"Li. Li. Let's take the taxi," she yelled over the din of buses, cars, and pedestrians.

He shook his head, waving with enthusiasm for her to come to the sidewalk.

She paid the driver, dodged several vehicles, and trudged up to Li who held a small worn bag.

"The fresh air will do us good, plus you need exercise. I see my time away hasn't made your clothes fit any better," Li said with a smile as he eyed her head to toe.

"You wear rags and tell me I look bad?"

"Clothes just hide us. Stop deceiving yourself with hair color and elastic clothes. The universe knows your age."

"Shut up and enjoy the walk."

The aging pair strolled along the tree-lined sidewalk as silent electric motorcycles with headlights off glided by in the dark.

The aroma of roasting chestnuts filled the air as the pair neared a stand near Jianghan University's Gate 1. Li stopped to buy a bag of nuts.

"Nuts older than the stars and yet you give me so few for 10 kuai. Robbery," Li said to the unresponsive vendor.

Hao faced softened as he offered her a chestnut.

"Why did you come back Li? You left the perfect job in Jingmen. You're back one day and already causing problems."

"Please, have a tasty chestnut. Oh, lazy farmers like your cousin just argue, ignoring wise words about farming. No interest in learning nature's way."

"That's not why you came back. What did you find?"

"I did find something interesting," he said with a surprised look. "A teacher, Wu Tong, saw your husband get thrown off a balcony for not accepting bribes to cheat farmers. The man feels guilty for not helping. He gave me a photograph of the killer. I will find and kill him."

"Old news. The man died in a plane crash years ago."

"The man's cousin saw him alive in Wuhan several years ago. He's not dead. I have his photograph," Li said. "Look."

She glanced at it and tried to hand it back to him.

"No. Study it," he said.

She took a second, longer look.

"Jun sliced the man's face with a knife, giving him a large scar before they threw him to his death. So he will have a large scar."

"My husband was a strong man willing to fight for what is right," Hao said, dabbing her eye with a tissue. "The man looks familiar but he's so young and the photograph so old. Maybe I just want to know him."

Li put his arm around the red-haired lady and pulled his wide-brimmed hat low to hide his face as they approached the Modena gate cameras and guards.

"Thank you for letting me stay here," he whispered into her ear while nodding at the uniformed guard.

CHAPTER 45

Tigers and Flies

DECEMBER 5, 2019

The Wuhan Communist Party Executive Committee, a 30-member group, handles issues facing the sprawling city. They gather each December to set the agenda for one of January's "two meetings."

Locals call the annual event the "two meetings" because the Hubei Province and Wuhan City Communist Parties hold back-to-back conferences to discuss pending issues.

Meetings' attendees discuss the past year and set the course for the coming year while providing channels for province and city residents to express the "popular will," or *minyi*.

"The two meetings must finish the last details of the disappointing World Military Games," Guo said to the committee. "Let's approve any final expenditures then move on. No point discussing the event's failure."

Hu Fong disagreed. His concrete company received none of the game's lucrative construction contracts.

"My honorable chairman, an examination of the games' expenditures must take place. Even bring in Beijing to assist. Corruption will be found. I'm never outbid that many times in a row. President Xi said to go after tigers and flies. I believe we have a tiger in our midst."

"A greedy old man?" Guo laughed. "Why waste Beijing's time crying over your failure as a businessman? The games cost Wuhan a lot of money. Let's just put our failure behind us like men and move on."

Hu folded his arms across his wide chest and grunted.

"Let's take a break," Guo told the committee. "Hu can I see you for a minute?"

Guo cornered the concrete man.

"I know you're upset over the game's bidding process. But picking at the bones does no one any good. Just let it go."

"I hate getting cheated."

"Be careful," Guo whispered into Hu's ear. "A recording exists of you bribing a city official. If Beijing gets involved, you'll be the tiger."

"Bribing a city official? I must not be any good at it if I didn't get any military game contracts. I think you're stealing money and want a fool to blame."

"You're on tape, not me. You want the committee to listen to it?"

"No, even if it fake."

"Let's look forward. A big highway project will be voted on soon by the development commission. Worth 10 of those stadium contracts. Maybe we can help you forget the past. Nothing illegal, just information to make a solid bid."

Hu just nodded.

"Excellent," Guo said with a smile, patting the short, squat man on the back.

"But if things don't straighten out, I'm causing problems. The tape's a fake."

"You know how Beijing handles local problems, shoot all the suspects. We don't want our death certificates to solve a problem," Guo said with a smile. "Keep your mouth shut and the tape will disappear."

The committee agreed after the break to no new discussions on the games or its expenditures on the Wuhan Communist Party agenda.

Guo then introduced a new topic.

"You're aware Yicai Financial ranked China's most commercially charming 338 cities into four tiers. Four cities were tier-one, Beijing, Shanghai, Guangzhou, and Shenzhen. Wuhan ranked as a second-tier city."

"A second-tier city? No, we should be ranked with China's top cities," a committee member said.

"Popular will requires the two meetings to discuss how to make Wuhan a tier-one city. The future of the city and Hubei Province requires a meaningful discussion. Nothing is more important," Guo said.

The committee unanimously agreed to Guo's suggestion, as members offered examples of Wuhan's exceptional attributes as a tier-one candidate.

The executive committee voted to make the issue the top priority of the two meetings before ending the day.

Peng waited outside the party offices with 29 other drivers. Guo came out last, his arm around Hu, as the two laughed at a joke.

"I'll be in touch about the highway project Hu. Bye-bye."

Guo jumped into the Buick's back seat.

"How'd it go? You two looked happy. No need to use the tape on Hu?" Peng pulled into the street with no regard for oncoming traffic.

"He's on to us. An unfortunate accident may happen soon. A suicide maybe. Shame over the report of his bribery plans with Jun. Think about it."

"Maybe a murder-suicide?"

"No. Hu deserves a sedate death. Quiet, dignified. I'll take care of Jun."

"Ok boss."

"One more thing. Please take care of that gardener Li. I'm tired of that asshole making me nervous."

CHAPTER 46

He Has a Scar

Modena's 1800 condos in 30 buildings hid a lot of people but Li wasn't one of them.

Farmers crave open spaces, a breeze, and the freedom to walk the land. Li escaped the four walls, venturing out to Taozhi Road where numerous shops, restaurants, and street vendors serviced 25,000 Jianghan students.

"Maybe I'll get lucky and see Peng," he reasoned while taking a deep breath of the warm breeze when walking past the guards.

The raggedy man walked by shops selling bread, bicycles, and fruit before coming upon a bus stop across from the university's main gate where a steady stream of green city vehicles transported students and workers throughout the huge city.

"Book learning, a waste. A bunch of bourgeoisie teachers filling kids' heads with junk. The universe teaches better than clueless parents who raise spoiled children and expect them to change the world. They couldn't grow a carrot."

The aroma of several food carts near the stop made Li's stomach rumble with hunger. He explored the area and found a nearby alley filled with fruit and vegetable sellers and small restaurants and shops. An almost-empty Muslim restaurant drew him in for lunch.

The waitress brought a menu along with cellophane-wrapped cup, plate, spoon, and bowl, along with a pot of hot water to wash the tableware.

The traditional Hubei Province menu included his favorite dish, lotus root French fries.

"Twenty steamed pork jaozi and a plate of fries. Don't be cheap with them," he said to the waitress who nodded.

The western Jianghan teachers liked the restaurant because it had dumplings, fries, beer, and English menus. Art and Daniel were the only other patrons that day as they waited for an order of fries along with two warm Snow beers.

"The police stopped me leaving your building," Daniel said as he watched Li enter. "They asked who I visited."

"I told you. What you tell'em?"

"Working on lesson plans with Jack who needed help with Chinese art history," Daniel said with a smile. "They seemed fine with it."

"What did you find out?"

"Guo Zhenqin is an important man. He runs the local party," Daniel said with a wince. "Not sure I want to know more."

"I know that guy," Art said, nodding his head toward Li who sat down at the table next to them.

"Who? That old farmer? How?"

"Had dinner with him. A family friend of Jun's. A bit of a hot head. Ask if he knows Jun FuMin."

"Excuse me," Daniel said to Li across the empty restaurant. "Are you friends with Jun FuMin?"

Li turned to look out the window.

"Excuse me. My friend says he had dinner with you at her mother's apartment several years ago. Do you remember?"

Li ignored Daniel.

"Sir, do you know Jun FuMin? We're friends and mean no harm."

"Jun FuMin," Art said with a smile.

The farmer's hand slid to his waist, touching something poking out beneath his shirt. "Yes, I remember. I've been gone for some time. My memory fails me."

"Have you talked to Jun? Is she well?"

Li sighed, looking sad but relieved as he pulled a plastic chair to the table.

"I remember your American friend. He loves Jun, as many do, including me. But some want to cut the April rose and put her in a vase rather than letting her grow as nature intends."

"Who?"

"Guo, the political thief, controls her with money and clothes. If he fails in some plot, he will kill her or put her in jail."

Daniel translated Li's words.

"Tell him I agree."

Li nodded with a crooked grin and reached across the table to shake Art's hand.

"My best friend, Jun's father, was murdered by a corrupt party official. The man who did it lives here. I will avenge the death, but it will take time. FuMin must solve her own problems."

"Ask him if he sees her often."

"Money hides her."

"Ask him how he intends to find the killer."

Li told the story of Wu Tong and the photograph before showing it to the two men.

"The man as a teenager. Now, he has a scar across his face from Jun LiJiao who fought to the death."

Art held the photo close. "A scar? This side of the face?" He traced his finger to where the scar might be.

Li's raised his eyebrows and spoke to Daniel.

"He wants to know if you know the man," Daniel said to Art.

Art nodded, bringing a smile to Li's face as the waitress put two plates of lotus root fries on the table.

CHAPTER 47

A Virus Has No Friends

DECEMBER 19, 2019

Jun picked imaginary lint off her new skirt as her driver inched along in seven lanes of traffic on the four-lane Wuhan expressway. The black Buick Regal headed toward Central Hospital when her mother called.

"Hey mom. How's Li?"

"Uncontrollable, like always. And all over you. That's why we had dinner with him years ago, to stop this fighting. You make our family life hard."

"Let's get through the next few weeks. New problems will chase away today's worries."

"What? The pneumonia? That's no big deal."

"We'll see. I'm at Central Hospital. I can't talk now. I'll call later."

"Try to calm these men down instead of exciting them. Ok?"

"I got to go," Jun said as she walked to the hospital's front door where Dr. Lui waited.

"Hello. You ok? You look tired," Jun said, peering at his worn eyes.

"FuMin, stop coming here. Just call. Please, put this mask on," the doctor said. "Hospitals are the most dangerous places in Wuhan. Another nurse came down with fever. She's on oxygen."

"Pneumonia?"

"I don't believe so. Could be SARS-related but this is not a research facility. We just treat changing symptoms. A few have died and more will unless we stumble onto a cure. We need help."

"No, not yet. You'll find a cure."

"Word gets out regardless. Everyone at the hospital knows the truth. Can't you explain to Guo that he trying to hide something that's in plain sight?"

"I'll try but don't expect the answer you want."

Jun's phone rang with an unknown number.

"Hello Jun. Art. I'm using a friend's phone since I'm blocked. Can we talk?"

"I'm busy right now."

"We need to get together for a cup of coffee then. Talk about old times. Got a great story to tell you."

"Let me get back to you. I'll call later and try to remember to unblock you," she said looking at the impatient doctor. "Bye-bye."

"Jun, leave now. If I need anything, I'll call. Just go."

"Don't think you'll keep me away. I'm your friend."

"I appreciate your friendship, but the virus doesn't care. It has no friends," Dr. Lui said.

CHAPTER 48

You're Special

DECEMBER 20, 2019

"Maybe a few minutes on Taobao," Jun thought after returning to her condo following the depressing hospital visit.

The site led to new Louis Vuitton purses where she went back and forth between three choices before buying them all.

Guo's military games' slush fund had paid her Taobao bills for three years, including this $2,000 purchase. "He'll never know or care. I deserve them."

Her father had stressed hard work over material goods to her as a child, "Work hard and get a good education. Rewards will come when you are old and can reflect on a productive life."

She obeyed as a 9-year-old daughter but times and attitude change.

"I'm not waiting to 2060 to live a little," she reminded herself every time she splurged on the Internet. "Dad died a poor man who never did anything but work hard for other people. I'll get mine now."

Her lifestyle required freedom and money which meant keeping pawing men away. She had let Art have her once, but he served a purpose.

"They just want to show me off to their friends like a farm animal. I won't be a marriage donkey, carrying the wishes of a useless spouse," she told herself. "Marriage and my baby will take center stage when I meet the right rich man."

Independence, however, requires unrelenting focus. Late-night buying binges of happy summer dresses, cute shoes, and trendy toe rings meant unwavering energy the next day to cover her tracks.

Guo knew her game but said nothing about budget irregularities.

"You're special, not like China's drones. Blend your beauty with intelligence so that fish sink and geese fall to the ground when you appear. You deserve more," he told her many times.

"I can handle it," she'd tell herself when a wave of guilt-induced panic hit. "Work hard but still enjoy life today."

Excitement flowed through her veins when a new delivery arrived. A brown box filled with finely stitched hems, smooth silk, or stunning high heels left her tingling.

But the nights brought tormenting dreams of the police putting her in jail for "bad choices" as an embarrassed family watched.

Each day the words, "I'm in control," came out of her mouth. But each night, Taobao and tainted money told her what to do.

CHAPTER 49

You'll Have to Kill Me

DECEMBER 22, 2019

A young delicate boy with fine features called for a servant. Two came running with great dispatch.

"You know I want warm hardboiled eggs. These are ice cold. Take them away! Cook them how I want or you'll be reeducated on a farm," the 10-year-old Guo barked.

His father entered the room, shooing the servants away, before sitting on his son's bed.

"Your mother's not coming back. It's for the best," he said with no emotion.

His father had told him several months ago that his mother went to Shanghai to visit family. She hadn't called or written to the young boy since that day.

A year later his cousin teased him about his mother "running off with a rich American to Shanghai." Guo broke the boy's nose with a ping-pong paddle.

"Ran off with an American," Guo said gazing at the Han Street Bridge glittering in the sun from his Reign Hotel suite. He picked up the phone.

"Jun, come to my suite tonight at 8 p.m. The project needs to finish strong with no mistakes," Guo's voice barked into the phone.

"Can't we discuss it over dinner?"

"The games are over. We're going to discuss money so it must be private. Room 2020. A most appropriate number," Guo said with a slight lilt.

"A single woman doesn't visit a man's room."

"That didn't stop you with the American. Be here," he said before hanging up.

A few seconds ticked by 8 p.m. as Jun stood mapping out her plan in front of the beautiful white double doors with gold trim.

"Keep quiet until you know what he wants. Then smile, entice if necessary, and get out. Nothing good happens after 20 minutes."

A plain knee-length black skirt, white dress shirt, cotton jacket, no makeup, and hair pulled back in a bun projected an all-business appearance leaving no misunderstanding about the visit's purpose.

A knock brought Guo's bodyguard to the door.

"Hello Wu," Jun said before taking a deep breath.

"You're not carrying a weapon like your farmer friend, are you? Search her Wu to make sure," Guo said without looking up from a laptop. "And don't miss anything."

"You sure you don't want to do this?" She raised her arms and twirled around with a schoolgirl laugh.

"Sorry," the bodyguard whispered as he patted her down.

"Greetings from my humble room," Guo said sitting at a French Provincial table covered in papers and several computers. "See, not the evil place you believe. Please sit down. Have a glass of champagne."

A large Louis XV armchair in the middle of the room next to Guo's table looked like a court-of-law witness chair.

"Hot water please. I'm working this evening."

"Ah yes, the hard-working professional. That routine fools a lot of people, doesn't it?"

"A good employee works hard."

"You, an employee? I'd hardly put you into that category."

A wall mirror let her brush back a few stray hairs on her head while speaking to Guo.

"We have a lot to discuss but Central Hospital needs help. Expertise, supplies, equipment. Dr. Lui doesn't think it's pneumonia but something worse. We can't let people die."

"The flu, nothing more. Focus on making Wuhan a tier-one city. Beijing thinks we're a bunch of farmers. Start building a nice boring case on becoming a tier-one city. I'll take care of the flu."

"What can you do?" She looked away from the mirror, giving him a quizzical stare.

"I told you three years ago at the right moment no one would care about the World Military Games. The time has come," he said with a laugh.

"The time for what?"

"Disease is a strange thing. Who knows where it comes from and where it goes?" Guo shrugged.

"Do you?"

"A big payday approaches and you wish to discuss the flu?" Guo waved with dismissiveness without looking at her.

Jun sat up straight, her mouth ajar.

"We'll request an army of doctors from Beijing after January 18 if necessary."

"Why wait? January 18 is three weeks away. Dr. Lui won't stay quiet."

"Then he'll be in jail, leaving his patients at risk. Bad doctoring."

"Dr. Lui is my friend. He's trying to save lives."

"Jun, the plan is in motion. It's pneumonia till January 18. End of discussion. You don't need to know anymore."

Jun shifted in her chair but said nothing.

"Now let's discuss our financial arrangement. Any leverage you had, shall I say, disappeared. If you're not aware, then I suggest listening to your poorly planned blackmail scheme." Guo shook his head with a smirk.

"You mean the tape?"

"Yes. Now, our previous deal is null and void," Guo said. "But let it be said, I am a generous man. Isn't that right Wu?"

"Yes, boss," Wu said, standing behind Jun with his hands resting on the back of her chair.

"Unfortunately, the treasury bonds are in your name. That's your pay. You can also have the Mercedes, the necklace, and all the purses and clothes you bought from the games' discretionary funds. I won't put you in jail for stealing that money unless you refuse to cooperate. We do have receipts."

Jun clutched her chair's arms, "You gave me the freedom to spend money to get the games. Looking good was a part of that."

"Tell that to the restaurant owners and hotels who lost money preparing for the promised crowds. They'll hang you naked in a cage in downtown Hankou."

Jun's face pulsed red for several seconds.

"Then our days together will soon end. Friends in Beijing have offered jobs. You'll miss me," she said with a coquettish smile.

"No, I don't trust you there. I'll kill you first."

"Kill your dream? Oh, you couldn't do it. Your life will never be complete until I open myself up to you. But our new agreement ends that hope."

"Still trying to blackmail me you little whore. I take what I want. I don't need your permission to do what I want to you right now."

"You will have to kill me first," Jun shouted, picking up an ashtray and throwing it at Guo's head a second before Wu grabbed her.

Guo ducked then gave a faint evil smile while nodding to his bodyguard.

"That impertinent act requires punishment."

Guo's face turned dark like a fast-approaching thunderstorm about to strike with fury.

"Throw her on the bed Wu."

The bodyguard grabbed her wrists, flipping her onto the bed with ease, exposing her backside.

"The best teachers know the value of harsh lessons," Guo said with an edge. "I should have done this when you were 13."

A worn whip made of long leather tassels came out of a drawer. Guo cracked the whip against the wall with a sharp snap. The woman screamed in terror, flailing across the bed as Wu held tight.

Guo spit out a hyena-like yelp. "Tighter. Don't let her move. She needs to feel this," he screamed as he brought the whip down on the bed inches from her backside.

Jun screeched in fear as she struggled to break free of Peng's vise-like grip on her wrists.

Guo grabbed the back of her skirt to try to rip it off, but he didn't have the strength.

"Stop it. She's not a 14-year-old whore. We agreed to scare her, not fuck her. Remember our goal," Wu said with force.

A bewildered look crossed Guo's face as the skirt lingered in his hand a few seconds before letting go to deliver numerous harsh blows to her backside.

"Ahhhh. Sex with an American you whore," he yelled in an orgasmic scream before dropping to one knee on the bed.

The bodyguard let go while keeping a watchful eye on Guo. Jun let out a low moan then curled into the fetal position on the bed, hiding her face with a pillow.

A now-placid Guo slowly stood as his eyes drifted toward the ceiling as he regained his breath before tenderly returning the worn whip to the drawer and entering the bathroom.

"Are you ok? I'm sorry it came to this," the huge, scarred-face man said to Jun who laid silent on the bed, breathing fast and shallow.

A composed Guo soon returned as if nothing happened.

"Now you know our new arrangement. Do what you're told or go to jail for theft," he said with no emotion.

Her body shook as she struggled with a broken skirt zipper. Wu stood between the two as if refereeing a wrestling match.

"Why don't you throw her out the window Peng?" Guo slid open the balcony's glass door. "Make it a family tradition."

The two both gave Guo a puzzled look.

"Let's think straight. She's important. She's learned her lesson so let's move forward," Wu said.

"She'll never learn Peng. You know suicide runs in her family," he said with a laugh.

Each stood still, waiting for the others to make the next move before Jun started looking for her shoes.

"Murder me like my father? I don't think so. You got what you wanted to satisfy your sick mind. But you know it's all about the money. Killing me doesn't work. Best to keep things quiet."

"Get out of here. Remember, I don't make deals with cheap women who screw Americans. You got a break, a second one's not coming," Guo said as he sat back at his table, fidgeting with papers on his desk.

She straightened her skirt, wiped her eyes, and brushed back her hair, saying nothing to Guo.

"Thank you, Peng," she whispered to the bodyguard as she left the room.

The service elevator took her to the employee entrance where she hailed a taxi.

"Take me to the Modena," she said through the sobs from the taxi's backseat.

CHAPTER 50

I Slipped on Garbage

DECEMBER 22, 2019

"What's going on?" Li rolled over on the couch, trying to shake the midnight sleep off as the doorbell rang nonstop.

He looked through the door's peephole to see a crying Jun.

"Now, now," Li said, awkwardly opening the door and patting her back like a child. "Come in. Sit down."

"I can't sit," she said, walking with stilted steps into the spacious apartment. "Please, let me think."

"What happened? Are you injured?"

"I slipped on garbage, but I'll be ok."

"Can I get you hot water?"

"That would be nice." She looked out the window for several minutes, thinking about her father's favorite question, "What did you learn?"

Questions about the bodyguard, Guo's plan, and getting thrown off a balcony left her sad and confused as warm tears rolled down her face.

Li brought the water. "Drink. It will help."

"Can I sleep here?"

"Of course, this is your mother's house. She left clothes in the bedroom on the left."

The bedroom mirror reflected a worn face, streaked in pain. She tore off her clothes, throwing them over the bedroom balcony where they floated into the courtyard where several women fought over them.

She flinched from a knock at the bedroom door.

"Hello. How's the water? Warm soothes the soul," Li said. "I met your American friend today. He knows who killed your father. A man named Peng. An older man with a large scar on his face. I have his photo as a young man."

"Wait." She put on a robe before opening the door. "Let me see the photo. Where did you get this?"

"Peng's cousin in YiChang saw the killing but had no idea what was taking place and did not participate. Peng's powerful Wuhan friends will kill him if he talks. But he's sick and will soon die. He needed to let it go."

"Who are the powerful friends?"

"The evil one, I believe. Do you know Peng?"

"Yes. We can talk tomorrow, I'm tired. Can I sleep in this room?"

"It's your mother's house."

She pulled sleeping pills from her Gucci purse as soon as the door shut.

CHAPTER 51

How Safe is She?

DECEMBER 23, 2019

Hao put several bags of groceries down to open her Modena apartment door to a silent living room.

"Li? Are you here? Li?" She shook her head as if chastising the silence.

A muffled moan drifted from one of the bedrooms. She put the groceries back down and carefully listened before walking toward the hallway. She opened the bedroom door to see a motionless Jun in bed.

"Jun. It's your mother. Do you know where Li is?" Her daughter didn't move. "Sweet baobao needs sleep. Working too hard. I'll make breakfast."

The water began to boil when Hao heard footsteps in the living room.

"Li, is that you? Don't go outside. Why hide if you won't stay hidden?"

"I was sitting in the garden. Nature protects me."

"I brought food, so you don't starve. The neighbor won't cook for you. Says you're mean. Can't you be nice to anyone?"

"That nosy neighbor can't cook and asks too many questions. Plenty of restaurants to walk to."

"When did Jun get here? Was she worried about you?"

"Late last night. She seemed strange. Very emotional."

"Does she have the pneumonia?"

"More upset than sick."

"I'll talk to her," she said, pouring ginger tea into a cup.

Jun still hadn't moved when her mother returned.

"FuMin, FuMin," she said, rubbing her daughter's back. "Here, drink some tea."

Jun curled up on the bed, tucking the covers under her chin. "Ohhh, don't."

"What's wrong? Are you sick? I told you not to go to the hospital," her mother said.

"Leave me alone. Let me sleep."

"I made tea. Drink some."

"Please mom, go away."

Hao saw the empty sleeping pill container next to Jun's head.

"You took this many sleeping pills since last week? Are you trying to kill yourself?"

Less than a mile away, Art and Liz drank cappuccinos at the London Bus Café.

"You feel OK Liz? You don't look good."

"I'm a little iffy. Crud's got me. Bad sore throat, cough, and no energy. Most of the teachers are sick."

"Yeah. My throat hurt for a couple days. Looks like a sick winter. Germs explode in those little classrooms."

"How's your Chinese girlfriend? You see her?"

"Found out about her past. Daniel and I met an old family friend. Jun's father was murdered years ago, and this farmer is trying to find out who did it."

"Charlie Chan on the case. It's good as solved!" She touched Art's hand and laughed.

"An old photo of a suspect showed some big guy with a large scar on the left side of his face. Remind you of anyone?"

"That slag at the concert? He'd off his mum."

"Ironic, huh. Killed her father and now protects her. How safe is she?"

"Going aggro to protect your woman?"

"The affair goes deep. Best to keep you in the dark."

"No, telling me is best." She moved her chair closer and leaned in with a smile.

"Well. She's being forced to skim money off the city with those guys."

"Forced? Really? No one's twisting her arm. She loves the pretty stuff."

"Liking nice clothes doesn't make you a crook."

"Hanging out with thieves usually does. Don't be a lovestruck prat."

"I know more than you think. I heard the tape."

"You know Chinese now? You know what Daniel told you. Hey brain, how do you say in Chinese, 'Anything you say or do will be used against you?'"

"I hear ya. I got to go."

"Don't go wonky on me, you douche bag."

CHAPTER 52

Just Being a Doctor

New viral pneumonia charts piled up on Dr. Lui's Central Hospital desk. The Wuhan Communist Party had yet come to the hospital to gather statistics on new patients to report the city's health commission.

"Chun, ignoring reality doesn't solve problems," the doctor said to the hospital administrator.

"Right now, orders are to not scare Wuhan."

"The people need to know. The spreading disease jumped from animals to man. I'm afraid to go home at night. I won't let blind party loyalty kill my pregnant wife and child."

"Let's hold tight. Don't cross Guo. I'll call my cousin and get us masks."

Dr. Lui picked up the phone. "Hello my treasure. I thought I'd call to see how you're feeling?"

"Fine. The baby has a small cough but seems ok. You never call from work. Everything ok?"

"Does the baby have a fever? Is he sleeping?"

"He's playing with a friend."

"Maybe the friend should go home. Don't want him to get the cough too. Keep an eye on his temperature."

"I'll take him home after lunch. You sure nothing's wrong?"

"No problem. Bye-bye."

"We need N-95 masks now," Chun said to his cousin. "Going

through them fast for some reason. They cost how much? That's nuts. I'll get back to you. Got to check the budget. Maybe we can work out a deal that helps both of us. Yeah. Bye-bye."

"Chun, four new viral pneumonia cases in the last hour. Three patients work at the Huanan Seafood Market, but one has no connection. That's not good."

"What do you want me to do? You're the doctor."

"Get us an infectious disease specialist now. Wuhan is not safe."

Chun, a seasoned political lifer, started as a driver for local party leaders before moving through Wuhan City government ranks to hospital administrator.

"Beijing wants us to handle it. Xi's projecting strength around the world. How would it look if our little hospital yelled 'fire?' Guo would have my balls."

"Nothing but dust if the virus spreads. No one is special. Bosses die just like workers."

"Hey, I'm trying to get masks. But no specialists. Let me know if things change."

The doctor shook his head as he walked into the hallway. Portable beds lined the walls as patients' coughs echoed off the walls.

CHAPTER 53

You're Soft

DECEMBER 23, 2019

A bay gives sailors a safe place to dock when life's waters get rough.

Peng's 900-square-foot Hankou apartment provided his respite from a stormy world, but he couldn't shake tonight's Reign Hotel scene.

His Tang Dynasty sancai ceramics usually brought serenity when work went bad. The 200-piece collection filled his home on North Liji Road near the confluence of the Han and Yangtze Rivers.

Tomb figures lined glass shelves in the living room and bedroom. The delicate one thousand-year-old collection consisted of camels and horses in glazes of brown, amber, green, and off-white.

Royal family members had put Tang Dynasty pieces, lead-glazed earthenware, into their tombs to carry wealth on the journey to the afterlife.

The dead wanted camels in the tombs because the animal traveled well, surviving harsh environments due to unique physical characteristics. Peng appreciated that ability.

Life as a large clumsy boy living with a single mother taught him the ways of the camel, carrying family belongings on his back from one bed or floor to another, with little to eat or drink.

The struggles created an unbreakable bond between mother and the man-child who protected her no matter the circumstances.

The ill-tempered camel grunts, swears, and spits but those who care for the creature treat the noble animal as a part of the family.

"I'm beginning to hate Guo for his violence toward young women,"

Peng told his only friend, Tu, a small, dark man who dealt in stolen goods.

"You're soft. Getting fed too often. He needs to starve you like a dog, so you'll rip people to shreds when let loose," Tu said as he sipped hot water.

"Everybody's an ass-kicker when it's someone else's fight," Peng said with a laugh.

Age mellowed Peng. He saw himself as an obedient negotiator instead of a thug.

Time softened his approach to shakedown targets who refused to pay what Guo said they owed, learning to intimidate with a presence and evil smile instead of a crack to the head. "Let's be reasonable" started every conversation.

"Finding young girls for Guo bothers me. I used to think they needed his strict hand. Now, I think he's sick."

"Again, the old, weak Peng comes out. Rich men become wealthy through strength. Weak people deserve punishment."

"She's just got cornered," he said, shaking his head trying to forget the same look of despair in her father's eyes when thrown off a YiChang balcony years ago.

"She's kind. Brings me duck necks and milk tea and snaps at Guo when he abuses me."

Guo's slip of the tongue, calling him Peng instead of his alias, Wu, worried him. A young, headstrong Peng killed her father. Wu had learned much since then and didn't want to disappoint Jun.

The young woman lying in fear on the Reign Hotel bed tonight, threatened by a cruel rich man, brought back memories of his mother. As a child, many men beat Peng for trying to protect his mother. Guo knew better.

"My mentor deserves respect. He pays me good money that allows me to live on Liji Road and buy Tang Dynasty camels. I obey, but no more."

A faded photo of his mother looked down with sharp eyes from the wall above the desk.

Peng dropped his head to avoid her disapproving gaze.

CHAPTER 54

What Determines Success?

Life's narrative trembles like an earthquake when the story switches from "other people die" to "I'm dying." The barrel of a gun, flesh-eating cancer, or a clutching pain in the chest suddenly shakes up the script on what's essential or irrelevant.

Jun's personal perspective flipped from a self-assured beautiful woman to a fearful and fragile soul when the ugly vision of a killer's whip crashed down at the Reign Hotel. Her closets full of dresses and shoes, the work calls and texts, and the shining sun struck seemed irrelevant today.

A tub full of hot water tried to wash away the terror from her body but fear had already sunk deep into her pores.

Her body quivered from the cool air when she stepped out of the tub. The bathroom's full-length mirror revealed a shaking and bruised body.

A voice caused her to jump.

"Are you ok?" Her mother appeared out of nowhere, red hair glistening in the sun shining through the windows high on the bathroom wall. "You're hurt. What happened?"

Jun wrapped the towel around her body, trying to move past prying eyes.

"We're going to the hospital. You need help."

"No. Too many sick people there. I'll be alright. Please go. Let me rest."

"Then maybe a massage will help calm you down. Let me see if the neighbor has any oil."

She left the bathroom door unlocked in hopes her mother would come to her rescue, like a child's scream when scraping a knee.

"She came in like I wanted. Now what do I say?"

A bottle of massage balm appeared in seconds.

"The neighbor opened her door as soon as I went into the hall. She gave me this oil. A nice woman who already hates Li. She did ask why we needed it."

"What did you say?"

"I don't know what happened." Hao stared at her daughter, seeing through her agitation to the child. "I'm not going to ask, but I'll listen."

"Mom, you don't need to know."

"Too embarrassed to tell your mother? I've helped many women heal from pain. I can lighten your heavy burden too."

"Dad never beat you, did he?"

"Your young father tried. The elders said, 'Beat a wife early in marriage, so they obey a new master.' His heart, so full of love, tried before apologizing and holding me for an hour. My prince. No beatings necessary."

"That is so sweet," Jun said, giving her mother a light hug.

"Now go lie in bed and I'll help you with your pain," she said, rubbing the massage oil on her hands.

The proud mother admired her young daughter's beautiful body stretched naked on the bed. Her body had been beautiful as well, but the years left it wrinkled, worn, but content.

"Life's winds blow us here and there. As a young woman I had no idea I'd end up in Wuhan with more money than 20 Jingmen farmers. But I worked hard to help people, and the universe blessed me," Hao said as she massaged her daughter's shaking legs.

"Dad had no money, but more people loved him than both of us combined."

"What determines success? Cheating people out of money so you can hide behind palace walls? No. Your father spread knowledge and kindness so others could succeed on their own. That is true success. I tried to follow his wisdom."

The daughter said nothing as her mother worked on her tense shoulders for a few minutes.

"Take a rest. I'll make ginger and chicken soup," her mother said, kissing her child's forehead before leaving the room in a hush.

CHAPTER 55

Listen to the Trees

DECEMBER 25, 2019

Mother-and-daughter talks need space, so Li left Hao's 20th-floor condo to explore the scenic Jianghan University campus across from the Modena.

The university's beautiful four-sided, 10-story administrative building sparkled in the sun as zombie-like students on the way to class shoveled noodles into their mouths from paper cartons.

A wooded path along Sanjiao Lake led to the school's library with its large public space facing the water. Ten skateboarders were doing jumps off the library fountains' short walls.

The farmer sneered at the colorfully dressed kids as he kept walking past the library to a set of 25 ornate concrete steps that led to an urban forest. A monument at the top of the stairs guarded a serene pond partially surrounded by swaying bamboo trees.

"A hidden oasis," Li said with a smile as his eyes told him he had the pond to himself. Solitude was a rarity in a city the size of Wuhan.

The bamboo trees appeared angry, creaking with force from a stiff December breeze. Li listened to the trees groan from a bench next to the pond.

After a few minutes, he asked the bamboo a question.

"My friend, Jun, makes bad choices, clinging to material goods like a kitten's paws on a cotton dress. How do you cure an addict?"

The wind stopped, silencing the bamboo. Li looked to the sunny sky with questioning eyes before closing them, waiting for an answer.

Suddenly a large hand grabbed his shoulder. A huge head with ugly eyes, a sly grin, and a scar running from the chin to the left eye peered inches from his face.

"Li, you shouldn't be here," the man said in a quiet, caring tone.

A startled Li struggled to brush away the intruder's grip, but the strong hand stayed firm.

"Leave me alone. What do you want?"

"What are we going to do with you?" His large head shook side to side.

The man sat down next to Li, embracing the old man's thin shoulder with a muscular arm while using his other hand to grab Li's knife resting beneath his baggy shirt.

He studied the knife for a moment before looking at Li. "My cousin in YiChang makes these. Does fine work."

The strong arm held tight despite Li's struggling effort. Peng pulled the thin man close enough to smell the garlic he had for breakfast.

"Important people want you dead. In my younger days, you'd be dead already. But let's be reasonable and listen to the trees, like you were doing. I like that. They'll tell us what to do."

Peng stared at the small pond, listening for several minutes to the creaking bamboo while Li kept turning toward the large man then away.

Two young female university students strolled up the stairs toward the men who appeared to be embracing. The girls stopped, whispered to one another, before giggling and heading up the hill on a different path.

"Smart kids. I love intelligent women. One we both love is Jun. My boss thinks Jun wants you to kill him. I don't believe it. If it is true, however, then both of you will disappear. Neither of us want that. Do we?" He squeezed Li. "Do we?"

"You killed her father, now you'll kill her too Peng Qiang."

An incredulous look spread across Peng's face. "Where did you hear that story? I'm Wu. Who's Peng?"

Li said nothing.

"The trees say, 'A reasonable man will head back to Jingmen on the 4 p.m. train.' You know nature strikes hard at those who ignore reality. Follow the advice farmer. Your job will be waiting. Let's write down a reminder so you don't forget."

Peng grabbed Li's hair, pulled his head back, and slashed the left side of his face with the knife.

"Blood brothers," he said with a hardy laugh. "At least no fruit will come out of your cheek. Knife cuts clean. Don't mind if I keep it, do you?"

Blood dripped off Li's chin as he tried to stem the bleeding by using his coat sleeve.

"Just a scratch farmer. You'd know if I wanted to hurt you."

Li let out a soft moan.

"Peaceful here. I'll come back. Hope the trees say, 'Li's gone.' If not, then I'll start by going to Hao's new apartment. Good-bye farmer. Let's not meet again for your sake." Peng stood and stretched before walking up the hill on a nearby path.

Li's sleeve soaked up blood as the two young girls walked down the hill, pointing at him as he staggered to his feet.

"Why kill him? He'll disappear like all old men, never to be seen again. Jun will like this good deed," Peng said with a smile as he slid the knife into his coat pocket.

Li stumbled away holding his sleeve to his face as the wind picked up again, letting the bamboo whisper new tales.

CHAPTER 56

Disease Never Sleep

DECEMBER 25, 2019

"I'm determined to strive to eliminate human suffering, enhance human health conditions and uphold the chasteness and honor of medicine. I will heal the wounded and rescue the dying, regardless of the hardships."

The last sentence stuck in Dr. Lui's throat, *"I will heal the wounded and rescue the dying, regardless of the hardships."*

The Chinese medical profession oath meant nothing to him 10 years ago, but today the words screamed "fraud."

Eighteen-hour days piled up as the viral pneumonia cases jumped by 30 in two days. New patients from the Huanan Seafood Market and the hospital staff made sense, but general population patients warned of big problems.

"Am I enhancing the human health conditions by staying quiet? Am I eliminating human suffering by letting my colleagues help contagious patients without masks?"

The oath seemed like an executioner dangling a guillotine over his head. Follow the oath by speaking truth to power guaranteed the blade would chop off his head in one swift motion.

"My pregnant wife and son will face problems if I'm in jail. And if they let me out, what kind of career will be left?"

He put his hands to a throbbing head and staggered to the office's couch hoping a 10-minute rest might ease the pain.

"Oh, here you are Dr. Lui. Sorry to interrupt you. Another viral pneumonia patient. I checked vitals. Temperature 39. A bad cough. Low energy," a nurse said in a quiet voice.

"Wear a mask when checking these patients," Dr. Lui snapped at the nurse without looking at her.

"Sorry doctor, we have no masks."

"Find a towel to put over your face." The young physician put his hands over his eyes and took a deep breath. "Sorry. Take mine. I haven't used it. I'll check the patient soon."

The nurse left and the doctor soon fell into a hazy trance.

Another nurse rolled a hospital bed into the room with a small body covered with a sheet. A black mask covered the nurse's face.

"Sorry to wake you but a child died from the virus. What should I do with the body?" She pulled the sheet back to reveal the dead child who resembled his son. Behind her stood more nurses with more beds covered by sheets, all seeking directions on disposing the bodies.

He screamed, "No!" The sound echoed in the empty room as his tingling body jumped up from the couch. The ticking wall clock showed he had been sleeping for just a few minutes.

"I will eliminate suffering, heal the wounded and rescue the dying, regardless of the hardships," he said picking up his phone to open his WeChat app.

He typed a short note to seven doctors, medical school friends working in Wuhan hospitals:

Thirty cases of contagious viral pneumonia or a virus spreading at Central. Take all precautions to stop the spread of germs. Wear masks in all interactions with patients. Will keep you informed.

Guo's words rang in his ears, "Keep quiet and take care of it or go to jail."

"Do I have the courage? Or will I always bow like an obedient child?"

The doctor read the message several times before his eyes wandered to a window overlooking the hospital entrance. A woman wheeled an old man into the hospital's front door.

"People come here to find answers, not die."

He pushed the send button to let the world know Central's disturbing secret.

CHAPTER 57

He'll Beat Me Now

DECEMBER 25, 2019

Whispers from the kitchen allowed Li to slip into the apartment without making a sound.

"Eleven thirty, time to pack, eat lunch, and get to Hankou for the 4 p.m. Jingmen train," Li thought entering his bedroom.

The mirror revealed an ugly slash across his face. A light door knock startled him.

"Li? It's Hao. Can I come in?"

"No. Go away. I'm busy."

"Please?"

"Alright," he said, turning his back to the door.

She glided into the room, shut the door, and sat on the bed.

"Shhh. Keep quiet. Jun's resting. She needs sleep."

Li turned to put several pairs of underwear into the suitcase.

"Oh my, what happened to your face? You've been cut."

"Nothing. A small scratch. Who needs to sleep before lunch?"

"How did it happen?"

"Did she tell you what happen?"

"She had a difficult night. Someone scared her," she said, examining his face.

"Bad spirits surround her."

"She didn't say who. She'll take care of it."

"I've got my own problems," Li said as he threw in a pair of dingy socks into the suitcase while Hao's eyes followed him.

"You're leaving? Is that wise?"

"The same people who scared Jun know I'm here. I can try to fight them in Wuhan or run back to Jingmen, pretending to be a man."

"I told you not to go out."

"They're watching your apartment," Li said, sitting next to Hao on the bed. "Guo's bodyguard threatened to kill me if I don't go back to Jingmen, cutting my face as a warning."

"Guo knows I'm hiding you. He'll beat me now."

Li laughed. "You make him money, nothing more. He's lusts after the daughter, not the mother."

Hao pushed Li's arm. "What? I'm not pretty enough?"

"Yes. And mean enough to beat," he said as his face turned red.

A defeated look crossed Hao's face as she patted Li's knee.

"I need to leave by 4 p.m. or get my throat ripped out. It's Jingmen or dead."

"Can't you stay?"

Li turned to Hao and put his hand on her hand.

"Why tempt evil? I promised to take care of you, not get you killed."

"I'd feel safer if you're here. I'll help if you stay."

"No," he said, looking into the mirror at an old man's slashed face.

CHAPTER 58

Risky Business

DECEMBER 25, 2019

"Blood in the water," Guo thought replaying the vision of a vulnerable Jun laying across his bed two nights ago. He shifted in his chair. "Time to attack."

A lunch of rice noodles and eel drew little attention but reminded him of his father's favorite saying.

"He who does not cultivate his field dies of hunger."

The front-page headline from the unread *Wuhan Morning News* blared up from the dining room table, *Wuhan seeks to be tier-one city*.

"Maybe Jun can be useful a bit longer."

He picked up his phone.

"What's going on with the deadbeats Peng? Coughing up the money?"

"A couple yesterday. Suppose to be a few more today."

"Stay on them. I'll handle the big money."

"Yeah, you get the easy ones. They never squawk because they just screw their subcontractors," Peng said with a laugh.

"Did you take care of the farmer? He better be gone."

"Try to find him."

"Ok." Guo hung up without a goodbye, dialing the Central Hospital administrator.

"The pneumonia under control?"

"Few more cases today, whatever it is. Can you get us masks? I got a few, but we need more to protect the staff from catching this shit."

"Masks send the message we don't know what we're doing. A healthy dose of fear will keep the people safe for now. The government will give hospitals its full attention in a month."

"Let's protect the doctors. We're screwed if they get sick. A SARS virus makes pneumonia seem like a cold."

"It's the flu. Nobody wears masks dealing with that. Keep me updated. If news gets out, then doctors won't need masks because they'll be in jail. Got another call."

Chun heard the click and sighed.

"What do you want? More money?"

"Bad news. The guys who released the virus got sick. They're in the hospital," Guo's Beijing contact said in a hushed tone.

"Risky business. Did they do their job?"

"People are sick."

"Then we got what we wanted. Does the price go down if they die?" Guo said while peeling a banana.

"Same price. Figured you'd want to know. From what I hear, people are getting real sick faster than we thought."

"People get sick. That's life. Only call me if the price goes down," Guo said with no emotion as he hung up.

Jun came next.

"Nice article in the paper today," he said listening to nothing but heavy, tentative breathing.

"Fathers know what's best for the family. I have been your father for many years. Your poor attitude toward elders brought the necessary punishment. Maybe if your real father lived, things would be different."

"Leave my only father out of this," Jun said through clenched teeth.

"I've decided to give you more money depending on your attitude. A little incentive. I set up a bank account in the British Virgin Islands with five thousand American dollars. Do your job and more money will go into it. Pick up the paperwork at the hotel. You're free to spend it, but I wouldn't recommend it."

"Send it to my apartment. I'll never go to the Reign again."

"Hard work determines success. Not crying like a baby when life gets tough. You'll thank me one day."

"Send the paperwork. I'll do my job." Jun hung up.

Guo smiled.

"Promise poor people money and they'll keep quiet," he thought while picking at a piece of eel with a turned-up nose. "Somethings never change."

CHAPTER 59

Jail Lets Them Reflect

DECEMBER 25, 2019

"Hello. Captain Yang of the Wuhan Police Department. Central Hospital's Dr. Lui sent a WeChat note yesterday to seven other doctors warning of a virus. Several forwarded the message."

Guo let out a low growl. "Arrest the doctors as soon as possible. Once in detention, let me know."

"Yes sir. Shouldn't take long. Thank you."

Guo called the Central Hospital administrator. "Dr. Lui sent a WeChat note to seven doctors. All will be arrested. I told you to keep him quiet. Disappointing. I should put you in jail too."

"What do you expect? We have a hospital full of patients," Chun said with a sigh. "Someone had to think about the other hospitals. Arresting doctors can't help."

"A citizen disobeyed Communist Party orders. Unacceptable. Jail reeducates. We won't keep them long, except for Lui."

"You're playing with fire. Arresting doctors for helping people?"

"Other priorities take precedent. Please tell the media that Dr. Lui's virus threat is an Internet hoax. Also say Chinese doctors are close to curing this mysterious pneumonia. Maybe in the next, say, two weeks?"

At Central Hospital, six doctors sought solutions to the facility's growing virus problem.

"Did we send virus samples to the lab yet? We need proof if it's related to the SARS virus," Dr. Lui said.

"Several days ago. No word," a doctor's said. "Any new patients?"

"None today," Dr. Lui said as three policemen entered the room.

"Dr. Lui?"

"I'm Dr. Lui," he said, jumping from his chair.

"You are under arrest for spreading false rumors on the Internet. Handcuffs aren't necessary, are they?"

"I'll go without trouble. Can I call my wife?"

"At the station."

"I'm sure Chun already knows. Divide my charts while we straighten this out. I apologize for adding to your busy schedules," he said to the assembled doctors before leaving with the police.

The efficient Wuhan Police Department tracked the doctors' phones to find them within a couple hours, detaining them at WuChang's Zhongnanlu Police Station.

Guo arrived an hour later to discuss the situation with Captain Yang.

"The doctors must be punished. No one, not even doctors, can disrupt social order using the Internet," Guo said.

"Social order is important but these doctors rank among Wuhan's best citizens. Do we want to punish them? We need them," the captain pushed back.

"Beijing gets upset when problems pop up in the provinces. They'll hammer both of us. Jail the doctors a couple days to send a message."

"We can charge them with disturbing the social order, which violates the People's Republic of China Law on Penalties for Administration of Public Security."

"What's the punishment?"

"A public reprimand. The police can punish violators without going through court trials for behaviors disturbing public order or hampering management of society but not serious enough for jail."

"A reprimand? Article 25 says 10 days in jail for spreading rumors. The 2016 Cybersecurity law says seven years in prison for manufacturing or spreading fake news disturbing the economic or social order."

"Was the doctor's message false? No. People are sick."

Guo grumbled at Yang's interpretation. "China's getting weak as America. Harsh punishment stops problems."

CHAPTER 60

Eat, Then Go, Coward

DECEMBER 25, 2019

Hao nipped her index finger mincing ginger. She dabbed the small circle of blood with the same napkin drying her tears.

"I'm set to go. Lunch ready?" Li sat at the table, covering the cut on his face with his hand.

Hao shuffled around the kitchen, cleaning the counter for the third time.

"Are you sure about leaving?"

"It's for the best."

"Running away solves nothing. What good are you in Jingmen?"

"You want killers watching your house? They can chase me in the countryside. Friends will hide me."

"Your Jingmen friends? Old men afraid of missing lunch. They're only brave when drinking rice wine. Li Shun hiding. Never thought I'd say those words," she said, shaking her head.

"I'm old and don't want to die. Can't a man live his final years without getting involved in things that don't concern him?"

"What? You're the detective finding clues about my husband's murder one day and not concerned the next. Who are you?"

"They'll forget about me. I'll come back to visit."

Hao slid the bowls of noodles and lotus root onto the table, "Eat, then go, coward."

His chopsticks dug into the food, finishing the meal in haste before grabbing his battered suitcase.

"Thank you. I'll miss your delicious food. I must go to the Hankou Railway Station to catch the 4 p.m. Jingmen train. I will call soon Hao. Good-bye," he said from the hallway before closing the door.

The neighbor's nose poked out, watching Li walk toward the elevator.

"You make weak and salty soup, you lazy foolish woman," he said passing the door while pushing the down button.

"You're a mean man. The police said they'll arrest you if you come back," the neighbor screeched through the crack before shutting the door.

The old woman shook with adrenaline as she dialed her phone from the living room.

"Hello. Is this Detective Wong? This is Hao's neighbor. Yes, he left with a suitcase at 1:30 p.m. like you said. He's going to WuChang, or was it Hankou, Railway Station to catch the 4 p.m. Jingmen train? Oh my, I can't remember."

"Doesn't matter," Peng said. "A vigilant detective. A well-spent 50 dollars. Now another 100 comes if you keep an eye on the apartment for the next few days. If Li comes back, then call. If the young girl leaves call as well. I don't care about the old woman."

"No one ever does. I won't miss a thing."

CHAPTER 61

You're a Dead Man
DECEMBER 25, 2019

"It's a police matter. Your participation looks inappropriate," Captain Yang said to an agitated Guo. "We're trying to protect you sir."

"As Wuhan Communist Party chairman, I want to make sure this Internet hoax gets handled the right way."

"I agree but noncriminal matters call for a reprimand, not court proceedings. These gentlemen disrupted the public order but nothing more."

"I'll listen to the discussion regarding this matter. Are they here?"

"Down the hall. Keep in mind, it's a police matter."

"Yang, this will not be the end of it," Guo said in a flat tone as the police captain walked out of the room.

Eight doctors sat in a tight circle in the police interrogation room.

"A SARS outbreak has been transmitted from animal to man. Numerous similarities," Dr. Lui said to his colleagues. "We need to determine where and how much transmission is taking place."

"That means trouble for Wuhan," a fellow defendant doctor said. "Medical staffs need protection and citizens quarantined."

"We have seen an uptick in similar cases," another doctor said as several others nodded their heads.

"Protecting doctors, nurses, and hospital personnel must be the first order of business. No needless exposure."

Captain Yang and Guo entered the room, dismissing the two guards who had been listening to the doctors while texting to family and friends.

"You have been treated well during this unfortunate situation?" Captain Yang asked.

"Unfortunate? Dr. Lui decides his opinion is more important than the Communist Party. That's arrogant, not unfortunate," Guo said with anger.

Dr. Lui's looked at Guo with indifference as the other seven doctors exchanged glances.

"Wuhan faces a high infection risk with a SARS-related virus. Not pneumonia. Hospitals need protection. Your policy makes the city vulnerable," Dr. Lui said.

"You disobeyed a direct order. Instead of wasting time on social media you should have been doing your job, not pretending to be a *New York Times'* reporter spreading false rumors."

"We will determine the proper punishment for disrupting the public order," Captain Yang said. "Violators of serious cybersecurity violations face court-ordered punishment up to 10 years in prison."

"Ten years in prison for receiving a WeChat message? No, no," one of the doctors shouted.

"Dr. Lui deserves prison time," Guo said, interrupting the captain. "The others no. They need to go back to work."

"Thank you for your honorable opinion, Guo Zhenqin, but while the defendants disrupted public order, they did it with the city's health concerns in mind."

"Spreading a hoax on the Internet in defiance of the Communist Party has no purpose but to get attention. Dr. Lui seeks glorification, not results for the people."

"Full hospital staffs are essential during the holiday season. I order the eight defendants to prepare public letters of apology for disrupting public order. Come back January 2 at 10 a.m. with your apologies. Can you manage to do this, do you understand? If so, you are free to go."

"The Wuhan Communist Party opposes the blatant disregard of

public order and stability. Justice must come to these criminals," Guo said as the doctors headed for the door.

"I'm sorry for this disagreement Chairman Guo. I meant no disrespect. I will write a letter," Dr. Lui said as he bowed.

"You're a dead man Lui."

CHAPTER 62

A Spreading Illness

DECEMBER 25, 2019

Li strode down Taozhi Road heading to the Metro with a confusing mix of emotions. His cut face stung in the cool breeze, but the pain and thrill of the last few days made him feel alive.

"When did life become so complicated? Just go to Jingmen and help stubborn farmers. Wuhan has never been my home," he thought trying to forget the last few exciting days living in Hao's home.

The farmer stopped at the chestnut stand at Gate 1. A peek over his shoulder spotted a man 50 feet behind who looked suspicious, stopping when Li turned.

"A bag of chestnuts. Don't be cheap. Give me a full bag."

"Here. A nice big bag of hot chestnuts for my friend."

"These nuts look older than your mother, yet you give me so few. Who are you saving them for?" The vendor turned away.

The suspicious man breezed by without a glance but was followed by a large man who looked like Peng. Li paid the vendor and began jogging toward the subway, brushing past couples holding hands or college girls locked arm-in-arm.

The Metro's long escalator to the underground trains allowed a glance back to see the man still following.

"That's Peng," Li thought. He pushed past several escalator riders before running down the final steps.

Metro security scanned the bags of a young college student as Li shoved past her friends, throwing his bag into the scanner while looking back.

"I can reach Hankou Railway Station either way with a transfer. I'll confuse him by heading south then change to the Number 6 train," he thought, running down a set of stairs to the subway platform.

The farmer weaved through the large crowd before hiding behind a recessed wall at the end of the platform.

"A good spot for the two-minutes wait." He peered down the platform searching for his pursuer.

A young boy ran up to Li, mimicking him by standing with his back plastered to the wall, looking like an escaped convict and grandson.

"Go away," he whispered to the laughing child who ignored him.

The southbound train pulled into the station. Li waited for the closing bell to sound before dashing into the front car. The young boy chased him, only stopping when an agitated grandmother waiting for the northbound train screamed.

No doors between cars allowed Li to see through a quarter of the train. The large man stood four or five cars away but began walking his way.

Li tried to hide by staring out the train's doors with his hat low.

A peek from under his hat showed the pursuer standing next to him causing him to twitch before realizing she was a large, short-haired woman.

He took a deep breath and leaned against a pole while watching darkness fly by in the tunnel.

He touched his knee several times where Hao had rested her hand as confusing thoughts drifted through his mind on the 45-minute ride to the always-crowded Hankou Railway Station.

The on-time Jingmen train arrived with few riders. Most wore masks while discussing a spreading illness.

"Why does everyone wear masks? I don't have one," he said to a young woman who sat next to him.

"A mysterious illness that kills people spreads in Wuhan. I'm going home to get away from it. Are you from the city?"

"No. I live in Jingmen."

"Here is a mask. Better to be safe from Wuhan people."

"Thank you." He put the mask on as a coughing old man nearby refused a free one.

"Death travels on the train," Li thought, shaking his head. "And I'm trying to hide?"

Li got off the train when it pulled into the first station outside Wuhan.

An expressionless clerk looked up from his phone.

"I bought a one-way ticket to Jingmen. I changed my mind. I want to go back to Wuhan."

"When do you wish to return?"

"On the next train."

CHAPTER 63

The Sun Does the Hard Work

DECEMBER 26, 2019

The old woman's phone rang as she sat in a large chair near the front door.

"Hello officer," she said hunched over, covering the phone with her free hand.

"Hello friend. What news do you have?"

"A quiet day since the mean man left. The young woman remains in the apartment while Hao comes and goes."

"Are you sure?"

"All I do is sit and listen. My muscles hurt from dragging my heavy chair near the door."

"It will keep you healthy. An extra 60 dollars if it's true. The blind masseuses across the street can work out the knots for that money."

"All I say is true. I expect 160 dollars from you but I will spend it as I see fit."

"Hao is there now?"

"Yes, making soup."

"Good. I'll be over in 30 minutes."

"Bring the money you owe me. $160."

At the same time, Li sat on a bench in the Modena courtyard about 30 yards from Hao and the old woman's condo building. The train brought him back, but the question now was where to go.

"The police will come again if you return." The old woman's last words to Li played over and over in his brain as he stared at the building.

"The police don't want me. Peng does," the farmer thought as he wondered if he made the right choice in coming back to Wuhan.

Thoughts about dying by a virus or at the hands of killers sounded brave on the train to Jingmen, but now he really didn't want to die either way.

The aching slash on his face sent him the message that his world had become a kill or be killed contest. Any blunder might cost him his life, but so would inactivity. The people chasing him never stopped and took no prisoners.

"If I go up to Hao's apartment, then the old lady will be sure to spot me. But does it matter? The Jingmen people will tell Peng I didn't show up by tomorrow. My ability to surprise him will not last long."

The low-in-the-sky 6 p.m. sun at his back still packed a powerful blinding punch as it shone between the forest of condos. The sunlight on his back made him think of LiJiao chastising him late in the day in Zigui County decades ago.

"The sun does the hard work, sending our farm life-giving light over millions of miles. We simply prepare our fields to receive the gift. The sun never complains about giving us a gift. Let's not complain about the good fortune of receiving it," his friend had said with a smile.

LiJiao's words brought a small smile to the farmer's face.

"Be prepared to receive life's gifts or they are sure to be wasted," he said as Hao's condominium glowed in the December sun.

Then, the split second of peace shattered.

"Peng!" The bodyguard's large, angular body strode past the Modena gate and its guards. Li sat frozen in the sunlight, watching the bodyguard turn left once past the gate and head toward him.

Peng put his hand up to his eyes to block the bright sunlight that engulfed the courtyard.

The farmer pulled his hat down low and folded his arms across his chest as Peng turned right, going up the steps to the entrance of Hao's condo building. He picked up the phone and within a few seconds the door buzzed to let him enter.

CHAPTER 64

He'll Kill Me Too

DECEMBER 26, 2019

Peng got off the Modena elevator as the old woman stood waiting for him.

"Hello Detective Wong. My money?"

"Shhh. Let's go into your home to discuss."

The old woman entered the apartment and sat in a chair blocking the door, causing the large man to maneuver around her into the living room.

"The Wuhan Police commend your excellent work. You deserve $200. In the future, I'll pay $100 for news of the young girl leaving or Li arriving."

"The police pay well," she said with a smile as she took the money from Peng. "I won't miss a thing. If you move my bed near the door, then I can listen at night too."

"Might look suspicious if Hao visits. Let's move the chair a bit. I'm sure you have the hearing and vision of an owl."

"And wisdom! It's exciting being an undercover policeman like you. Don't worry about moving it, no one ever visits me."

"I believe you won't miss a thing," Peng said with a laugh. "But please, sleep in your bedroom. Now I'm going to visit Hao and Jun. Don't open the door for one hour. Undercover cops need to lay low at times."

Peng slipped out of the apartment without a sound, waiting several seconds before ringing Hao's bell.

Hao opened the door as the scarred man waited with an awkward grin.

"Hello Hao. I'm Wu. We've met before. I'd like to talk to you and your daughter."

Hao squinted at the bodyguard's damaged face before touching her own face with a fearful blink.

"Jun's gone. Please leave," she said, trying to close the door.

His large arm stopped the door. "I know she's here. No harm will come to you. Just want to talk for a few moments," he said brushing past the shaking Hao.

A door creaked.

"Please Jun, come out. We need to talk," Peng said in a loud voice.

"Hello Peng," Jun said with cool detachment entering the room. "Don't worry mother. It's ok."

"Peng? You know my name is Wu."

"Liar! You killed my husband." Hao ran at the large man with swinging fists, punching with wild blows that he deflected before grabbing her arms.

"Calm your mother so I can talk," he said with a smile.

Jun put her arm around Hao, leading the sobbing woman to the couch.

"I'll be honest. My name is Peng. I worked for the YiChang Communist Party when your father died but I did not kill him."

"More lies! Your own cousin, Wu Tong, accused you. You threw my husband to his death," Hao said, pointing at Peng. "Killer."

"Wu, a scared little man, will die in fear for his part in the killing. I wasn't home when Wu killed him. He got paid and now blames me."

"If you weren't there," asked Hao, "then how did you get the scar on your face?"

"I'm a bodyguard. My job can be rough," Peng said with a smile.

"So, you're here to kill the rest of the family," Jun said without emotion.

Hao jumped off the couch and ran screaming into the bedroom, locking the door.

"Why do you frighten your mother? You need to be a good Chinese daughter. I'm not killing anyone. I saved you from Guo at the hotel. He wanted to tear you apart. I let Li leave town yesterday instead of killing him like Guo wanted."

"Li's probably dead. You'll wait till the two meetings end before forcing me to visit Guo one last time. Now my mother knows too much."

"Here's the truth. Guo killed your father to steal farmers' money to fund Baixin. He tastes blood again. He wants all the games' money and no witnesses. He'll kill me too. Neither of us are safe."

"If I could only trust you," Jun said with downcast eyes and a slight shake of her head.

"Oh, you can. I'd do anything for you. Anything," Peng said as he spread his hands apart and leaned toward the young beauty.

"Anything? I don't feel safe around Guo. Will you protect me if he decides I'm not needed anymore? If so, I promise to do the same for you. I've always thought of you as a friend," she said with a shy smile while avoiding eye contact.

"We need to work together if we want to live," Peng said. "I will always protect you. My family owes that to your family to make up for my cousin's murder of your father."

"Let's not talk of my father. Will you protect Li as well?"

"That depends on him. If he threatens Guo, I'll have no choice but to stop it. I don't think he will. Do you?"

"No, he won't. And if I threaten Guo?"

"You know better. Your friend is not that smart," he said with a smile. "Let's just agree to protect each other."

"How are you going to stop Guo if he wants to kill me?"

"Sit and I'll tell you a story."

Peng sat down and closed his eyes for a few seconds before opening them with a faraway look.

My mother and I walked through a village searching for food. I was 12 years old. Scraps of disgusting dumpster garbage and an occasional rat had been our only food for a week.

A restaurant owner swept in front of his shop. We stopped.

"Please kind sir, we have not eaten for many days. We will do anything for food," my mother said, begging from her knees.

"Anything, heh. Ok, I have a few chores. But you must do them before beggars get fed. Boy, you sweep the restaurant floor. One grain of rice will get you beaten instead of food. Woman, you come with me."

A door leading to the man's meager home closed behind the two while I cleaned the room with great intensity, dreaming of huge fish, lotus soup, and a big bowl of steaming rice from the nice man.

Hunger soon sapped my energy, so I laid on the cold floor, falling to sleep in seconds. Then, my mother screamed.

I jumped up and ran to the door.

"Stop it. Stop it," I said pounding on the locked door. Many men had beaten me over the years for interfering with them trying to take advantage of my mother.

"Please, kill me," I heard my mother say as the sound of pounding flesh echoed through the door before a tremendous blow brought silence.

"The mother tried to seduce me while the boy stole food," the owner told the local village leaders. "The woman fell and hit her head trying to escape."

The court lauded the owner for keeping the community safe from thieves before sending me to my uncle's house.

I returned to the village three years later with my Red Guard troop and hung the owner outside the restaurant.

"The capitalist roader deserved to die a thousand times," I told the troop, spitting on the swaying corpse.

I promise to never fall asleep on you.

Peng stood and walked to the couch where Jun sat.

"It's OK. I won't let anyone hurt you. I'll protect you." Peng gently brushed her hair before walking out in silence.

CHAPTER 65

Guo Will Protect Us

DECEMBER 27, 2019

"What's that?" Hao leaned up in bed with her ear pointed toward the door listening for the sound of danger before pulling the covers over her head.

She curled up into a tight ball. Out-of-control fear assured a scarred-faced killer would soon come busting through the door and slice her to death.

The elevator stopped on her floor. She propped herself up on her elbow when the sound of footsteps echoed.

She shivered in fear as a bead of sweat rolled down her forehead.

A creak at the door brought a shout of "no," before she scurried out of the room and into bed with her daughter.

"I'm afraid. Noises keep me awake."

"It's just your imagination. Peng thinks the fear will keep us quiet," Jun said to Hao whose eyes remained riveted on the door.

"I'd feel safer if Li and his knife were here. I want to go back to Baixin."

"You can go but I want to stay here. It doesn't matter. Guo tracks our phones wherever we go."

"He supported us for 26 years. Why scare me when he can just say what he wants? It makes no sense Jun. He's not the problem."

"You fail to see the real Guo."

"Peng killed your father. I believe that. Guo was working in Wuhan with no idea what that evil man did."

193

"You foolish woman. He knows everyone's business and wants a cut. Father refused, paying for it with his life. Peng couldn't find his ass with his two hands."

"Guo will protect us. I'll call tomorrow."

"Do whatever," Jun said, gently rolling away, "but go to sleep."

Hao called her boss the next morning.

"I'm sorry but I need to talk about an urgent matter."

"Of course. I am always available Hao. In fact, I'm glad you called because I have a matter to discuss as well."

"The man who works for you killed my husband. He threatened Jun and me yesterday."

"Your husband died many years ago. A suicide I believe. Who is the man? Many work for me."

"Your bodyguard. He says his name is Wu, but his name is Peng. He pushed his way into my new apartment at the Modena yesterday, threatening to kill Jun and me. I'm terrified of him."

"Why did he come?"

"I'm not sure. First, he said his name was Wu, then Peng. I accused him of killing my husband. He denied it. Said you ordered the killing. I don't believe him."

"How do you know he killed your husband?"

"My friend, Li, talked to his cousin who was at the apartment when they threw him off the balcony. The cousin said powerful friends in Wuhan wanted my husband dead."

"The death, always a mystery. Peng said his cousin and another man watched your husband kill himself after a disagreement. What's the cousin's name?"

"Wu Tong. You don't believe your bodyguard killed him?"

"At the time, no. But this story worries me. I'll look into the matter."

"Can you keep him away from us? And my friend, Li, too? He had to go to Jingmen because of Peng's threats. We are frightened."

"Back to Jingmen. Sorry to hear that. Very sorry. No one will bother you. Now, I'd like to discuss Jun."

"She's angry with you for beating her. A very harsh punishment."

"You know Jun's the daughter I never had."

"You have been kind."

"Children need discipline. They fail to understand their place, acting in selfish ways. You have seen it?"

"Jun can be difficult."

"The party needs to accomplish much in the coming weeks. She needs to focus on completing her work without the need for recognition. She now will, thanks to my efforts."

"I hope you are right, but she wants revenge."

"That's good. I don't want to break her spirit. How are the plans coming for the family reunion banquet on January 18? Will it be the biggest ever?"

"Forty thousand family representatives expected. A world's record."

"Excellent. Now Jun doesn't know but she will greet the banquet attendees instead of the mayor. She grew up in Baixin. Who knows where this may take her? A prestigious honor, indeed."

"That is too kind."

"Say nothing. Discipline has its rewards. Now I must go."

"Oh my," she thought putting down her phone with a smile. "No threats from Peng, plus Jun speaking at the banquet. And, who knows, maybe it will be safe for Li to return?"

CHAPTER 66

Service to the People

DECEMBER 27, 2019

The young doctor tapped a pen on a blank piece of paper.

"Guo puts me in jail if I don't apologize. If I do, then back to fighting a deadly virus, with no expert assistance or supplies. Jail's safer."

Chairman Mao's philosophy of "service to the people" floated into his mind.

"My WeChat note tried to protect my friends while failing to warn the thousands of doctors, nurses, administrators, and support staff in Wuhan's eight hospitals who face danger too. A selfish act," he said to the blank page.

"I'm a coward for informing a privileged few, the bourgeois. I need to apologize for failing to eliminate human suffering and uphold the chasteness and honor of medicine for all people, regardless of the hardships."

His two-year-old son crawled around his legs in the small apartment as the doctor struggled to find the right words.

"Will you, my young son, find the courage to do the right thing?"

The boy grabbed for the paper, wanting to tell his story by putting it in his mouth.

"No. That's daddy's paper. Here, play with this," the father said, trying to give the toddler a ball. A wounded scream echoed through the room.

"Don't cry," he said, then stopped. "No son, yell so everyone hears you. Stand up to the powerful unlike your father who remains silent."

He gave a sheet of paper to his son before writing, "Dear Captain Yang: I apologize for my selfish WeChat message to my seven colleagues."

CHAPTER 67

Planting Fear
Never Hurts

Peng sipped latte outside a Starbucks on North Liji Road next to a large suitcase filled with cash.

"Li needs to go. I'll protect Jun. The farmer's a hothead who'll just get in the way. I can make it look like an accident once I find him. He's not in Jingmen so where is he?"

His China Mobile contact offered no help.

"Appears Li's phone has been turned off for several days in a Baixin apartment," he told Peng. "I'll let you know if it changes."

A warm December breeze blew leaves past his feet when his phone rang.

"Shit, Guo," Peng said before answering.

"I just got a distressing call from Hao. You visited her and Jun?" Guo stopped.

"I needed to talk with Jun about an account."

"Hao told a different story, saying you blamed me for her husband's death. Now, we both know I didn't want to know how you dealt with that farmer. You decided to throw him off the balcony. I thought I could trust you?"

"A confused old lady. I didn't blame you. She brought up your name. I said he jumped."

"I see. She said the farmer's back in Jingmen. Didn't you tell me he was taken care of? I hope that is true."

"That's true. He had an unscheduled detour on his way to the train station," Peng said with an unconvincing laugh. "My visit might keep Jun in line."

"Planting fear never hurts. I should have suggested it. Why didn't you tell me?"

"Just seemed the right thing to do."

"Leave it for now. Don't make any more visits. Got it?"

"Yes boss."

Peng let out a sigh as the phone clicked off. Guo didn't believe him, but he didn't care.

"Nothing matters to him but money and the screams of young girls," he thought as his bony fingers tapped on the table.

In the alley shadows 50 yards away, a tall thin man watched the animated Peng squirm.

"Now who follows you Peng Qiang?" Li's motionless body hid a racing heart.

The sun had provided Li a shining gift yesterday. He followed Peng on the Metro to his Liji Road home then rented a hotel room nearby. The next morning Li followed the bodyguard when he came out of his apartment carrying a suitcase.

Peng visited several construction companies before finishing the day at a nearby small sign shop. The owner argued with him outside about paying such "high fees," saying he took his profits.

"Don't do something that upsets us both," Peng said, lifting the small man off the ground with his shirt.

The frightened man handed Peng a stack of 100-dollar bills who walked away laughing as the man screamed obscenities.

"In a cat's eye, all things belong to the cats," Li said as he watched the large man sip latte. "Until they don't."

CHAPTER 68

Just Helping a Friend

DECEMBER 28, 2019

"Egos never solve problems," Jun LiJiao said to his daughter the day before he died. "Study the facts without prejudice. Set aside personal opinions or potential gains. The truth cares little for what you get out of life."

Soaking in a tub of hot water let her mind drift to heroic stories of Chinese leaders like Sun Yat-sen and Mao Tse-Dong and the strength to rally during bleak moments.

"Success takes energy. I'm not sure I have it," Jun thought as the water line rested on her chin.

The phone rang. Jun hesitated, then picked up.

"Jun? Is that you? This is Art. I'm using a friend's phone. You sound weak."

"Under the weather. Sorry for not getting back to you."

"I'm worried about you. Can we meet? I'm going to Cambodia in a couple weeks. Want to see you before I leave."

"What are you doing now?"

"Not a lot. Just working on student grades. Where are you?"

"I'm near your campus. Let's meet at Rock Pizza across from Gate 1 in an hour."

Five days of non-stop work calls and a mother's smothering attention had the walls closing in on her. She needed a friend.

A black Dolce and Gabbana short wool double-breasted peacoat with a Peter Pan collar and silk-lined wool pinstriped black pants hung in her mother's closet. A sense of femininity returned.

The next-door neighbor peeked out as she left.

"Hello. How are you?"

"Not well. I hurt from sitting too long."

"Why don't you get out? Meet a friend. That's what I'm doing. Going to lunch at Rock Pizza."

"Too old and poor to waste money on bad western food. I have a call to make. You said Rock Pizza?"

"Yes. Bye-bye," Jun said, pushing the elevator button as the old woman closed the door.

"Jun! Good to see you," Art said minutes later, trying to give a hug which she fended off.

She lowered her gaze with pursed lips.

"Thank you for coming," she said in a whisper, running her hand through her hair several times.

A young Chinese waiter looked up from his phone as the two entered the empty western-styled restaurant that served pizza with Chinese toppings like dragon fruit and shrimp with the shells still on.

"A booth or a table? We have our choice," Art said with a smile.

"A booth please," she said, brushing the back of her pants.

"Been wanting to talk. I ran into your friend, Li, at a small restaurant up the street. I was with my friend Daniel, so we could talk."

"Li mentioned it."

"Did you see the photo? It's the same guy who was with the old man at the Qintai Theater."

"I do, a bodyguard for the elder gentleman."

"You really work with guys who killed your father?"

She said nothing, shaking her head to blink away a tear.

"Shit, back home someone would shoot him."

"Art, there's much you don't know. As I've said, don't get involved in Chinese politics. Arrangements have been made."

"Just trying to be a friend. Do what you want."

"This has been a, ah, delicate situation. Is that the right way to say it?"

"That's correct. Delicate means sensitive or easy to break. You've never seemed that way to me. More like a brick wall," he said with a laugh.

A tear rolled down Jun's face as the Eagles' *Hotel California* bounced through the empty restaurant. Her beautiful hair tumbled down as she stared at the table.

"Jun, I love you. The one night we spent together never leaves my mind. I want to marry you and have a family."

"Oh Art," Jun said, shaking her head. "If it was only that easy."

"I know Chinese politicians shouldn't marry Americans, but love conquers all!" He patted her hands as she stared out the window.

"I need to tell you something that I should have long ago." Jun bit her lower lip.

"Wait. Before you do, I have a present. I know more about your problems than you think."

Jun remained silent, giving Art a blank stare.

"I'm a friend now. I have something for you. Might help, might cause trouble."

"What?"

"A copy of your original tape," he said, setting it on the table.

Jun's eyes widened. "The tape?"

"I hid one in case something happened. Daniel and I listened to it. Couldn't help it. The guy mentioned a plan. Is that the old guy from the theater? You involved?"

An alarmed look crossed her face. "Put it away. But keep it down."

"Why?" He followed her eyes out the window to see Peng standing outside. The large man smiled and waved, then walked away.

"He's dangerous," Art said, giving a fake laugh while sliding the tape back into his bag.

"Don't worry. If he wanted us, he'd already be here. Probably looking for Li. Hide the tape. Can you trust Daniel to keep quiet?"

"Who knows? Could be a cop for all I know."

"Send me his name. I'll find out. I don't want anything to happen to you."

"Happen to me? Nothing's going to happen to me or you, Mrs. Iron," he said, grabbing Jun's cold hands from across the table. "What did you want to tell me?"

"Nothing important. I'll tell you later. Let's keep in touch while we can."

CHAPTER 69

That's Insane

JANUARY 1, 2020

"Any lab results from the Hubei Province Health Commission? They should have completed the testing," Dr. Lui asked his assistant on the morning of January 1.

"Strange news. The health commission ordered us to stop testing samples and destroy existing virus samples."

"Destroy the samples? That's insane."

"Called a friend at the commission. A similar virus to 2003 SARS, but higher ups said to stop testing. I guess they'd rather spread the virus than bad news."

"Wuhan has a world-class coronavirus clinic, and they tell us to destroy samples? I don't understand the logic?"

The assistant shrugged. "I really don't know. My friend won't say anything more."

Dr. Lui sunk in his chair, staring at an ever-increasing number of new virus patient charts. He picked up the phone.

"What's going on Chun? We can't report new cases and now the health commission won't let us test for a SARS outbreak. They're telling us to destroy existing samples."

"Relax. The province remains sensitive to bad news. They want to make sure it's serious. Monitor the situation until the two meetings end. We'll see where it goes."

"So do nothing for 18 days but watch people die or get sick! We might be dead."

"Let's hope not. Are you 100 percent sure it's SARS?"

"We'll never be 100 percent sure with no testing. Why?"

"The provincial and local party believe it's an Internet hoax started by agitators trying to embarrass them before the two meetings. That won't happen."

"So, let's pretend it doesn't exist while people die? That's the message?"

"Easy Dr. Lui. You got off light with the apology. Guo wants you in jail. He's thinks you're the agitator."

"People tend to get agitated before they die."

"Guo's adamant. No discussions."

CHAPTER 70

I Can. I Understand.

JANUARY 2, 2020

Captain Yang walked into the conference room where eight Wuhan doctors waited.

"Good morning. I hope you didn't wait long."

The captain pulled out a folder as the doctors fidgeted in silence.

"To make things easier we wrote letters of apology. That was this morning's delay. This way everyone says the same thing."

The captain gave each doctor a personalized letter admitting to disrupting social order and promising to stop "illegal activity."

The letters of apology asked two questions.

The first question: The law enforcement agency wants you to cooperate, listen to the police, and stop your illegal behavior. Can you do that?

"I can," Lui wrote under the question.

The second question: If you insist on your views, refuse to repent, and continue the illegal activity, you will be punished by the law. Do you understand?

"I understand," Lui answered.

"Sign the letters and return to your normal lives as long as you abide by the terms," Captain Yang said with a cold smile.

The doctors avoided eye contact with Yang as they left in silence. The captain grabbed Dr. Lui by the arm, pulling him aside.

"I didn't want to do this, but orders are orders. Hey, my uncle doesn't feel well. He has a fever and a cough. Do you think he has pneumonia?"

"He's lucky if he does, but I don't think so. Get him to the hospital with a mask but don't let him cough in your face."

CHAPTER 71

It Doesn't Exist

"Quit feeling sorry for yourself and get back to work," Guo said to Jun in a flat tone over the phone. "The two meetings start next week. We need your expertise."

"I understand. I'm feeling better."

"You know what to do. Work with the four newspapers to promote the good work we've done. The party hopes for a prosperous 2020."

Jun worked for years with the *Hubei Daily* (the official organ of the Hubei Communist Party), the *Chutian Metropolis Daily*, the *Changjiang Daily* (the official organ of the Wuhan Communist Party), and the *Wuhan Evening Post*.

"I've been told the papers need to fill 150 pages during the 11 days of meetings. That's a lot of information we'll need to provide," Guo said.

"Should I focus on Wuhan becoming a tier-one city?"

"Yes. The agendas are set. Talk about how wonderful Wuhan is but not one word about the pneumonia during either meeting. The illness doesn't exist. We want the meetings to finish on time."

"So, your plan unfolds. But people are already talking about pneumonia and SARS."

"Good. We want them talking about the pneumonia as much as possible. That just means no one will be talking about the military games. We want them distracted. Fear is the point."

"Why not discuss it? The hospitals delegates can prepare us if things get bad."

"That's the advice of our technical support. We'll get all the support we need after January 18 when the Wuhan Games' discussion is complete."

"Technical support people? What are they doing?"

"A special project. No need for your involvement," Guo said.

CHAPTER 72

No One Is Behind the Scenes

JANUARY 5, 2020

Fifteen hundred people waited in a Wuhan drizzle outside a crammed Central Hospital. Each had a simple question: "Do I have pneumonia?"

The hospital's hallways resembled a triage as employees tried to separate the sick from the worried.

"If you're not sick, then please leave immediately. It is not safe," a loudspeaker blared, but no one left.

Weibo and WeChat posts talked of hospitals full of sick relatives and friends. Wuhan City Hall seemed the only entity not concerned about the growing problem.

"Look at that line," Dr. Lui said to Chun pointing through the administrator's window. "Every person from here to YiChang with a runny nose, cold, or upset stomach wants to be told they're ok. How many healthy people will die coming to the hospital?"

"Death is our business," the administrator said without looking up from his desk.

"They're overrunning us. Can't we separate the sick from the not-so sick somewhere else?"

"That's the plan. Community centers will diagnose and send us the sick. Then we'll barricade the hospital at the street."

"Does that start today?"

"Not yet. Changes will take place once the meetings go for a few days. The meetings start tomorrow."

"We can't wait."

"Four or five days. We can make it," Chun said.

The doctor took a photo of the large crowd and sent it to Jun before calling her.

"Get us masks. The hospital's being overrun with people, threatening the staff. Hundreds of people waiting together guarantees the virus will spread. The government needs to act now."

"I understand. We're working behind the scenes to take care of the situation. The rollout begins soon."

"No one's behind the scenes here. We're all on a dangerous stage."

"Please be safe. We'll talk soon. I'll check on masks." She hung up, coughed, and felt her forehead.

CHAPTER 73

Our Silence Helps the Tiger

JANUARY 6, 2020

"Chun! Hey," Guo shouted across the expansive entrance to the Han Theater.

Chun approached a grumpy-looking Guo who ignored his outstretched hand.

"Mr. Chairman, a glorious pleasure to greet you on a spectacular January 6. Again, thank you for my appointment as chief healthcare delegate."

"I didn't appoint you to drink tea and gossip. You're my point person to the other 15 hospital delegates. You know your task?"

The hospital administrator had heard his Wuhan Communist Party's marching orders several times.

"Mr. Chairman, not one word about the pneumonia."

"Your reeducation will be cleaning bed pans if I hear anything. No help from the government until the meetings end January 18," Guo said before another delegate grabbed him to whisper in his ear.

Chun stuffed his hands back into his pockets, looking for his ticket to enter the Han Theater.

The $350-million theater, next to the 20-story Reign Hotel, resembled a giant red lantern.

The grand theater's main attraction was the Han Show. The show started with the theater seats sweeping back to allow 2.5 million gallons of water to fill the auditorium for 95 aquatic performers. The water drained away at the show's end in an amazing technological feat.

Chun pulled out the January 6 edition of the *Changjiang Daily* from his coat pocket. Two stories ran on the front page. The story below the fold said:

The Wuhan Municipal Health Commission reported yesterday that a viral pneumonia of unknown cause involves a total of 59 cases. Laboratory test results ruled out respiratory pathogens, such as influenza, avian influenza, adenovirus, the Severe Acute Respiratory Syndrome coronavirus, and Middle East Respiratory Syndrome coronavirus, as the cause.

"Easy to rule out SARS when you don't test for it," he thought before glancing at the story above the fold.

The story trumpeted Wuhan's effort to become a first-tier city, raising its profile to equal status with Beijing, Shanghai, Guangzhou, and Shenzhen.

"Chun, you don't have a fever, do you?" The administrator from Wuhan Number 1 Hospital laughed before sitting next to his friend.

"I know people who do. What can we do but let the politicians handle it? Do me a favor, don't speak of it in a public setting, ok? Otherwise, you'll never see me again."

"I've been warned over and over. If I say something, we'll disappear together. This theater hides more than water today."

"How's your hospital?"

"More patients than we can handle, so I'd rather be here. No masks or protective gear. Help's coming after the meeting next week?"

"That's what they say. Guo's up to his eyeballs keeping this quiet. All I say is, 'Yes Mr. Chairman, we can handle it till the 18th.'"

The 15 healthcare delegates from Wuhan No. 1 Hospital, Wuhan No. 6 Hospital, the Union Hospital of Wuhan Medical School, the Wuhan TCM Hospital, and the Respiratory Clinic from the Wuhan No. 1 Hospital joined Chun in keeping the virus quiet at the meeting even though countless delegates asked in whispers for updates for "family members."

The hospital representatives gathered at the end of the Wuhan meeting to congratulate themselves for following orders.

"I appreciated your cooperation on the virus during the meeting. This deadly tiger came out of nowhere. But silence always helps the tiger," Chun told the representatives before returning to overwhelmed facilities.

CHAPTER 74

The Fix Is In

A fearful wind blew through Wuhan City as the Hubei Province's 1,346 leaders crowded into the Hongshan Ceremonial Hall for the second of the two meetings. Many wore masks.

Six days of fierce debate over "why Wuhan is as good as Guangzhou" filled the auditorium and newspapers while little was said about the city hospitals' losing battle with the virus.

Jun worked at city hall preparing tentative plans for quarantining Wuhan in case the hospitals' struggles spiraled out of control.

Her phone rang. "Where are you? I want you here for the opening of the Hubei meeting," Guo said in a loud bark. "The US, France, and Great Britain are here but you can't make it?"

"I did my part. The fix is in. The politicians are free to worry about Wuhan being a tier-one city while the locals worry about a mysterious pneumonia. You walk away with $200 million in the confusion. Congratulations. You win again," Jun said.

"No courage to cross the finish line with me? C'est la vie."

"You just want to show off some arm candy to your old men friends. One last bit of free advice. Party orders, bribes, or threats won't stop the tiger so watch out."

"I've succeeded a long time without your advice."

"The doctors say the pneumonia loves the elderly. What a waste if you die now. All this work for nothing. Remember me in your will."

Her phone clicked off.

CHAPTER 75

Talking Doesn't Cook the Rice

JANUARY 15, 2020

Hens shuffled, scratched, and squawked in stacked cages as bats and rodents defecated on the birds from above at the Baixin wet market.

"Which lovely chicken wants to receive the honor of being boiled for my family banquet chicken soup? That one looks plump," Hao said to Wei.

The chickens pecked at the cage floor, avoiding the red head's hungry-looking gaze.

"My chicken soup brings people to the banquet just like a mother's cooking. Maybe that one," Hao said.

"Too skinny. We're sure to see dozens of plates of eggs or squash decorated as rat families. Year of the rat always brings them out," Wei said.

The banquet brought out the artist in many attendees. Hao's assistant worked nights preparing an elaborate dish of squash and cucumber carved into seven large orange and green birds. The detailed plumes of feathers stood two-feet tall.

Hao and Wei had swapped banquet stories for so long that they rarely listened to each other's tales.

"My traditional Hubei Province dish of steamed WuChang fish always gets praised," Wei said to her friend.

"For weeks people ask me if I'm making my soup. Twenty years in a row and it is still popular as ever because of its wonderful flavor," Hao said as Wei waved her hand at the comment.

"I'm sending photos to my daughter in the United States so she can see the fish she's missing," Wei said.

"The wet market fresh hens create a better flavor than the grocery store's frozen meat, a richer taste for the soup," Hao said as she stared at the caged chickens. "This will be the best yet."

"Aren't you worried about the news of the doctors' internet hoax," Wei said. "Everyone talks about it. Have you discussed cancelling the banquet?"

"Jealous and destructive people want to tear down my success."

"My friend's cousin works at Central Hospital. The growing numbers of sick people there has everyone nervous," Wei said. "Maybe delay it a few days?"

"Never. People want to celebrate the New Year holiday. Cancel because a few people have the flu? That makes no sense. Jun will speak at the banquet, such a great honor! She'll ease people's concerns."

"Sounds like your family needs the banquet," Wei said with a smile.

"As does my boss. He'd never cancel."

The banquet committee met the next day to discuss the issue.

"Many buy wet market chicken and fish. Maybe we should not allow dishes with such ingredients? You know, the government closed the Huanan Seafood Market," a concerned committee member said.

"People will lie about where they shop if we ban wet market food, plus cooking kills any germs," Hao said with an air of confidence.

Yu Tong, a mean-spirited man who disliked everyone, according to Hao, asked her a question from the audience.

"You are a scientist as well?"

"Cooking chicken for a long time kills any germs. Even the dim-witted understand heat kills germs." The members smiled, nodding in agreement. "That's why we drink hot water."

The discussion ended with a plea for unity.

"Isn't the risk of getting the patriotic virus worth the price of feeding those who cannot feed themselves? Disease doesn't stop our responsibility to serve the people," Hao told the committee.

"Our great leader, Xi Jinping, will cancel the event if necessary to maintain social stability. He has said nothing," a committee member said in support of Hao.

"All in favor of the banquet as planned raise your hand," Hao said to the committee.

All voted yes as Yu left the room shouting at the committee. "You vote to kill our friends and family. Baixin will remember this sad day for a long time."

"The banquet proceeds. Buy your expensive fish for your daughter's hungry eyes," Hao told Wei with a laugh later that day in the community's courtyard. "Go to the Baixin market now or all the best fish will be gone. The crowds get large today then the prices go up and you'll pay twice as much for a skinny one. They'll still have fat ones with 13 ½ bones if you go now."

"I'm on my way," Wei said as she pursed her plump red lips.

"Yu called me a killer for having the banquet. I need to report him to Guo," Hao said to her friend.

"A weaseled-faced man who argues, drinks alcohol, and gambles like a fool at mahjong. He won't attend or eat any food from the banquet, yapping like a dog about his nephew who he says is a Tianyou Hospital doctor. He's probably a janitor," Wei said, causing both ladies to laugh.

"All false Internet rumors spread by the eight doctors who apologized for their lies last week."

Yu, a tall man with rounded shoulders and a pointed chin, loved to discuss politics in the garden. His fiery rhetoric enticed others to join the conversations.

"A mysterious virus burns like wildfire for weeks yet our government acts if nothing is wrong," Yu said to his friend as he moved a mahjong tile. "Maybe there's more to the mystery?"

"Talking doesn't cook the rice," his friend said grinning w_th shyness. "Maybe they work in silence."

"What they keep silent worries me. Just don't eat any banquet food. Hao will strong arm one of her single friends to bring us fish and cakes. My nephew says eat the infected food and end up a dead farmer."

Hao and Wei walked by soon after Yu lost 50 dollars in a close mahjong battle.

"Hello neighbor. You look thin as a starving ox. Wei will bring you her delicious steamed WuChang fish from the banquet to show you the food is safe. When can she serve it to you?" Hao smiled at the man.

"I'd eat the slop pigs refuse before touching fish from the banquet. Your committee and the Baixin thieves will be in jail for poisoning our community," Yu said without taking his eyes off his mahjong tiles.

"Lies. Nothing but lies. I will inform Guo of your traitorous behavior."

The ladies walked away from Yu, glancing over their shoulders as he patted his friend on the back and laughed.

Hao noticed a tall man wearing a large-brimmed hat covering his face following her and Wei.

"An associate of Peng's? Maybe," she thought, picking up her pace toward her office.

"Hao. What's the hurry? You look like you're running from a tiger," Wei said with a laugh.

"Late for a meeting at my office. Go now to the wet market," she said to her friend while looking back at the man walking behind with his head down.

"Sorry to slow you down. I'm going. If you weren't busy, I'd ask you to join me."

"And I would go but not now. Bye-bye."

A reflection from a condominium window showed the man right behind Hao as Wei walked away. She pulled out her phone, but the man grabbed her arm.

"Come here," he said, pulling her behind a garbage dumpster in the alley.

Hao froze, wanting to scream but fear kept her silent. She grabbed the mace button on her keychain.

The man took off his hat, giving Hao a smile before covering his face with his hands.

"Even a rabbit bites when cornered. You're not too afraid I hope," Li whispered with a smile.

"What's wrong with you? You frightened me. What are you doing here?" The red head smiled, playfully hitting his arm.

"You need help, so I came back."

"I've been so afraid. That scarred man who cut you, Peng, came to my apartment threatening Jun and me. I was so scared I called Guo."

"Your neighbor works with Guo and Peng to watch your apartment. Did he do anything to you?"

"Nothing yet but I'm afraid he'll return. I won't stay there anymore. He frightens me."

"Not for long."

"What are you going to do?"

"Don't worry but tell no one I'm here, including Jun. I'll let you know if I need anything."

"I'm glad you're back." Hao grabbed Li by the arms, looking into his eyes before leaning forward to kiss him on the lips.

CHAPTER 76

Next Week Is Too Late

JANUARY 17, 2020

"Life's about to get bad in Wuhan," Jun said to Qin as they drove to Terrace Park Gardens to meet Art. "Go to the Sichuan Province and stay with your parents. You might still be able to make it."

"Why? The pneumonia?"

"The two meetings finish tomorrow. The city will find out it's not pneumonia but something much more serious."

"I'm going home for the New Year celebration. I can wait a couple days."

"It'll be too late then. Hubei Province delegates are spreading the news. Villages aren't allowing cars with Wuhan license plates through. They're guarding their borders and turning them away. Afraid they'll bring the virus to their towns. That means only one thing, a quarantine."

"What does that mean?"

"No one into Wuhan. No one out. The government will restrict people to their apartments. No transportation. Food distributed in communities. The military patrolling the streets. Foreigners leaving, fearing China's disease. It will be bad."

"Art will leave?"

"Of course, why would he stay?" A mist formed on her black eyes. "He doesn't know yet. I bought a going-away present but let's not call it that."

"He'd stay for you Jun," Qin said. "He loves you."

"It's complicated. Better for both of us if he goes home."

The ladies waited for Art at the subway stop next to the park's ticket gate. They planned on eating dinner at the restaurant then viewing the park's New Year light show.

"Hello ladies. Strange ride on the subway. Not many people but they all wore masks. Maybe there is something to this virus rumor," he said with a wry smile.

"Don't you have one? You should wear a mask on the subway," Jun said with alarm.

"I'll be fine."

"I'm not so sure but thank you for coming. I wanted to see you before things change. Let's eat before touring the gardens," Jun said, grabbing his hand as they entered the park's restaurant. "I haven't eaten in a day."

Qin and Art chatted, eating fish soup and tofu in a brown sauce while Jun talked on the phone in agitated tones, stopping only to let out a soft cough.

The two ladies spoke Chinese several times between calls, discussing the hospitals and police, but Art didn't understand much more as the two spoke too fast for his limited Chinese. He asked about the calls but sensed he didn't get straight answers.

"You seem busy. Does the subway and all these calls have to do with the old guy's plan?

Jun looked at Art but said nothing.

"Let's postpone the walk till next week. No fun watching you talk on the phone," Art said.

"Next week is too late."

"Too late for what?"

Another message buzzed in from city hall.

Jun's narrow deep-set black eyes fixated on the text for several seconds before looking up at her companions.

"Let's walk while we can," Jun said.

Jun's gloom lingered over the trio's 90-minute stroll while young children yelled, ran, and danced around large colorful dragon and animal balloons like the Macy's Thanksgiving Parade.

"Let's rest," Jun said near the end, sitting on a park bench. She let out a soft cough and closed her eyes.

"Are you well?" Qin touched Jun's forehead, giving a concerned smile.

Qin, a young wife with attractive golden skin, spoke excellent English with an open attitude in contrast to Jun's exacting, all-business approach.

"Yes, yes. I'm fine. Art, I want to give you something," she said, pulling a beautiful box wrapped in hand-painted paper from her purse.

His face softened as he carefully opened the package to find a small red rubber ball.

"It's what my father gave me. I want you to have it," she said looking away. "Be careful what you put into it."

"No. No, I can't take a family heirloom," Art protested, trying to hand the ball back to her.

"Art, we've already put something into it together," she said with a shy smile. "But let's just enjoy tonight."

He pulled on Jun's arm to make her face him. "What have we put into it?"

"The moon's beautiful tonight. Does it shine this bright in America or only in China?"

"Become my wife and find out," he said with a nudge. "We can put something real into our world. What's life without love?"

"When men speak of the future, Buddha laughs," the slim woman said as the moon hung above her head. Art put the gift into his pocket.

The three stood outside the Metro stop outside the park's gate. Jun put her arm through Art's, pulling him close.

"Life's moments bloom and fade away, never saying hello or goodbye. But if we dare to trust our hearts, another moment may sprout again. Maybe we'll have the freedom to love in America one day?"

"What are you talking about? Are you going somewhere?"

"Let's sit again before you go. I'm so tired," Jun said, slumping onto a bench.

Art draped his arm around Jun, pulling her close as young parents lumbered by carrying sleeping children.

"You're warm. You getting sick?"

"I'm ok. My coat's too heavy. Makes me warm like the children." Red puffy eyes and a soft cough told a different story.

Her high cheek bones and black eyes glistened in the cool air as the blue Metro lights reflected off her pale face, giving it a sickly, greenish glow.

"Please be careful on the subway. Sit in a car with the fewest people," she said to Art as he rose to leave, her eyes coming alive for the impending embrace.

"I know. Maybe it won't be too crowded," Art said with a laugh. "Go see a doctor tomorrow."

"Tomorrow's busy. I'm giving a speech at the Baixin Family Potluck Dinner. They want to break a record with 40,000 families attending. My mother organized it. The mayor asked me to speak. I must be there."

"Thousands of people meeting with a virus spreading? That's a nutty idea," he said, rolling his eyes. "Go when it's over. Ok?"

Qin flagged a taxi as Jun turned to Art.

"Wuhan will suffer soon. Go back to America now before the airport closes. Beijing will shut the city down for who knows for how long. Please go. We'll meet again. Goodbye, Art."

"Wait a minute," he said but she slipped out of his grasp and into the taxi. The cab's red taillights soon disappeared into the traffic.

CHAPTER 77

Get off This Train

Art glided down the subway's escalator scrolling through his phone while thinking about Jun's strange conversation. A *New York Times'* headline flashed in front of his eyes.

"Three US airports to check passengers for deadly Chinese Coronavirus."

"What the hell? Oh my God." His now-wide eyes quickly scanned through the article.

The story pointed a finger at Wuhan as the culprit in spreading a dangerous virus around the world.

He glanced up from his phone at the subway platform to see everyone in the station wearing masks and standing apart from each other. His fingers worked fast to see if the Associated Press had reported a similar story.

The AP, Reuters, and the BBC all carried similar stories about the mysterious Wuhan illness. Each doubted the city's pneumonia diagnosis.

The incoming train rushed into the station with windows showing masked passengers spaced apart. He tried to shake out the tingle rushing down both of his arms.

"Trapped in a subway with a deadly virus circulating. How am I the only person who didn't know? What a moron."

His Cleveland Browns' sweatshirt provided cover to his mouth and nose, blocking out the invisible enemy as the train pulled out of the station and into the dark tunnel. An empty row of seats in the back of the car allowed him to sit alone.

Nervous passengers traded furtive glances in the Metro car. Coughs and flushed faces drew glares before the scared moved to another car, not wanting to take a risk three days before the beginning of the Chinese New Year.

"Now the tape makes sense," Art thought. "Why worry about the games with a killer virus running wild. What else don't I know?"

The foreign teachers had a long history of distrusting the secrecy of the Chinese people. Antoine, a brilliant scientist from Cameroon, summed up China one night after five shots of whiskey.

"No Chinese person is your friend. Don't be deceived into thinking they are. They'd cut your dick off with a razor blade to help China."

"I had high hopes for my penis's future," Art had replied with a whiskey laugh. Now Antoine's warning sunk in as the woman he loved hid a life-threatening virus from him.

He had no one to blame for not having a mask. Virus rumors started flying on campus last week.

Whispers circulated about a leak at the Wuhan Institute of Virology. Now the media says the virus started at a wet market.

A university teacher from Poland said in hushed tones in the cafeteria that a Warsaw source said the Chinese released the virus on its own people to test its impact for future biowarfare.

His Chinese boss at the university pushed back in assured tones. "Americans brought the virus during the World Military Games to kill us."

America poisoning the Chinese was a popular Wuhan talk-radio topic. Several months before numerous callers accused the USA of selling poisoned corn to the country.

"If Americans brought anything to the games, it was whiskey," Art replied but his Chinese friend didn't laugh.

The world press focused on various scenarios concerning a Hankou wet market selling bats for human consumption.

"I heard virus clinic employees sold infected chickens to the wet market to make a few bucks instead of destroying the chickens as ordered," Art's brother from Los Angeles told him.

How anybody knew the facts baffled Art. "Last week no one outside China knew Wuhan existed. Now people in Warsaw and LA are telling us what's going on here. Just a lot of crazy clickbait."

Chinese social media reflected the seriousness of the virus with few buying the "mysterious pneumonia" story. Art's Chinese friends and students posted on WeChat and Weibo the need to donate masks and sanitizer to local hospitals.

"The AP says 300 sick people in Wuhan. Three hundred? Jun said eight hospitals were full," Art thought as he quickly scrolled through the article.

News reports said fever accompanied the virus. Jun's warm body alarmed him.

He texted her. "Seek immediate medical attention. You may have the virus."

"I feel better. My coat made me warm. Don't worry so much."

"Am I next? I hugged her!" A trickle of sweat rolled down from under his hat as he clutched his stomach.

The Hankou open-air wet market receiving blame for the virus stood minutes from the Terrace Park Gardens.

"How many people on this train work at the market?" The faces of the subway riders now all looked guilty of carrying the virus. He pulled his hoodie over his head.

The city's numerous markets went back thousands of years. The never-changing markets sit on concrete slabs in aging buildings about the size of a big-box retailer.

Many farmers' markets provide no modern conveniences like cash registers, air conditioning, or heat. Running water makes them "wet" markets.

Vendors sell a wide range of products including fruit and vegetables, rice, home-made noodles, meat, fish and other seafood, household products, and toys like a 10th-century WalMart.

The fresh meat booths, in the back of the markets, held live animals such as chickens or bats in stacked cages, with bigger animals on the bottom.

Knife-welding shop owners slaughtered smaller animals for customers, hosing pools of fresh blood down floor drains.

Tanks of fish, snakes, turtles, and frogs, in various stages of life, lined market walls where young children tapped the glass, looking to get a reaction from the trapped creatures.

Art squirmed when bored workers brushed flies off large pieces of crudely butchered hogs hanging on hooks but was glad the Wuhan markets didn't hang skinned dogs like in southern Chinese cities like Guilin.

"Wet markets, nothing but squawking animals, thousands of arguing customers and sellers, and crying babies. What a perfect place to plant a clinic virus," Art thought looking into the dark subway tunnel. "They'll never figure it out."

Nervous commuters eyed one another as Art transferred from the Number 7 line to the Number 3 line at the busy Wuhan Business District Station with hundreds of masked passengers.

The packed Number 3 subway held 50 passengers standing or sitting shoulder to shoulder in each of its 30 cars.

"God damn it. I need a mask," Art said as he looked out the subway's window while holding his breath for one-minute intervals.

The life-or-death game occupied a troubled mind as the train neared his Sports Center stop.

"Sixin Boulevard. Only two to go," he thought as the subway glided into the station only to see Ninja soldiers lining the platform.

"When men speak of the future, Buddha laughs," Art said as a Ninja soldier with a bullhorn entered the train.

CHAPTER 78

Today is Victorious

JANUARY 18, 2020

"Red aprons. Buy your red apron here." Wei stood at the Hankou Auditorium entrance hawking commemorative items as thousands of excited patrons flowed into the noisy banquet hall.

"Not now. Too busy," Hao said to several women trying to resolve seating disagreements between families.

"Always the same complaints, please tell the Wu family not to sit at the Wong family's table," Hao said to Wei. "How are sales?"

"We need more aprons. Women want more than one for gifts."

"Have you seen Jun? She said she'd be here by now."

"The speech isn't till 1 p.m. It's only 11:30."

"Not too many masks. See, I told you people aren't concerned about getting sick." An elderly woman passed the two, coughing with force without covering her mouth.

"Some cough but not too many," Wei said with a forced smile while gripping a mask stuffed in her pocket, not wanting to disappoint Hao.

"You're strong for not wearing a mask. We can't look weak."

"I guess so," Wei said without much enthusiasm.

"The local government believes the banquet must go on. They see no danger to the thousands who want to celebrate our great anniversary."

Families flowed by as mothers carried dishes of food, grandfathers held children's hands, teens obeyed grandmother orders, and men smoked cigarettes in front of No Smoking signs.

"Beautiful red aprons. Only 10 dollars. A great gift," Wei said to the enthusiastic holiday crowd. "Put it on. Show your support."

Five women laughed helping each other put aprons on over winter coats in the unheated auditorium. The animated women attracted more buyers.

"Don't be foolish. Wear a mask if you must attend," Yu Tong said outside of the auditorium to a family pushing past holding eggs dressed like rats. "Illness threatens us all. Don't spread it to your family."

"Quit trying to scare my children old man," a mother barked with a look of disdain.

"The so-called patriotic virus kills. Your family is in danger. Stop! Go home. One hundred Wuhan doctors dead from the virus."

Yu's warnings grabbed Jun's attention as she hurried through the crowd.

"Yu Tong, your speech made me stop. It's me, Jun FuMin, Hao's daughter. I'm speaking at the banquet today."

"You wear a mask. Good. You understand the danger. I wouldn't go inside if I were you."

"I'll tell the people to be careful about the virus. It may help."

"How foolish to think you won't get sick. Are you more powerful than nature?"

"We're all fools whether we dance or not. Thanks for trying to warn our friends. Now it is my turn and 100 Wuhan doctors have not died. Truth must not wander in the chaos."

She walked away as Yu shouted to the large crowd, "One-hundred-and-fifty Wuhan doctors dead."

Jun looked back to Yu when she spotted Peng leaning against a wall. A stony smile crossed his face. She paused before approaching the large man.

"Hello Jun."

She said nothing but gently smiled.

"You look nice."

She lowered her head.

"Nothing going on with Guo," he said. "Collecting money is it."

"Please let me know if anything changes," Jun said, giving a light brush on the large man's hand.

"You know it could have been anyone's father. I just didn't want to go to bed hungry again. I'd do anything for the people who fed me real food, not garbage and rats."

"Guo feeds both of us."

Peng nodded as sadness spread across his meaty face.

Jun closed her sad eyes and took a deep breath. "I loved my father. A man I never got to know."

"He died a brave man."

"Brave men die. Heroes like him live forever. Are you a hero? You said we can work together. Can I trust you? I need to know," she said, moving close to him while staring into his eyes.

Peng's face turned red. "Oh yes. Please trust me,"

"The meetings end today. Wuhan will soon be in quarantine. The police will be worthless. If something happens, it's going to be soon. Keep me informed on what you know, and I'll do the same," she said with a twinkle in her eye.

"Yes. Yes, I will," Peng said with energy.

Yu's voice pierced the cool January wind. "Doctors dead from virus. Save yourself. Go home."

Jun snapped to attention, turned, and walked toward Hankou Auditorium.

"Over here. Hello, Jun," Wei said, while giving change and an apron to a lady while her husband stood holding a dozen century eggs. He coughed and spit on the auditorium floor.

"Wei. I'm glad to see you but wear a mask. The virus is real," Jun said, her head going back and forth to watch streams of people enter the auditorium.

"I forgot to put it on," Wei said, pulling it out from her coat pocket.

"Put it on now. For me?"

"Your mother's waiting near the stage. Go find her," Wei said, stuffing the mask back into her pocket as Jun walked away.

Jun checked her appearance in a mirror, sweeping a hand through her hair before entering the packed hall.

Hundreds of tables lined the chilly auditorium decorated with red lanterns and posters wishing everyone a happy 2020.

"I haven't been to this banquet since I was 17. A scared little girl to a scared big girl." She laughed while scanning the room from the back of the auditorium.

"The price of pork makes me angry. Why did it jump 20 cents last week? I can't feed my family," an old woman complained to her table.

"My back's been killing me. Cupping did no good," her friend said.

"Just don't get the pneumonia. That killed my cousin last week, I think," a third woman said. "We shouldn't be here except we're old and what else do we have to do but die?"

Tiny fragments of long-ago Saturday mornings where a young Jun passed out brochures boiled up at the sight of the familiar but aging faces.

"I no longer remember their names," Jun worried as a table of 12 waved to her.

"Please come here," an elderly woman shouted.

Jun blushed with youthful nervousness approaching the smiling family.

"Hello. You don't remember but we're the Ming family. We moved here in 1998 because of a beautiful and kind 12-year-old girl named Jun. You changed our lives."

"I loved your dog, Bao Bao," Jun laughed, surprising herself by remembering its name.

"She loved you," the lady said with a sweet smile.

"My family owes you for belief in a young girl. Your happiness fills my heart with joy," Jun said before moving onto others who waved while whispering to grandchildren, "I knew her when she was your age."

Love replaced anxiousness as friends long forgotten welcomed her home.

"Wear a mask," she said when giving a greeting.

"Yes, yes," they replied but few followed the suggestion.

"Congratulations, mom," Jun said when reaching the stage. "The event looks tremendous. Everyone is so friendly."

"You could have picked a better dress. And do you have to wear a mask?"

Hao turned to check the reactions of those near the stage. "You'll scare those who believe in such nonsense."

"Mother. The virus is dangerous. I've been busy. I'm only here for you."

"Don't wear the mask when speaking. People want to hear. A policeman wants to talk with you. He's over there," Hao said, pointing to Captain Yang, who smiled and waved.

"Captain Yang, hello. Surprised to see you. What can I do for you?" Jun peered at the officer while brushing her hair with her hand.

"I want to hear your speech and thank you for the masks. I don't know how you got them, but we needed them."

"Oh, I sold an old car I don't need any more and bought them with the money. I'm glad to help."

"We appreciate it," he said with a slight bow. "Don't let me keep you. Good luck with the speech."

Jun exhaled after leaving the policeman's side.

"What did he want? No trouble I hope," Hao said.

"Not sure why he's here?"

"He can watch that monster and my neighbor who talks too much. I wouldn't say anything to her if I was you," Hao said, pointing out Peng who chatted with Hao's neighbor.

Jun shook her head.

"I'm telling the officer if he does anything," Hao said with a sneer.

"Ever since a child, I knew Baixin was the greatest community in Wuhan thanks to each of you," Jun said as audience let out a low murmur of appreciation.

She told several stories about her young days and the kind families she met passing out brochures before finishing.

"Today is victorious. I thank my mother and banquet organizer, Hao Gui, party chairman Guo Zhenqin, and my family along with you, my Baixin family. I want to thank my father, Jun Lijiao, who helped me grow, teaching valuable lessons of choosing right over wrong, that service to the people is our greatest gift, and family and health matter more than gold or silver. Stay safe and wear a mask."

The huge gathering rose, roaring its approval as a masked Guo greeted her off stage.

"Wonderful job. It made Baixin happy."

"I love them. Hardworking people who love family and country. I'm unworthy to speak to them."

"You're not common like them. Come with me. I'm leaving Wuhan for Los Angeles next week. Building a house in a beautiful community, Manhattan Beach. Come with me and live the life of a rich California woman. Together, we have no limits," Guo said, shuffling his feet like a scared teenage boy.

"You're leaving China? Are you an American citizen now?"

"I have no country or home. Only money. But a small investment in America and the next thing I'll be taking pictures with the president," Guo said with a laugh. "Marry me and you'll be in the picture too."

"If I say no, then Peng takes me on another trip?"

"You never let your guard down, do you?" Guo shook his head. "It's always about you."

"Said from the best. Maybe we do belong together." Her eyes lowered. "Marrying a rich man and moving to America was the dream of a young farmer's daughter, but she died."

"Maybe the farmer's daughter died but the dream lives on," Guo said with a wide smile. "You love money too much. You're a California girl. We belong together. I live in you, along with Louis Vuitton and Coco Chanel."

She wrapped her arms around a Gucci purse and held it to her breast.

"You can't give me what I want," came out of her perfect red lips in a soft, uncertain tone.

"But I can buy it. Think about it. You'll know where to find me. I'm going to need someone with refined Chinese taste to decorate an expensive American home. It's the only way you'll get your share."

Jun took a deep breath.

"Listen. The virus is worse than we've been told. It isn't pneumonia after all. Leaving is the best way to avoid illness or even death."

Jun's eyes flared.

"What we've been told? What you wanted us to believe. You put a city in crisis and want me to flee while friends and family die? I can't do that."

"What's people got to do with money? Make it and you can take care of them later."

"If they're still alive. I can't take that chance with my mother and she's not leaving."

The old man shrugged. "If not you, plenty of beautiful California women who'll pretend to love a rich man."

"I can't fake it. I'll make my own money."

"My leaving may create problems for you. I'll do what I can to help."

"Help me?" Jun let out a small laugh. "You've taught me well. Just take the money and don't screw me."

"Ah, That's another negotiation. We'll have it."

"Peng seems nervous. What did you tell him?"

Guo smiled but said nothing.

"My mother will continue at Baixin after you leave?"

"Of course, she's the only one I trust. You'd be dead if it wasn't for her," Guo snapped. "Try to be a good Chinese daughter."

Jun ran her hand through her hair as she scanned the audience. Captain Yang stood watching them with a steely gaze.

"You need to cover your face," Guo said, touching his mask.

"Now masks are important?"

"No point getting sick this close to the end. The virus is dangerous. I don't want to take it to America," Guo said with the look of a scared old man.

"I understand. Come with me behind the curtain, I want to give you something in private. It's from my family," she said, stepping out of the view of the audience.

She led him offstage to a dark corner before turning around and putting her two long toned arms around his neck to pull him close.

"Masks? I don't think we need them now, do you?"

Guo's greedy eyes sparkled as he eagerly pulled down his mask. She engulfed the slim man with a long, deep kiss as his arms wrapped around her thin waist.

She then pushed away with an aggressive shove.

"That's the only taste you'll get. And, it's worth more than all your money," she said before coughing in his face, putting on her mask, and walking back on stage.

A smile crossed his face for a second before rubbing his mouth and spitting on the ground.

Phlegm came from deep in Li's chest as he spit on the floor when Guo and Peng strode by on their way out. Neither looked at the farmer who waited a moment before following the two men.

CHAPTER 79

Wuhan Winds Change

JANUARY 19, 2020

A crush of shop clerks and shoppers pushed out of the Line 1 Metro on North LiJi Road, heading to Wuhan's massive 100-block wholesale district where sellers and buyers argue prices in a free-for-all setting.

Li Shun walked out of the Liji Road station looking for a 7 a.m. breakfast of sesame noodles, Wuhan's favorite dish. He found a fast-food restaurant selling them near Peng Qiang's home.

A smelly alley dumpster provided cover for Li as he ate the meal served in a bright yellow paper container.

"Don't break a noodle. No bad luck today," he thought, using his chopsticks with care as he slurped down the noodles.

Peng emerged from his eight-story condo building at 8:15 a.m., wincing as a strong north wind blew a light mist into his face.

"Hello fruit seller," Peng sung in a lyrical voice to the old vendor who stood protected by an umbrella in the January drizzle. "Will it rain all day?"

"No. My bones say the rain will soon stop. They are never wrong," he said with a stern shake of the head.

"Good. I want to sit outside today. Take care," Peng said with a wave of the hand.

"No suitcase today. Where's he going?" Li threw the carton into the dumpster and followed behind at a safe distance.

Peng entered a large office building to buy a latte from a lobby coffee shop as he had the past few days. Li hid behind a tree as people carrying babies, work buckets, and backpacks hurried past on the typical busy Sunday morning.

The bodyguard sipped coffee while taking the short walk under the elevated Liji Road Metro tracks.

"Yesterday a trip to Han Street and the fancy hotel before driving Guo to the Hankou Auditorium and the banquet. Maybe Modena today?"

Peng took the Metro south to Zongguan Road, a connecting station between the elevated Line 1 and the underground Line 3. He got off the train and began walking toward the underground lines.

The bodyguard's huge mane allowed Li to easily follow behind in the huge crowd on the long walk to the Line 3 trains.

"He's either going to Jianghan or Hao's apartment," Li thought. "Nothing good happens if he goes to Hao's."

Line 3's doors opened, letting a mob of aggressive passengers bounce off Peng like ping-pong balls. "Be patient. We'll all get to where we're going," he said with a smile.

"Maybe the old lady tipped him off about Jun going somewhere? Or maybe he's going to kill her?"

Peng stood near the door in the train's last car, letting several ladies take an occasional empty seat with a gracious wave of the hand. Li stood ready to get off several cars in front when the train pulled into the Sports Center station. Peng squeezed out of the crowded Sunday train and headed up the escalator.

Li fell 20 paces behind the large man, his face hidden with a large hat pulled low and a mask.

The escalator dropped Peng off on the station's main floor. He stopped to look in both directions.

"No! Keep moving you animal," Li mumbled as the escalator moved him too close for comfort.

Peng turned right after the few-second delay toward the Exit D escalator that led to Taozhi Road and the short walk to Jianghan University and the Modena.

The winter drizzle had stopped like the fruit seller predicted but many colorful umbrellas remained open as the tree canopy dripped on the busy sidewalk. Peng's red one stood high among the others.

Li had forgotten his umbrella, so water ran off the brim of his large hat into his eyes when a shout came from behind.

"Hey, wait up," a voice yelled.

Peng stopped, turned back to Li, and started walking toward him. The farmer rubbed the water from his eyes before going to one knee, pretending to fiddle with a shoe.

"Stay, do not show fear, keep your head down or you're dead," Li thought as the mighty Peng walked past.

Peng's voice rang out, "Hello. How are you?" Li snuck a quick peek over his shoulder.

"Wu? Is that you? How are you?" A brutish man gave Peng an aggressive handshake and pat on the back.

"An accomplice? I cannot handle two large men."

Li pushed forward like a sprinter off the starting line, jogging to the bus stop enclosure next to the chestnut stand at the university's Gate 1.

"Hey farmer. Come here and I'll give you a big bag of roasted chestnuts," the vendor shouted to Li.

Li shook his head, trying to ignore the vendor who walked over to him.

"Here, a few free chestnuts. Just made them. Very fresh," he said with a wide grin.

The red umbrella started moving again as the two large men walked together.

"Leave me alone. I'll buy some in a few minutes."

The umbrella covered Peng's eyes as it neared the bus stop. Li leaned back into the bus enclosure as Peng walked by, then stopped.

Li stood unhidden two feet from Peng, but the big man looked toward the stand.

"I'm going to get some chestnuts. Nice seeing you," Peng said to his friend who walked away.

"A bag of chestnuts please," Peng said. "They smell wonderful."

"Thank you. I think so too but rude people like that farmer over there always complain," the vendor said, pointing toward Li.

The bodyguard began to turn but the vendor handed him his change for a 100-dollar bill as a brisk winter wind blew leaves past the stand.

"The breeze makes a good day to listen to the trees," Peng said to the vendor.

"Ah, Wuhan winds suddenly change like an angry woman, blowing this way and that," the man said with a smile.

"Yes. I agree. Thank you for your kindness and wisdom," Peng said. He turned and walked past the guarded gate onto the sprawling Jianghan campus.

Li lingered at the gate, watching the big man close his umbrella then cross the school's 30 outdoor basketball courts.

"He's headed to the coffee shop. Maybe then to the bamboo trees?"

"A college campus, so full of young hope," Peng thought as he entered the London Bus Coffee Shop. "Maybe the wise bamboo trees will direct me to a bold new life."

"The time has come," Li said heading straight to the bamboo trees, a 10-minute walk past the coffee shop.

Li pranced up the ornate stairs across from the library like a schoolboy. His eager eyes surveyed the pond and the bench near the thicket of bamboo.

"My friend, Jun LiJiao, what better place than in the bamboo where uprightness and perseverance live through harsh conditions. Those who fail together, grow together."

The farmer dropped to his knees in the thicket of trees behind the park bench. He dug his hands into Wuhan's moist soil, throwing the red dirt into the air with energy.

"Yes, the trees protect well," he said, as a large knife's silver blade appeared in the crimson soil. "Three days in the ground did little to dull it," he thought, giving it a bright shine by wiping it on his dingy pants.

He dropped to the ground and crawled to get a clear view of the bench through the low-hanging trees. The knife rested in his hand with the point facing the sky.

"All is set," Li whispered, brushing off the mud clinging to his pants.

"Original Tang Dynasty pieces, over 1,000 years old and rare. Royal family members took them to the grave to carry wealth to the afterlife," Peng told two Chinese history majors in the cramped coffee shop.

"Why do you collect camels?" The male student appeared interested in Peng's collection while his girlfriend played on a phone, looking distracted.

"The most regal and loyal of the animals, eating and drinking little while carrying great weight for long distances for its master. Underappreciated in importance to Chinese history. I have photos on my phone."

The girl tugged her boyfriend's coat, rolling her eyes while tilting her head toward the door.

"We must go. Maybe we can meet again to talk more about the Tang Dynasty and look at your phone," the polite young man said.

"I would like that very much." Peng wrapped his two massive arms around his chest and smiled as the young couple inched away. "My lifelong dream has always been to teach college students about the importance of camels in Chinese history. A poor boy's fantasy."

"Why did you talk to that scary-looking man?" The young coed looked over her shoulder at Peng who waved from inside the shop.

"What could I do? The shop's small and he's so big. He was alright. He looked tough but acted like a child," the young man said.

Peng stretched before nodding to the owner while walking out into the stiff breeze. The serene Sanjiao Lake path cleared his mind as he headed toward the bamboo trees.

"Guo can enroll me in Jianghan. My dead uncle would smile. How many times did he say, 'Never stop learning.' The gentlemen trees understand perseverance. Maybe they will approve."

Peng stopped to admire the flower garden at the foot of the silent stairs before heading up to the isolated pond. The bench, tucked into the bamboo trees, beckoned.

"Good, no Li. The last person I want to see today. Let's forget about Li, Guo, and all the craziness for the next two weeks. I need a vacation."

The swaying bamboo trees waved hello from across the languid pond, promising a lengthy discussion of coming changes.

Li's heart pounded into the cold, red clay at the sight of Peng.

"Stay calm, like LiJiao. Breathe." He stuck his face into the soil, waiting until he heard the bench groan under the large Peng.

Peng grabbed a couple chestnuts from his pocket and took a deep breath as his imposing arms spread wide on the bench with his back to the thicket.

"Tell me bamboo trees, what does my future hold?"

A tree-bending gust of wind turned Peng's head to the January north. A rush of air blew past as the bamboo creaked in a thousand unintelligible voices. Then, the wind suddenly stopped, silencing the gentlemen.

Li squirmed in the red soil. "No more wind? He'll slice me to pieces with my knife if he hears me."

"The wind died without warning?" Peng glared at Wuhan's foreboding sky as if trying to intimidate nature. The bamboo remained taciturn.

"Maybe I should go? A hard rain's going to fall," Peng thought as he stood for a few seconds before sitting back down.

"No not yet. Let's give it a chance. Nature needs patience. I need to get use to killing time."

The breeze soon picked up again.

The red soil ground into Li's gloves as he pushed up to a crouch in slow motion.

"Take a rest. The rain will chase me away in a few minutes," Peng said as he chewed another chestnut.

Li slithered out of the bamboo thicket through the short grass behind the bench, looking right and left for witnesses. He saw none.

A weeping mist began to fall as Peng dreamt about graduating to an enlightened life, an existence denied to young poor boys.

"People can change. I can change," Peng said as the bamboo trees let out a soft moan. "Ah, the gentlemen agree." He smiled.

Li raised his arm in silence.

A clean, deep slice cut Peng's throat in one easy motion. His head turned sideways as he tried to grab Li. Blood and half-chewed chestnuts spurted onto Li's pants and the red soil.

Peng clutched his throat before falling off the bench, moaning and thrashing on the ground for a few seconds. He then stopped, his wide eyes looking to the dark clouds.

The dying man's writhing stunned Li for an instant before throwing the bloody knife into the pond.

The wind blew hard at Li's back as he jogged toward the stairs. One last look showed Peng's still body next to the swaying bamboo trees.

"You can now rest in peace Jun LiJiao," Li said as tears streamed through the red dirt on his brown face.

CHAPTER 80

Crazy Old Fool

JANUARY 19, 2020

"Wu had his throat slit at Jianghan. Kindness killed him. The stupid son-of-a-bitch let the killer, your farmer friend, go when he had his chance."

"Peng dead? I can't believe it," Jun said in a whisper over the phone.

"I should pay the farmer because I was going to pay Peng. No big deal. He was getting soft. Come to the Reign for a drink in his honor?"

"You can't be serious?"

"I understand. He did kill your father. More important things to worry about than the dead. I need to wrap things up before I go to Beijing and then California. You haven't changed your mind about coming with me, have you? I can work out the details."

"No, no," she said. "I'll see you in America but on my terms."

"Make sure you're available. We may need to meet one last time."

"One last time? Why?" But Guo had hung up, leaving only the echo of her words.

She called her mother. "Peng's dead. Someone slit his throat."

"Li?"

"I don't know but Guo will pin it on him whether he did it or not. Guo may have had him killed."

"Why would he do that? He worked for him. I don't like that."

"Where are you?"

"Modena. Cleaning the apartment."

"Let me know if Li contacts you. He needs to get out of town," Jun said before hanging up.

"Li killed the scary man for LiJiao and me. Crazy old fool." Hao smiled moping the kitchen floor and singing a Chinese love song.

The elevator opened on Hao's floor as the old lady's door opened, exposing her nose.

"Your job is done old woman. The man who lied about being a policeman won't be back," Li said in a monotone whisper.

"They'll arrest you soon," she said before slamming the door.

"He's not going to answer," he shouted.

The noise sent Hao running to the door. "Li! Come in quick."

The agitated farmer pushed into the apartment and headed straight to the window overseeing courtyard.

"Did you kill him?"

"Kill who?"

"You need to clean those pants and shoes."

He gagged at the sight of the splattered blood.

"Go into the restroom and take those clothes off. I'll find something for you to wear," Hao said.

"I've been walking for hours," Li said in a breathless whisper. "I, I …."

Hao grabbed him by the arms. "Don't say anything. Jun LiJiao and I thank you."

Sobs exploded from Li into Hao's shoulder. "I can't believe I did it. He had to die but now I just want to forget it."

"No more said. You must leave Wuhan today."

"No. I'm not a coward."

CHAPTER 81

Give a Little, Get a Little

JANUARY 19, 2020

"A tragedy," Captain Yang said to Guo who sipped tea in his Reign Hotel suite. "The police department apologizes for the loss of your employee."

"I won't let disturbing violent acts threaten Wuhan. Find his killer or killers now or you'll be gone."

"I understand," the captain said with no emotion. "Did either of you have enemies who would want to do such a thing?"

"I have many enemies, but my guess an insane farmer named Li did it. He recently threatened me with a knife at Baixin. Somehow, he knows the mayor's chief of staff, Jun FuMin. Maybe she's mixed up in this?"

"Do you know the connection?"

"Jun's father and Li were Zigui County friends. Her father committed suicide years ago. Li had the crazy idea Wu killed him, confusing him with a man named Peng who died in a plane crash."

"I see. Jun's mother works for you, right?

"Many years. She knows the truth."

"The dead man's fingerprints show a discrepancy on who he was, but your information is helpful."

"I know him as Wu. Regardless, I suggest you arrest Li and Jun today."

"Thank you for your time. Contact us if you have more information or feel threatened. The hotel does a good job protecting guests so you should be safe while staying here."

"I'm well aware of how the hotel works Captain Yang."

The department commander drank hot water behind a large desk when Yang returned to the office.

"What did you find out?"

"A farmer named Li had a motive and the means. Guo wants to link the mayor's chief of staff, but I know her. Not a killer but might have a motive too. Not sure who the dead man is. Guo knows but won't say."

"Find Li and bring him in. Talk to Jun but don't threaten her. She's busy enough."

Yang walked back to his office. A wrapped parcel with a note saying, "To Captain Yang from a loyal party member" sat on his desk.

"Someone left it while I was at lunch," his secretary said, pointing to the package.

"Call security and get it checked."

"Already have. A recorder with a tape. Nothing dangerous," the secretary said.

Yang pushed the play button. "Yes Hu Jin, this in Jun FuMin, and you know I have been processing contracts for the city."

"Yes, and from what I hear you are a fine employee," Wu said.

"Have you ever wondered how I have all these fine clothes? I know many people have. Fixing city contracts is quite easy and I've done it for years. If we work together, I believe anything is possible considering the number of contracts for World Military Games' construction coming up. We can make a lot of money together."

Yang smiled in his small windowless office before heading back to the commander's office.

The two listened in silence before the commander spoke. "What do you think?"

"Done by amateurs considering the way the details get laid out. It's not her."

"Serious charges. We need to inform the party."

"That's what someone wants. Guo will make sure they both disappear," Captain Yang said.

"Let the tech people listen to it. Get a voice sample from her. And thanks again for talking to Guo. He can be difficult."

"That's my job. Give a little, get a little," he said with a smile.

CHAPTER 82

What's Your Life Worth?

JANUARY 20, 2020

A cold 6 a.m. wind blew Dr. Lui into Central Hospital on January 20. The hours ran short for the 34-year-old as an increasing number of patients filled the hospital's corridors and a sick two-year-old son rested at home.

Fifteen new patients in portable beds crowded the hall outside his office.

"Have these patients been cared for this morning?" The young nurse who wore no mask shook her head in silence.

"Please see they are. And find a mask to wear."

"Only one mask left in supply. You should wear it," the nurse said in a quiet voice.

"I'm leaving soon. You wear it. I'll find some before I return," he said covering his mouth with his coat sleeve before entering his office and picking up the phone.

"Masks Chun. Masks. Where are they?"

"Good morning my early-bird doctor. I'm not at your speed as I lie in bed next to my plump wife," a sleepy Chun said.

"Get up and find some. We need them now."

"A fruitful conversation last night with my cousin in Shenzhen. He can get them, but the price is ridiculous. One hundred dollars per 20 masks. Last week it was 100 masks for 20 dollars. Robbery."

"What's your life worth?"

"I'll work something out this morning."

"Let me know. Fifteen patients with no masks sit outside my office. No one is safe."

The new patients' charts resembled previous clients, older people with pre-existing conditions, along with a few younger, healthier people. The mix confused him.

A knock on his door interrupted his thoughts.

"Dr. Lui, sorry. A new patient wants to see you, a friend with someone you know," the head nurse said.

The doctor looked at his watch. "I have little time now."

"A determined man. Maybe for just a minute. He is making a disturbance."

"Give me a minute. I have the charts here. What's his name?"

The patient's name did not ring a bell, but he had serious symptoms.

"How are you? How do you feel?" The maskless doctor tried to keep his distance from the feeble man on the portable bed but the patient grabbed his arm to pull him close.

"Sick doctor. Very sick. Please stay with me," the old man said as he struggled to breathe.

"You know me?

"I'm friends with Guo Zhenqin. He said to ask for you."

He pried the old man's hand off his arm. "I have an important meeting but will return soon. Until then the nurses will care for you."

"No nurses. Guo said you must help me," he said in a loud, demanding voice as spittle sprayed over the doctor.

"Sorry. That's not possible. Good-bye."

The head nurse tried to wipe the spit off Dr. Lui.

"Leave it be. Put him where he won't disturb the other patients like in the basement. I'll be back as soon as possible."

CHAPTER 83

What Do You Think?

"Hello Mr. Chairman. I'm sorry to call you again but a new issue has come up. Police business never stops."

"Of course, Captain Yang," Guo said, pouring a glass of French champagne as he looked over architectural plans for his new California beachfront house. "I was hoping you were going to tell me you arrested my trusted employee's killers."

"Not yet. I'm sorry. A mysterious recording showed up at my office. The tape's information indicates that Jun FuMin may be involved in illegal activity regarding the World Military Games. Do you know anything about it?"

"No, but quite unfortunate. Wu's murder, now this. She seemed such a loyal party worker when giving that wonderful speech at Baixin. But often those are the ones to watch. Such activity needs severe punishment. The party must step in on this matter."

"No one has been charged. The tape may not be legitimate. We need to look at the financial records involving the games' expenditures."

"That makes sense. But I've seen the records. They appear in order. The two committees just reviewed them without complaint. I can get you the information. Why would anyone submit a false tape? That makes little sense."

"Someone trying to be a little too smart. We're bringing her in for questioning. I wanted to let you know."

"I appreciate the update. I heard a tape existed weeks ago."

"Really? That's interesting," the captain said. "If I may ask, who told you?"

"We stand ready to come down hard on those who betray our trust whether they're flies or tigers. How is the virus progressing in the city?"

"Not good. The hospitals are struggling. Many don't believe it's pneumonia. We'll see. FuMin did help the department with masks. She sold a car to buy them. Quite a generous effort for a fly."

"Getting rid of evidence is my guess. She should be arrested as soon as possible."

"We'll talk to her first. Thank you, Mr. Chairman. I'll keep you informed."

Captain Yang smiled as he buzzed his secretary. "Can you let Jun FuMin in?"

A tired, pale woman walked into the office.

"Please, sit at the table."

"Thank you," she said, just loud enough to hear over the rumbling of the room's heating unit.

"An excellent speech you gave. Quite moving. Can I get you something to drink?"

"Hot water, please." Jun coughed behind her mask as the captain handed her a cup.

"Are you ok?" The captain's eyes showed concern from behind his mask.

"A terrible headache. Too much work on the computer," she said rubbing her head. "How can I help you?"

"An anonymous tape came to us implicating you in a scheme to defraud the government with regards to the World Military Games. What can you tell me about it?"

"I've heard the tape. Someone trying to scare me into doing something I don't want to do. It's fake," she said without looking up from the steam rising out of her cup in the cold office.

"What do they want you to do?" The captain looked hard at the frail woman as if searching for a lost ring at the beach.

Jun's gaze drifted up until their eyes met. "What do you think?" She shook her head. "I won't do it."

"I understand. A voice sample will determine its authenticity. Our tech guys think it's fake but that will ensure it."

A light exhale came from Jun.

"Another question," Captain Yang said. "Do you know where Li Shun is? We know he's a family friend. We want to talk to him about yesterday's killing of a man at Jianghan University."

Jun took a small, shallow breath as her head turned back to the captain. "Who was the man killed?"

"Not sure. His identification said his name was Wu, but the fingerprints don't match. We're still trying to determine who he is. You might know him as Guo's bodyguard."

"Peng. His name is Peng Qiang. He killed my father many years ago. He worked as Guo's bodyguard."

"Records show your father committed suicide. Li knew your father?"

"He was murdered. Li was his friend in Zigui County. The party sent us to Wuhan when they took our farm for the dam. I haven't seen Li in several weeks. I thought he went back to Jingmen to work."

"Ok. I'm finished for now. Let us know if you see him. A tech will come for a voice sample. Then go home and rest. I'll get a car to take you home."

Jun stared at the steam rising while saying nothing.

CHAPTER 84

I'm Sick

JANUARY 21, 2020

Dr. Lui slumped in a chair across the desk from the hospital administrator. Sweat rolled down his forehead from his matted hair.

"I'm sick, Chun. I think the virus got me too," Dr. Lui said, putting a hand to his forehead.

"You're fine, but go home if you need to." Chun picked up a mask from his desk to cover his mouth and nose, making Lui wince.

"Ten minutes too late for that. You know I can't go home. That's the last place I want to go anyway. I'll survive," he said without conviction.

"Just get better. We need you to work. Too many sick people around here already," Chun grunted.

Dr. Lui continued to spiral downward during the day. Central Hospital admitted the doctor as a patient at 6 p.m.

"I'm sick. So far, the virus impacts older people more than the young and healthy. Things will be better in a couple days," the 34-year-old doctor told his nervous wife over the phone. "How's the boy?"

"I'm worried. Can I see you?"

"No, too dangerous. Nothing but sick people here. Stay home. I'll be in touch."

"Not good. He's struggling," Chun whispered into his phone. "The night did not treat him well."

"What? He's young and healthy," Jun said in disbelief. "He's going to be ok, right?"

"We'll see. I'm going to check on him now. I'll let you know."

Chun entered the doctor's room and saw a sick man flirting with death.

"He needs a ventilator," the attending doctor whispered to Chun. "Sinking oxygen levels. Not a good sign."

A pale, thin Dr. Lui looked scared lying on the same hospital bed that held thousands of his Central Hospital patients over the years.

"Don't waste a ventilator on me," Dr. Lui said to Chun. "Others need them."

"Doctors make the worst patients because they can read our minds," Chun said to the other doctor, laughing without a response.

"You'll get the best care possible Lui. Let us diagnosis. Take a rest," the doctor said, giving Chun a head nod to leave.

Chun hesitated, looking at his friend, before heading to his office.

"How many times has she called?"

"Ten times in the past 20 minutes. A lot of tears," Chun's secretary said, wiping her own away.

A silent Chun waited a few minutes before dialing the number.

"Hello. This is Chun Fang. How are you?"

Chun's face tightened as Dr. Lui's wife sobbed for 30 seconds while a child cried in the background.

"It's going to be all right. Your husband is young and strong. He's receiving oxygen to help him breathe. A doctor's with him now. Now don't worry. We expect a full recovery."

"I need to be there," Dr. Lui's wife said between the moans.

"Sorry, no visitors. It's best. The virus is very contagious. You don't want your son to get sick, do you?"

"When can I see him?"

"No visitors allowed. Sorry, hospital rules. We'll keep you informed."

"Please. Please," the young wife said in a weak voice. "I can't live without him."

"I understand. Do you have help at home? We could send a nurse."

"No, my mother's here. Thank you."

"Good. Let us know if anyone begins to feel ill. We'll be in touch. Take care. Bye-bye."

Chun looked out the window. His secretary buzzed, "National Health Commission on Line 1."

"This is Zhang Nanshun of the National Health Commission in Beijing. The commission will come to Central Hospital tomorrow with a team of experts for an on-site investigation into the prevention and control of the pneumonia virus."

"Where were you last week? We needed you then."

"China's health issues keep us busy. We do our best. I trust we'll receive your cooperation."

Zhang rattled on about his team's needs as Chun half-listened while scrolling through his phone's messages. One stopped him.

"The Wuhan Municipal Health Commission pneumonia outbreak briefing today. As of yesterday, January 18, Wuhan had reported a total of 62 confirmed cases, including 19 cases discharged after recovery, eight cases with severe symptoms, and two deaths."

Chun laughed. Central Hospital had at least 62 cases as did his colleagues at Wuhan's other seven hospitals. "Not a surprise when the party reports the cases. At least help's coming," he thought.

Guo called seconds later.

"Chun. The full force of the powerful Chinese government will come to Wuhan to attack the virus outbreak, showing our might as a nation. High-level sources in Beijing believe the United States released a coronavirus in Wuhan during the World Military Games."

"I heard from the NHC. They'll be here tomorrow. Why did they wait two weeks?"

"Tomorrow President Xi Jinping will require party committees and governments to make thorough plans to curb the virus's spread. China will not let America poison Wuhan citizens. Health and safety will be our top priority."

"Thirteen days to make an announcement? Xi discussed the epidemic on January 7. Why did they wait so long?"

"Priorities Chun. Priorities."

CHAPTER 85

No News Today?

JANUARY 22, 2020

The black Buick Regal's tinted window slid down two inches as Liz approached the car. A white string came out of the car.

"Put this mask on and get in the back seat," Dean Zhu Huang said in a cold, abrupt tone.

The holiday season brought temporary staff changes to the *Changjiang Weekly*. The newspaper needed Liz and Zhu, the Jianghan's International School dean and a party member, to fill in for the day.

"Nice to meet you dean," Liz said as she put on the mask.

The Columbia University graduate grunted as he looked at her in the rearview mirror.

Liz let out a raspy cough as she put her mask in place. Zhu shot a mixed look of anger and fear.

"You sick? Maybe you should stay home," His left hand covered his mask.

"I smoke. I hack every day. Don't worry," Liz said with a wave of the hand. The dean remained silent, afraid to open his mouth or even breathe.

Her occasional smoker's cough kept the dean's eyes riveted on the rearview mirror as if watching stopped it. The two played the uncomfortable cat-and-mouse game for the 45-minute ride to the Hankou office.

The dean walked up the 10 flights of stairs to the newspaper office rather than enter the elevator's enclosed space with Liz.

Liz entered the combined Chinese and English newspaper office to find reporters gathered in groups, speaking in hushed tones. No one was working.

The English newspaper's Chinese editor sat at a cluttered desk when the out-of-breath dean walked into the office. He immediately let loose on her with an agitated rant.

Four masked men with tanks on their backs entered the office, spraying a nasty-smelling disinfectant throughout the large room without saying anything.

"Jesus Christ that shit stinks," Liz said as the reporters scattered, covering their faces.

The spray ended Zhu and the editor's conversation. "No edition today. Let's go," Zhu said to Liz. "I'll see you at the car."

"Quick acting. Yesterday no virus problem. Today, the office gets sprayed, and the news cancelled," Liz said with a lilt to Zhu.

His head shook no, keeping his lips sealed behind his mask.

"Pass these out to the teachers," Zhu said as he handed her a box of masks as the Buick pulled up to teachers' apartments at the university.

"Righto. Thanks," Liz said with a smile as the doctor opened all the car windows as he drove away.

Art carried a bag of garbage to the dumpster as Liz walked to her apartment.

"Back so soon. No news today?"

"Very sketchy place. The editors called off today's news. The Chinese can do that," Liz said as she lit a cigarette.

"The school cancelled today's teacher holiday luncheon. Instead, the apartment manager passed out a week supply of dumplings, rice balls, masks, and hand sanitizer."

"Nothing says 'Happy holidays' like masks and sanitizer," Liz said looking up to blow out smoke.

"The school's message did say we won't starve to death if things get bad."

"They said that? Good news, I guess. We'll die coughing with full bellies and our boots on."

"Don't even look at today's news. CNN reported most countries issued essential-travel-only orders to the now-notorious Wuhan. The U.S. State Department has concerns over the Chinese government lack of transparency."

"What? The Chinese government hasn't been straight with us? I'm gobsmacked," Liz said as she shook her head and waved goodbye.

Bad news continued throughout the day. A disturbing afternoon Internet rumor began circulating:

"Attention: Today in Wuhan at 5 p.m. up till 9 p.m. please do not go out, as people affected by the disease will be moved to the hospital that has been prepared. And from 5 p.m. until 9 p.m. the Air Force of the central theater will begin to spray disinfectant powder over Wuhan. Please close your doors and windows and don't go out! If you have any friends or relatives in Wuhan, then please inform them."

"The Air Force is dumping disinfectant over the entire city? That's insane," Art texted Liz.

"Let's just hope the planes carry only disinfectant," Liz said.

CHAPTER 86

Didn't Kill the Birds

JANUARY 23, 2020

The disinfectant-carrying jet planes never arrived or someone came to their senses, but the Wuhan Communist Party did drop an Internet bomb on the city on the evening of January 22, 2020:

"Party committees of district units, accredited offices in governing organs: According to the spirit of emergency meeting of the Municipal party committee and municipal governments on the evening of January 20 and emergency meeting of the management committee of the industrial and commercial commission on the morning of January 21, all personnel are not allowed to leave Wuhan from today until the outbreak is relieved except under special circumstances."

Art read the obtuse language of the Wuhan Communist Party's bulletin's several times trying to figure out its impact.

He texted several teachers looking for a simple answer to a difficult question: "Does this mean they shut down the city?"

"I heard from a Chinese friend that the Metro, buses, taxis, businesses, the airport, and life in general has stopped in Wuhan," Liz responded.

"Wall us off and see how many of us die," he wrote back.

"That's the game. Sounds cozy. How'd we get here? Or, better yet, how do we get out?"

Liz's question was on everyone's lips the next morning.

The chirping of birds woke Art on January 23, 2020. He rolled over to put a pillow over his head while staring at the dull gray paint on his bedroom wall.

"Well, the virus didn't kill the birds, that's good," he thought as the reality of being trapped in a quarantined city sunk in.

The daily din of the usually crazy-crowded Taozhi Road roaring past his bedroom window was silenced, leaving only the warblers' tunes.

The songs waned as early-morning light sent the birds searching for breakfast. He pulled back his bedroom curtains to reveal low gray clouds trapping a stark funeral-like stillness.

The school sent a 7 a.m. message.

"The school has closed all gates to the campus except for number two and number five. Staff and students can enter the campus using their ID card. All people must wear a face mask when entering the campus."

"Well, I can go out. Let's check out history." He left his apartment with a yellow paisley bandana wrapped around his mouth and nose.

He saw no one on the 25,000-student campus. The only sound was the raspy scratching of dead leaves blowing across the basketball courts. A 20-minute campus walk past two cafeterias, the administration building, the library, and the medical center turned up no people. A masked guard sat in a small, closed booth at Gate 2. He waved Art on without looking up from his phone.

The stark silence of Taozhi Road, the always-busy thoroughfare with its sea of black hair, jarred the teacher.

"The end. Frightened people hiding in closets waiting to die. What a world," he thought as he spun in circles on the barren street.

A car horn beeped as a taxi headed down the street.

"Another person," Art said with a smile. The car ran several red lights before flying by Art. The driver wore a hazmat suit.

Five minutes later an emergency vehicle pulled into the university's hotel parking lot across the street. Eight people in hazmat suits got out.

A 10-minute conversation among the safety workers took place before they mustered the courage to enter the hotel wearing their puncture-resistant, airtight suits.

His phone constantly beeped with WeChat messages from students about the new world:

"McDonalds artificial customer said the Wuhan store is not expected to reopen for three months. I can't imagine living without McDonalds for three months. It's too painful."

"Wuhan, hold on and refuel."

"Ignorance is not an obstacle to survival. Arrogance is. More terrible than panic is pride."

"Do you have a good way to persuade the elders to wear masks?"

"I have to say the price of face masks on Taobao have gone up fast, fast, fast. The price for 25 paper masks is close to $100 USD."

"Is my throat getting sore? Maybe."

"Yesterday I had a low fever. I felt like I lost all hope. I was scared to death."

"The Hankou Railway Station is deserted."

"The village chief took the doctor to my house for special 'sympathy' by giving me a thermometer, a mask, and a warning not to go out. Am I in quarantine?"

"Please stay away from Wuhan people. Just don't want to bring panic to those who still care about us."

"My mom ran upstairs and knocked on the locked bedroom door and called my dad and said, 'Why don't you open the door?'"

"Let the weak be strong. Let the pessimist go forward. Let the forward go on."

Xing, a young Chinese friend, sent a note:

"Today is the first day blocking the city. People are crazy, going to the supermarket for everything. Can a quarantine city feed 11 million people? Will food riots break out?"

Liz sent a text. "Wondering if we should go to WalMart to see if it's open? I'm going to need alcohol and smokes."

"We're thinking alike. Meet me at the dumpster in 20," Art replied.

An old Chinese woman in a straw hat dug through the teachers' dumpster looking for plastic and cardboard when Art walked up to Liz.

"Let's check out the quarantined world," Art said. Liz nodded without a word.

Four maskless Chinese men strolled down Taozhi Road laughing.

"No masks for the prats," Liz said.

"A big problem if it gets to America," Art said. "Nobody can tell ME what to do. I have my rights!"

"Bloody Americans," the British woman said. "A lot of arrogant pricks who think they're above everything."

"And damn proud of it. I think it's in the Constitution. In order to form a more perfect union, we will establish justice and ensure domestic tranquility by having a mask-free country."

Liz shrugged before letting out a spastic cough forcing Art to inch away. "Xing says people are going nuts."

"Just cigarettes and booze for me," said the leggy, rail-thin Liz who looked like she survived on those two staples and a couple daily spoons of rice.

WalMart anchored the Wanda Mall, a four-story facility with over 200 stores and restaurants.

A few people walked outside the mall but only one bakery and WalMart remained open as the dimmed lights and gated stores painted a post-apocalyptic scene.

The bakery employee refused to touch Art's cash as if poisoned. "Card," the man spit out, leaning away from the money.

A masked WalMart employee met shoppers at the entrance. She took temperatures with a gun-like device pointed at foreheads, turning away the sick.

"Wasn't sure you'd make it wanker," Liz said with a relieved laugh.

The unfazed shoppers showed no panic-buying tendencies unlike a chaotic American pre-hurricane stampede of hoarders.

The shelves remained well stocked with plenty of meat, fish, eggs, fruit, milk, and liquor. Only green vegetables didn't survive the run.

The store manager ran a checkout register, answering questions from numerous employees while scanning beans, fresh fruit, and yogurt for the long lines.

"Lawson's is open. I can get my cigs there," Liz said as they left the mall.

Liz entered the convenience store outside of the mall and immediately let out a smoker's hack. Everyone froze except for three customers who ran out of the store. Art followed them out.

Erick, a Polish photographer who taught at Jianghan, waited for photo opportunities near the mall's closed Metro entrance.

His Canon camera dangled from his neck with a Chinese girl standing at his side, looking like two cats ready to pounce.

"Hey, can I ask a question? You nervous about the quarantine?"

"A little. Liz and I stocked up so we're good for a week."

"The quarantine scares me. I smoke so the last thing I want is a lung virus. I don't want to see anyone till I'm out of fags," Liz said, standing 10 feet away, looking ready to run.

"People seem calm. Maybe this insanity will pass in a week or two," Art said with a shrug.

Erick snapped a few uninspired shots of the skittish Liz before spotting a beautiful Chinese lady in a yellow dress. His Chinese assistant approached the woman.

"See ya," he said over his shoulder as he consumed his next victim.

"Fucking muppets," Liz said over her shoulder. "Pythons squeezing victims."

A depressing reality of long, solitary days stretching into an unforeseeable future engulfed Liz and Art on the silent 20-minute walk back to campus.

"You want to get together later for a drink? The days are going to get long," Art said with hesitation when reaching the apartments.

"Not sure that's a good idea. Bye," Liz said out of the side of her mouth, scurrying off to safety with little more than a wave over the shoulder.

The apartment's steel entrance door swung open then slammed shut with a cold, hard echo like a 1940s' prison movie.

"Going to be doin' some hard time," Art thought as he trudged up the concrete steps to his second-floor flat. "Not sure what I'm going to do if I get sick."

His small kitchen window showed an empty campus. Gone were the usual scenes of drum-pounding soccer matches, military parades, dancing Africans, cricket-playing Indians, Chinese women jogging in dresses, and lovers caressing.

"How did this happen?" He shook his head as a shaky hand poured a drink from the new bottle of Johnny Walker.

CHAPTER 87

Bad Science Fiction

Ugly news mounted as the Associated Press reported the virus had killed 17 and hospitalized 440, an alarming discrepancy compared to the Wuhan Municipal Health Commission numbers.

Scary stories filled the Internet. An online story circulated about a married Wuhan couple in their 40s who fell ill. The hospital admitted the husband while releasing the wife.

The man began to recover the next morning, telling his wife by phone about a planned afternoon release. His noon death changed those plans.

The distraught wife waited hours outside the hospital for the body's trip to the morgue. She held up a handmade sign declaring "I'll love you forever," when her husband's body sped by in the truck carrying the dead.

Dying in China worried Art. Brett, an English teacher from Arkansas, had died of cancer at Jianghan several years earlier. The Chinese held the body for a six-week investigation then let the university hold a small service before turning it over to the American authorities.

The teacher's wasted-away corpse had no eyes and smelled revolting. Those gathered held their breath as they circled the body three times before setting off fireworks in a Chinese ceremony.

"That was awful," Art told the American government representative who collected the body following the ceremony.

"I've seen worse," he replied with a cold stare.

"No signs, investigation, or firecrackers if I die," Art thought in his lonely apartment. "Just another body in the incinerator."

The media soon became his only contact with the outside world. An American friend told *The New York Times* about him being in Wuhan. An interview with the paper led to an onslaught of media requests.

CNN, the Washington Post, NBC Nightly News, CBS Morning Show, Fox News, and the Los Angeles Times filled his email or Facebook accounts with interview requests.

"I'm the trapped miner in a tunnel collapse," he thought as reporters ended telephone interviews with "thank you, best of luck, and goodbye" in hushed tones. He laughed off the "you're so brave" comments.

"Worried and alone, sure, but not brave. That requires action," he told the reporters. "I'm sitting in an empty apartment hoping I don't die today just like everyone else."

Art tried to call Jun after four lonely days.

"Hey, you unlocked my number. How are you? Keeping the city safe?"

"Hello Art. Yes, I thought you might need help," she said, sounding tired before letting out a cough.

"Have you been to the hospital yet? You're sick."

"On my way now. The mayor forced me. No one wants to be around anyone coughing. I think I just have a cold. How are you?"

"Surviving. Very strange with no people on the streets. Seems like bad science fiction. I live alone so no one can get me sick. Your friend's plan worked too well."

"The government's investigating all the possible causes including America releasing it during the World Military Games. When are you going back to America?"

"Suspects always blame the other guy. Who said I was leaving?"

"America will send planes for its people. You need to be on one."

A pause between the two lasted several seconds before Art sighed. "It's confusing. What about us?"

"Water now flows from the in to the out. Perhaps it will flow in again. I must go. Take care Art."

"I love you Jun."

CHAPTER 88

My Yellow Dress

JANUARY 31, 2020

The dirty hospital window let in a dull gray light, creating a somber atmosphere in the private hospital room.

Jun squirmed on the hard bed, shifting positions every few seconds to help her breathe.

The cool air encouraged coughing, so she pulled the worn hospital blanket up to her chin which increased her body heat.

She struggled with pain as the virus strangled her lungs. A nurse checked her into the room four hours ago. No one had come since.

"Nurses are people too, with families to protect. They need to stay at home," she told herself while buzzing the nurses' station for the eighth time.

The room's door opened 20 minutes later.

"How's Central Hospital's favorite patient? I made sure the mayor's chief of staff had our best private room," said the hospital administrator, looking uncomfortable wearing a N-95 mask while standing far away as possible.

"Where are the doctors and nurses Chun? Four hours and no one has seen me."

"Well, it's a busy day. You'll get care soon. Today's small staff is due to no public transportation. Tomorrow will be better, I hope."

A nurse entered the room with food.

"The mayor wants you to receive our best treatment and here it is,"

Chun said, sweeping his arm like a game show host toward a prize. The nurse had a towel tied around her face.

"No masks? How long have you been out?"

"A day or so, but more are coming from my cousin's supply house in Shenzhen if we can get them here. He didn't cheat us too bad. Sickness and war mean big profits for some," he said with a lilt. "How are you feeling?"

"Tired, my head hurts, and my wind is not good. How is Dr. Lui?"

"Nice room," he said, examining the small hospital room before looking at a silent street. "Amazing, no traffic in Wuhan. Hard to believe."

"Chun, what happened?"

"I'm sorry but Dr. Lui died today," Chun said turning to the thin woman lying in bed. "A sad day at Central Hospital."

Jun moaned, curling into a ball on the hard hospital bed.

"Doctors face challenges. A difficult profession. Get rest. I'll make sure a doctor checks on you," Chun said, waving to Jun before leaving.

The fading sun left a few dim streaks on the light brown wall when a doctor entered the room.

"How are you feeling? What symptoms do you have?"

"Did you know Dr. Lui? Tell me something nice about him," Jun asked.

"A very nice man. We'll miss him. Now let me listen to your lungs," the doctor said with no emotion. "Symptoms?"

The doctor's anxious eyes glanced toward the door.

"This doctor had the next 10 years planned. Now, his friend's dead and he might be next. We're all so foolish," she thought.

The exam finished within a minute. The doctor looked at his shoes while mumbling he'd return tomorrow before rushing out.

Jun's misty eyes mindlessly stared out the window until noticing something partially hidden by the curtains.

The sick woman staggered out of the bed, finding a pair of round glasses and a photo near the window.

"His glasses," she said, remembering the doctor's red face from her teasing 15 years ago at Wuhan University.

Jun wiped a thin layer of dust from the lens before looking at the photo of a laughing father pushing his two-year-old son on a park swing. A happy moment captured like a fish on a hook.

"So quick, so final. I deserve to die, but him?"

She knew how the son would feel when visiting the photo on special occasions, searching for forgotten memories.

"Small squares of paper with yellow dresses and swings can't bring back brave and true fathers."

The photo fluttered to the floor as the young woman crumbled onto the hospital bed, legs dangling in space.

"My yellow dress. I want to wear my yellow dress," she yelled at her mother.

"It no longer fits you. I made a new one that's very pretty."

"No! Daddy loves my yellow dress. I want to wear that one."

The pretty yellow dress enlivened the dull hospital bed before it disappeared with a cough.

A wavering breath ushered darkness into the room.

"Let me go see daddy now," she whispered.

CHAPTER 89

It Wasn't the Bats

Life and death fought a fierce battle inside Jun as she clutched Dr. Lui's glasses.

Hazy doctors mumbled unintelligible words to her, but Jun only saw panic oozing from small, scared eyes.

Jun asked each, "Is that you Dr. Lui?" Each said no.

Young China asked questions as well about the now-dead doctor. His arrest to suppress the virus news now enraged the young.

A hard and fast reaction hit the country's social media sites.

Two top trending hashtags emerged, "Wuhan government owes Dr Lui an apology" and "We want freedom of speech" before being censored.

The young Chinese then posted under the hashtag "can you manage, do you understand?" The reference came from the letter Dr Lui signed when accused of disturbing "social order."

The online comments reflected anger and confusion.

"It wasn't the bats that killed him."

"Do not forget how you feel now. Do not forget this anger. We must not let this happen again."

"The truth will always be treated as a rumor. How long are you going to lie? Are you still lying? What else do you have to hide?"

"Tearful nephew of the virus, there is no hero from the sky, only the ordinary who must stand up."

"Although the world is not worth it, the angel really came."

"I thought a miracle would happen. I thought God would leave a light on the earth. Some people die trying to make up lies. Some people will die trying to tell the truth. Ridiculous, pathetic, pathetic. Rip."

"Thank you for trying to save the planet. A hero all the way."

"The trust built up in the book is now cut by this reality."

"I have never been afraid to presume the Chinese with the worst of evil, but I do not expect, nor do I believe that it would be so brutal. In memory of Dr. Lui who tried to sound the alarm but was silenced for 'spreading rumors.'"

"If his warning was not silenced how many lives would have been saved?"

"There is not "if" in history."

"Truth should never be silenced again!"

"Praying for a miracle. Good people don't deserve to die like this."

"At this time, the selfishness and ugliness of human nature are fully reflected."

"I'm going to shut my eyes for now and float in the darkness of my expectations."

"It's too fucking hard."

"Love does not forget. And don't forget… That is what you look like."

CHAPTER 90

Hiding their Crimes

A private jet idled on a Wuhan Caidan General Aviation Airport runway, waiting for clearance for a flight to Beijing. The new airport had no problem allowing the Wuhan Communist Party chairman to fly during the quarantine.

"Leaving Caidan now. Should be there in three hours. Yeah, we're set," Guo said before letting out a soft cough.

A stewardess brought a glass of Chateau Lynch-Bages 2014, a decent French Bordeaux.

"I know it's hot right now. Who knew the doctor would die? People die every day. But this works well. I'll resign as chair and apologize, then disappear. You'll never see me again. Everybody gets paid. Ok. See you soon."

The chairman leaned back into the seat, sipping the wine. His lips smacked together before smirking.

The jet's engines roared as he made another call. "Captain Yang? Hello, Guo Zhenqin."

"Thanks for returning my call. An update. The unknown assailant who killed your assistant left no fingerprints on the body. No weapon recovered. We'll drag the pond when we can, but the quarantine shut us down. We'll follow up on the farmer, Li, at some point."

"Sorry to hear that. Murder should not be so easy to get away with. You'd think this was America."

"Questions about Wu still exist. How long did he work for you?"

"Over 20 years. He came from Xi'an. Or was it Chongqing? His references checked out."

"Any contact information in your files? Might be helpful. A vita or family member?"

"I'll check but I'd be surprised. I heard his cousin just died in a house fire but no other family that I know. Who keeps records that long? The second item?"

"Jun tape's a fake. Voices didn't match. Another note, she's in the hospital. Very sick and Dr. Lui died of the virus."

"Oh. That is too bad. Yes, the poor doctor," Guo said in a raspy voice as he let out a soft cough. "No visitors for Jun?"

"Not on that floor. Did you have close contact with her in the past few weeks? If so, I'd get checked."

"No," he said, clenching his fist.

"Didn't you two talk following her speech."

"I was wearing a mask. Why would someone fake a tape?"

"Trying to hide their own crimes. If criminals weren't so stupid we'd never catch one," Yang said with a laugh. "We dusted everything for fingerprints. Got a few."

"Anybody we know?" Guo gripped the wine glass.

"Still checking."

"Good. I'm sure you have much to keep you busy. Thank you for the updates. Goodbye."

Guo stared out the jet's window. "Stewardess, please get me a cup of hot water and ginger and take this wine away. It has no taste."

A smiling Yang entered his supervisor office.

"We found Peng's prints on the tape's package, but he's dead and I'm not arresting Guo."

"No, let's not bark up that tree. Just let it fade away," the supervisor said. "We got enough troubles."

"I agree. Policemen don't do well in prison," the captain said with a laugh.

"Follow up with Jun's mother. See what she says," the supervisor said.

"Hao Gui? Captain Yang of the Wuhan Police Department. We met the other day at the banquet."

"How are you?'

"I'm sorry about your daughter's illness. I hope she recovers soon."

"Jun is strong like her father. I'm worried but believe she'll recover."

"Are many people sick from the banquet? Reports blame the Baixin banquet for leaving hundreds sick or dead."

"No more than other developments. We did what the party leaders thought right," Hao said with an edge. "Guo Zhenqin insisted we move forward with it."

"Many are upset. Newspapers around the world call it a criminal event and want those responsible arrested, but we don't have the time or manpower."

"Nothing but false reports to justify beliefs. Yes, people are sick but who knows from where? Maybe the Metro, right? I'm fine, my friends are fine. Thank you for your opinion."

"Let me know if things get worse. Ah, one more thing. We're still trying to track down a person named Li Shun. I believe you know him?"

"For many years. My late husband's best friend. I don't know where he is. How would I know where he is?"

"I have to ask. We have a few questions to discuss with him, but the quarantine has us responding to only emergency situations. If you hear from him, please tell him to give us a call."

"Of course. Anything else?"

"No. Thank you for your time."

Hao hung up. "The police want to talk with you, but the quarantine is keeping them busy."

"Did they sound angry?"

"No. He's angrier at me for holding the banquet. I think you should stay here. I'll cook food for you," Hao said touching his hand.
"I'd like that."

CHAPTER 91

A Vast Practical Joke

Jun's phone glistened with sweat from her shaking hand.

"Hello Art," she said in a weak voice.

"Jun? I can barely hear you. How are you?"

"Sick Art. I thought I died last night. But the fever broke. They put me in the room Dr. Lui died in. It's terrible," Jun said, twisting in the hard Central Hospital bed.

"That's awful. I hope you're feeling better."

"Oh Art. I keep reading a passage from your book, *Moby Dick*."

"There are certain queer times and occasions in this strange mixed affair we call life when a man takes this whole universe for a vast practical joke, though the wit thereof he but dimly discerns, and more than suspects that the joke is at nobody's expense but his own."

The phone line remained silent for several seconds.

"Life, a sad joke at my expense. No heroic journeys. No changing of the world. Just a cold universe," she whispered.

"Jun, we all chase something, safety, money, family, fame, or just fun. But life ends up laughing at most of us. I chose to move to Wuhan. Now that's hilarious."

"When are you going back to America?"

"Jun, I love you, but I'm leaving in a couple of days. America may not be any safer, but it's home."

"Yes. Family's a priority. Now that the games are over, I need to take care of our family. We hope to visit you in America one day, but who knows? I love you Art."

"Who is going to visit? You and your mother?"

"No Art. Our family. We have a three-year-old son."

"What? You're kidding, right? It's a joke."

"No, it's not. I'm so sorry for not telling you. My mind complicated things. My father's death hurt very much," Jun said. "I wanted a son in his image. It left no space for you."

"How could you do such a thing? What's his name?"

"Tie LiJiao, after his father and mine. Tie means iron in Chinese. But I call him Arthur."

"Does he look like me?"

"Yes. Light brown hair and blue eyes. I'll send a photo."

"I can't believe this," Art said, taking a deep breath. "Is this a half-baked scheme to have an American child? Did you finally figure out he can't be an American without me?"

"No Art. I'm aware of American citizenship laws. But I also know the Chinese government will never let him go to America without my approval."

"Wait a minute. Before we get in a custody battle, is he ok? Where is he?"

"He already knows English," Jun said with an unconvincing laugh. "My relatives in Chongqing take good care of him."

"Says who? You? How often do you see him?"

"Every few months. I plan on moving there."

"I don't believe it. How can a mother just leave her baby for three years? That breaks my heart. Do you treat all men the same?"

"Art! Don't be so mean. The games took a lot of time. Chinese relatives often care for others' children. I'll make it up to both of you. Just remember I love you. I'll find you."

"No, you don't. The baby, clothes, money, it's all the same to you. A zero-sum game. You win what others lose. You don't love anybody but yourself."

"We'll be together in America one day, you'll see. I can't talk, the doctor is here. I need to go." The line went dead.

Art's return call went straight to voice mail.

CHAPTER 92

The Long Game

FEBRUARY 2, 2020

A bottle of Johnny Walker and Liz seemed a good idea. Minutes later Art stood in front of her door.

"Open up. Let me in, I need to talk," he yelled from the hallway.

"No. It's not safe. Go away. I'm not letting you in," Liz said from behind the door. "I can't chance getting the crud."

"Well then I won't tell you about my 3-year-old child."

"What?" The door opened a crack.

"I just found out I have a child."

"Meet me on the roof," she said shutting the door.

"Bring two glasses."

Liz smiled as she walked onto her apartment's roof five minutes later, seven stories above an empty Jianghan campus.

"Now don't do anything stupid like get close to me," Liz said as she lit a Chinese cigarette. "Now what's all this rubbish about?"

"I slept with her three years ago. One time! Now she says we have a child. Jesus Christ you can't trust women."

He poured two healthy Johnny Walkers as the warm February sun reflected off her pale but beautiful face. He handed her a drink.

"She just told me. Said she didn't have space for me in her fairyland."

"Fairyland, huh? When did she tell you? Before or after you told her you're leaving?"

"After. Once I told her she had to tell me."

"She lying. 'Don't go Art. We have baby,'" Liz said in a bad Chinese accent. "A smart femme fatale keeps her options open. She's playing the long game."

"The long game? What are you talking about?"

"She may need you down the road. Where's the baby? KuMing?"

"No. Chongqing."

"You're a pair of red, white, and blue shoes to her. She'll pull you out of the closet to match her outfit when the time's right."

"She sounded distraught," Art said while shaking his head. "Why would she lie?"

"Oh, you silly lad. You don't get it? You're her 'get out of China free' green card. Who wouldn't want to get out of here? Especially with what she's been up to. I give her credit, she's quite a tidy hustler."

But she's sending a photo. That'll prove it," he said before taking a long drink.

"Oh, you'll see a hapa baby. Just not yours. When the wedding day comes so will the excuses. 'Oh he's sick' or 'I left him in Chongqing so we can have a romantic honeymoon.' Just don't send money."

Jun curled on the Central Hospital bed as the doctor finished his examination.

"I believe you'll recover. Get some rest," he said before scurrying out.

Jun listened for more visitors before grabbing her large Hermes Birkin purse sitting next to the bed. She opened the clasp.

Delicate fingers unzipped a pocket and opened a fine Cartier case without a sound, letting the sunshine reflect off the diamonds to create a blinding glitter.

"Oh, how spectacular," she whispered before quickly closing the case and stuffing it back into the purse.

"This and the treasury bonds will tide me over for a while. Then to LA to shake Guo down with a couple smiles. He'll miss me," she said with a laugh. "Then it's off to my green card. The best of an American world, a young husband and an old man's money."

She began scrolling through photos of a three-year-old boy before attaching one to a text message.

"Tie LiJiao looks like you! So sweet. He promises to be an obedient son. Maybe you'll see him one day if you let us come live with you every day as an American family. I love you so, Jun." She nodded then pushed send.

Art's phone buzzed. "See. I told you she loved me. Look at my baby! I need to get some cigars," Art said to Liz.

"Hustlers feed off hope," Liz said as she pulled out a Chinese cigarette.

Art swayed back and forth on the seventh-story ledge examining a photo of a child. He picked up his Johnny Walker and took a long sip.

CHAPTER 93

When You Leaving?

FEBRUARY 4, 2020

Liz's apartment rooftop became an oasis from Wuhan's virus.

Warm and sunny weather brought more teachers out of isolation as they accepted the premise that drinking and eating grilled chicken outside wouldn't kill them. A few held out, glumly waving from adjacent apartment windows.

The sunshine-splashed conversations revolved around one question: Are you staying or leaving?

A few teachers remained steadfast to remain in Wuhan, each protesting they had nothing going on in hometowns of Mexico City, Green Bay, Melbourne, or wherever.

But the phrase "my county is sending a plane," shriveled the resolve in most as the virus's long-term threat remained a mystery.

Teachers from Pakistan, several African countries, and Poland had already left with bleary-eyed waves and promises to keep in touch.

"When you leaving, you wanker? Soon, I hope. I'm tired of looking at ya," Liz laughed as she blew cigarette smoke toward Art.

"Tomorrow," Art said sipping his drink and gazing over the empty campus.

"How you getting to the airport? I heard the Pakistan government organized a bus to take their citizens," Liz said.

"America told us to get our own ride. No problem, the airport's only 50 miles away in a city with no public transportation." Art laughed.

"Going to take some bloody American ingenuity, huh smart boy?" Liz gave him a sad smile.

"Done. After six years, the missionaries are finally doing a Christian thing. They're taking me," Art said. "I'm chaperoning some kid."

"Speaking of kids, what about your phantom child? Thought you'd have a crew by now."

"No, nothing," Art said, turning his palms to the sky as Liz shook her head.

"Just get out of town before the family moves in with you."

CHAPTER 94

Don't Leave Me Behind

Scattered remnants of escaping were strewn across Art's small apartment floor. Piles of clothes, assorted kitchen utensils, stacks of textbooks, and garbage bags littered the room.

The U.S. rescue plane allowed one suitcase per person so most of his stuff had to be left behind.

"The building manager will look good wearing my Cleveland Indians' sweatshirts," Art said with a laugh, knowing the apartment would be combed over minutes after he left.

A toaster oven, blender, and wine glasses had already been given away to a couple of teachers staying behind. A pair of cowboy boots and a box of chocolate sat on his table, waiting for Liz to show up.

Slow footsteps and a muffled sound headed up the stairs. Art opened the door to see Liz crying, holding a computer.

"I'm having a strop, can't get on the fuckin' Internet. Can't verify my airplane seat to England," she moaned. "Don't leave me behind."

"I'll try but don't have much time," Art said, looking at his watch. "The Chinese always block it when international news makes them look bad. Let me see what I can do."

Five minutes of distracted fiddling led to the inevitable parting of ways.

"I got to go. I have two miles to walk to catch my Christian ride. Those people won't wait," he said with tears in his eyes. "Maybe someone else can help?"

"No, don't worry. Get out while you can," she said, trying to regain her composure. "I know it's dodgy. I'll take care of it."

"I feel bad leaving you behind," he said, dropping his head.

She put her finger to his lips and smiled.

"Shush and give me a snug you arse." A silent embrace ended after 30 seconds when she whispered in his ear, "Come to London sometime and we'll go mental." She waved then walked out with her new pair of cowboy boots.

Art scanned his small Chinese home one last time before grabbing his suitcase and shutting the door on six years of a strangely beautiful existence.

Lisa, the Chinese building manager, waited downstairs with her small, white poodle.

"Here is my key. Thank you for all you've done for me," Art said, knowing she understood little English other than phrases like "no electric, three days."

Her small black eyes reflected the same sadness others had the past few days. The teachers and Chinese staff had formed a team and now an unknown virus broke it up without time for proper goodbyes.

An awkward pause took place between the two before Lisa embraced Art.

"I love you," she whispered into his ear in broken English.

"I love you too." Art stared into her eyes for a second before turning into the bright afternoon sun as tears streamed down his face, feeling like he was escaping while others were left behind to fight alone.

He took several steps before Lisa shouted to him, "Teacher Art, you have mask?"

"What? Oh, I forgot it."

Lisa handed him one.

Sounds like Hell

FEBRUARY 5, 2020

The high-pitched whine of a cold, dirty 747 cargo plane ground to a halt on San Diego's Miramar Marine Base tarmac.

Excited chatter and the unbuckling of seat belts filled the cabin as 150 exhausted passengers exhaled from a grueling 20-hour Wuhan flight.

A "we made it to a Covid-free America" joy trumped concerns over the constant coughing on the plane.

Thirty minutes later four people warily entered the plane. A tall thin man in a blue blazer and light brown pants stepped out front as the other three stood near the open door.

"I'm Dr. Thomas Christopher, deputy director with the U.S. Centers for Disease Control. Welcome to everyone. I'm sure you're very tired and hungry. We will work to process you as quickly as possible. You will be in quarantine here for two weeks."

Art watched a small red rubber ball roll in a circle in his hand as the doctor tried to appear knowledgeable about a virus no one knew much about.

Confused Chinese passengers who spoke little English worked together in whispers to decipher Christopher's words.

The doctor finished with a pointed warning aimed at the bewildered Chinese.

"This is a working military base. If you take any photographs or video of military activities or equipment, your phone or camera will be taken and destroyed. We'll get you off the plane soon. Have a nice stay."

The four emissaries quickly left the plane, with Dr. Christopher glancing back.

Passengers immediately formed a line at the door with suitcases and fidgeting children in hand.

Dr. Christopher's promise to get people "off the plane soon" dripped past 90 minutes. The passengers spoke less and less until the only sound was nonstop coughing.

"Jesus, what's going on." Art pushed past the queue to the stairs outside the plane's door.

Dr. Christopher stood on the stairs reading a notebook.

"Hi. I'm Dr. Christopher."

"Hello. Art Iron. Hey, when we getting off this plane? It's been 20 hours. I could use a cocktail."

"Soon. The CDC's in charge of the passengers' health and well-being but the military controls operations like the buses. Were you threatened trying to leave China?"

"Armed military stopped us outside the airport. The soldier in charge was wearing a Kobe Bryant Lakers' jersey in honor of his death yesterday. He didn't want to touch our passports, but he smiled," Art said. "That was kinder than being trapped on a plane filled with overflowing port-o-johns and sick people."

"We'll get you off soon. The good news is you won't have to wear that mask here. The CDC believes stay six feet away and all is well," Dr. Christopher said with the assurance only a doctor can give.

"Everyone's wearing a mask in China," Art said.

"Well, we believe we're right," the doctor said.

"Tell that to Dr. Lui."

The doctor gave the tired man a perplexed look. "I have a question. Why didn't more people come back? Neither of the planes were full."

"A lot of reasons. You try to get to a Chinese airport 50 miles away in a quarantined city. Others needed the job or didn't have $1100 our government charged us for a rescue plane seat. The cost of freedom, huh?"

The doctor shrugged.

"The breeze feels nice," Art said, looking out at the picturesque Santa Rosa Mountains east of the airport. "Jun would love San Diego. And maybe Arthur?"

"So how was it in Wuhan?" The doctor's piercing eyes looked for clues.

"A lot of great people but scary in the end. Just happy to be home. Strange stuff going on there. People will never know the truth. But I got a pretty good idea."

"Sure you do," the doctor said with a softened look. "We'll have people to talk to if you need help."

"People who never been to Wuhan telling me how to feel? No thanks, sounds like hell. Just get us off this plane doc," Art said with a wan smile as he pushed past the coughing, masked passengers.

An hour later, Art descended the 747's stairs, ending the bizarre 42-hour journey since saying goodbye to Lisa.

While the smooth Miramar tarmac felt solid and safe, the American military treated the passengers like radioactive escapees.

Armed soldiers stood 50 feet away from the coronavirus refugees pointing to a bus no one wanted to drive.

A sergeant in the driver's seat stared straight ahead, smacking his hands with force on the bus's steering wheel when his dangerous passengers entered.

"Hello. Great to be home," Art said to the masked driver who grumbled an obscenity and jumped off the bus.

Constant coughing by an aging Chinese woman kept the bus's passengers wondering if the trip to America protected them from the disease after all.

Art curled up into the seat, pulling up his sweatshirt to cover his masked mouth and nose. He reached into his pocket for his red ball.

Tears clouded his eyes as his head pressed against the bus's window.

He tried not to breathe as his stomach rumbled with hunger and the red ball rolled in circles around his palm.

"Man, the world got smaller in six years," Art thought as he shivered in his seat.

He picked up the ball with his forefinger and thumb, placing it in front of his right eye while closing his left eye. Jun's gift blocked the huge California sun from his vision.

The lifer jumped back on the bus. "Here we go. Next stop quarantine," he barked as the bus engine roared. Art shoved the ball back into his pocket.

About the Author

John McGory lived in Wuhan, China from 2014 until February 5, 2020, when an American rescue plane took 150 U.S. citizens to San Diego. The journalist and teacher worked as a language editor at the *Changjiang Weekly*, Wuhan's largest English newspaper, where he covered the city leading up to the outbreak.